THE G[...]

"I love this book. The haunting les[...] [...]
the legacy of war cannot triumph [...] [...] Where there is
love and humanity, the human spirit triumphs. Read it."

Sandra Dallas, *New York Times* bestselling author of *Prayers for Sale*

"Mustian writes relentlessly, telling his haunting story in brief bursts of
luminous yet entirely unsentimental prose."

Library Journal

"Why are war stories so often truly love stories? Because, as Mustian
proves in *The Gendarme*, love in the face of war gives testimony that love
endures our savagery, our violence, our hatred. In this powerful retelling of
the horrible crimes committed against Armenians at the beginning of
World War I, *The Gendarme* is a beautiful, haunting tale of survival and
resilience."

Julianna Baggott, *New York Times* bestselling author of
The Madam and *The Miss America Family*

"Ahmet Khan's spiritual transition to Emmett Conn is emotionally reso-
nant. This is an important and unique journey told with compassion and a
stirring sense of humanity."

Atom Egoyan, award-winning director of the films
Ararat and *The Sweet Hereafter*

"Mustian...tells a story that probes a timeless array of life's general ad-
versities: the tricks of memory that enable us to carry on with our daily
existence; the brash decisions and subsequent regrets of the young; the
ever-present need for forgiveness; the way a single event can be subject to
many interpretations."

The New York Times

"[An] ethereal examination of love and memory."

San Francisco Chronicle

"Mustian takes us through this horrendous period of history with objectivity. He does not assign blame. What emerges is a love story, one that transcends the misery of the human condition, forever changing everyone it touches."

Florida Times Union

"The novel effectively captures the human capacity for survival and redemption."

Publishers Weekly

"Every decade or so, I find a novel that I sense, just by reading the basic description, will become unforgettable; after reading only 20 pages of *The Gendarme*, my impression was confirmed with great force. For this decade, and this reader, *The Gendarme* is that extraordinary, unforgettable novel..."

Bookpage

ABOUT THE AUTHOR

Mark Mustian is an author, attorney, and city commissioner. He lives with his wife and three children in Tallahassee, Florida.

THE
GENDARME

Mark Mustian

ONEWORLD

The Gendarme

First published in Great Britain and the Commonwealth
by Oneworld Publications 2011
This edition published by Oneworld Publications 2012

Copyright © Mark Mustian 2010

Published by arrangement with Amy Einhorn Books,
a division of G. P. Putnam's Sons,
a member of Penguin Group (USA) Inc.

ISBN 978-1-85168-839-5

Typeset by Jayvee, Trivandrum, India
Cover design by David J. High, highdzn.com
Cover photograph © Steve McCurry / Magnum Photos
Printed and bound in Great Britain by

Oneworld Publications
185 Banbury Road
Oxford
OX2 7AR

Learn more about Oneworld. Join our mailing list to
find out about our latest titles and special offers at:

www.oneworld-publications.com

For Bern

To the Roaring Wind.

What syllable are you seeking,

Vocalissimus,

In the distances of sleep?

Speak it.

—WALLACE STEVENS, *1917*

THE
GENDARME

· 1 ·

I awake in a whispering ambulance.

Attendants huddle, a gloved finger withdraws.

Memory makes its way back: the crush of the headache, the darkness. I am cold now. My face is numb.

"Can you hear me?"

Başım . . .

"What is your name?"

Speech half forms. In English? At length, "Em . . . Em . . . Emmett Conn."

"Where do you live?"

I think. "Twenty-three fifteen Wisteria Court. Wadesboro, Georgia." The words flow easier.

"When were you born?"

I pause, for I do not truly know. "The year 1898." This is what I have said, for many years now. "I am ninety-two years old."

A light shines in my eyes, twisting the headache's slow thrust.

I smell alcohol. Metallic voices flutter. The siren rises—did I not hear it? Then silence, except for a buzzing sound, and darkness. Sleep falls. Is this it?

A sudden burst of coldness comes, then nothing.

I wake. A chill shakes and leaves me, a great wind rushing past. The headache remains, confined now to a solitary spot, perhaps a single nerve ending. I touch my face. A television speaks somewhere, perhaps in a different room. I see no window, no natural light. I am . . . where?

A rustling sounds next to me. Shapes form and dissolve into a woman, a voice.

"You're awake."

For a moment I think I am back there, injured. A prisoner. Unidentified Patient Number A-17.

"How are you feeling?"

I close my eyes. I was a soldier. My injury left me without memory, of the war or much before it.

"A neighbor saw you collapse," the woman whispers. "You had a seizure. They're going to run tests."

"For what?" I try to still myself, even my pulse.

She pauses. "A stroke. Or a brain . . . something."

I attempt a smile, for there is humor in it. A brain something. I shift in her direction, the headache stabbing its response.

"I am an old man."

"They're calling your daughter," she says. My daughter who stays away.

This woman—nurse?—pulls the sheet. "Where are you from?"

I sigh. My foreignness, found at just a few syllables. Despite all the years, all my efforts at English.

"I am an American." I say this. The woman nods.

"We're gonna set you up for an MRI."

She says something more, but a tiredness creeps over me. Arms become elbows become joints, PVC pipe. Plastic tubing spawns hair. I think, How have I lived, for so long now?

I sleep.

Coldness again, and wind. This time I can see—a long, wind-swept plain, and a train, an ancient steam locomotive, spewing black smoke tossed sideways by the wind. The smoke smells vile and heavy, not the sweet odor of burning wood, but harsher, more primitive. The oddness of smell permeating a dream tugs at me. The train sways. I do not recognize the surroundings.

It looks to be late afternoon, maybe spring or summer. The wind rushes across the plain, barren except for the train and a few dusty trees. The train is barely moving; in fact, I seem to be moving faster, in the same direction, bobbing my head like the mast on a ship. In the distance to my left, at the far end of the plain, red and violet mountains merge with the horizon. The sun stands on my right in what appears to be a sinking posture, placing my bearing as southerly. I hear nothing, which makes it seem surreal, even otherworldly, except for the train, and then the people.

A black line of humanity, several hundred long, trudges in the same direction the train moves. I wonder why I hadn't noticed them before—perhaps the languidness of their pace, perhaps the way they mesh with the shadow. They look to be pilgrims of some sort, dressed mostly in black, with the high collars and shawls of those who seek comfort from the past. A few ride on mules, and here and there a wagon breaks the uniformity of the line, a line that sweeps out to the horizon, longer than I had first noticed, thousands instead of hundreds, maybe more. Figures on horseback pace beside them, erect, dipping, like dogs nudging a herd. I reach down, recognizing my buckle and weave as that of a rider. My hand strikes the hardness of metal and wood, the elongated form of a rifle. For a moment it feels so familiar. Then it trails away, in a blast of cold and wind, the chill condensed to a pinpoint, like after the first headache. Then gone.

The gurney glides along the polished floor. A surgery sign, a black arrow. Post-Op, an arrow. Rumbling, rotating, a large vessel's slow movement. People passing, speaking. Oncology, arrow. Radiology, arrow. A final turn, a slowing.

A heavyset nurse runs a hand through red hair.

"Are you able to sit?"

Lights blink and shimmer. The headache has nearly vanished, a tenderness in its place like a newly formed bruise. It hurts if I move my head quickly, or if I look at the overhead light. I move slowly, cautiously. I lift a hand to my face.

The nurse prods me onto another gurney, this one attached to a large machine.

"Lie down here, with your head on this headrest."

I move to comply, a man with his fragile egg-head. I think again—I cannot help it—of before, of the hospital. Seven decades before. Almost a year to remember my name. I should have died then. Without Carol I would have.

"Let's scoot you up a bit."

My memory is fine from the hospital forward, but before is still darkness, only speckles of light. I remember almost nothing of the war, the Great War. I rarely dream.

"Lie as still as you can." The voice comes through an earpiece. A plastic object is placed in my hand. "Use the panic button if you need to."

The bench slides inside the machine. The apparatus whooshes and clicks. The machine accelerates to buzzing, then clanging, loud to the point of pain. The earplugs rattle and bounce in my ears. I wonder again at the purpose of this—to add a few breaths to my life? Carol is dead, dead now three years. I am alive. Ninety-two years have passed—for what? For *what*?

I finger the panic button. Then, gently, release it.

The horse sways under me, the wind back in my face. It is dark. The light of a campfire flickers off to my right. Sounds carry on the wind, yelps of pain, guttural grunts and moans. Words snap and volley: admonishments to be quiet, directions to get up. A faint sobbing crescendos and lessens, stops. The word *gâvur* sprouts in front of me, hurled as an accusation. *Bahşiş. Sigara.* Groupings of consonants, vowels, clips and snorts strung together as symbol, as communication. Snarling, human conversation.

It dawns on me, even through the depths of the dream, that I know this language. I have always known it. It is odd, this, to dream and recognize the dreaming, to dangle beyond the vision like a watchful ghost or god. For an instant I see myself astride the horse, bundled against the wind by a mottled wool blanket, my face scruffy and bearded, my hair long and free. Young, maybe seventeen, thin and upright, dark eyes, heavy brow. Then everything swirls, like a rotating camera, until I find myself back atop the swaying animal, pulling and prodding, peering through darkness at gray things below.

A man straddles a prone form, his bare rump visible in the dim light. He looks up at my approach, smiles in recognition, decouples, extends his arm toward the object beneath. A young girl lies below him, her face darkened with mud. I shake my head, declining, observing his gap-filled grin, his filthy beard, his still-erect *kamış*. Izzet is his name; I knew him somewhere before. Then he is on her again, grunting, the girl whimpering, the slapping sound of flesh on flesh mixed with the wind. I wonder at it a moment, at why I am here, why I seem to know this place yet not to know it, why I understand this language but cannot place it. I smell the smoke of the campfire, hear the shouts and the groans and the rustles. I feel the wind. I touch my own mouth. A certainty strikes that I have been here before, that I have ridden this horse, spoken these words, borne the same silent witness, watching and waiting. And then it is gone, leaving only the dark and the cold, and the wind. I pull the blanket tighter around me, and continue on through the night.

A man fingers my face. I do not know my surroundings, my name. Liquid drips on a hard surface, metal rattles, the smell of medicine floats—all familiar, all strange. Am I among enemies? My hands shake, my body tensed in protection, until the round, smooth face of Dr. Harry Wan registers, like a key clicking true in a lock. I recognize the hospital's bright lights, the static intercom announcements, the smells of plastic and urine. I am Emmett Conn. I am in the United States. It is April 1990.

"How are you this day?"

The dream still tugs at me, the coldness and wind. I smell the sweat of the horse.

"Can you understand me? You may nod yes or no."

I nod affirmatively. My head is sluggish, not my own.

"Good!"

I remember that Dr. Wan is perpetually cheerful, prone to elaborate bows and exclamations of "wonderful." He and I are Rotarians, one of the things Carol tossed me into to acclimate me to Wadesboro. That effort failed, but I remain a member. The others have become used to me, or at best feign indifference. I am an outsider—a Yankee, a foreigner. A transplant. An old man.

"You have what looks to be a brain tumor, Mr. Conn." He smiles as he says this, as if I have won a big prize. "A glioma. It is about the size of a pea, located at the base of the left parietal lobe. We will do a biopsy, confirm the best course of action. We may want to try radiosurgery. It is something new."

He stops to let this sink in. My daughter Violet leans forward, her frown transformed and whisked into a smile. The edge of her mouth curls like Carol's, her mother. I haven't seen her in . . . months? For this I blame myself—we have long had our difficulties. We are in ways so alike. I am pleased she has come now, even under these circumstances.

"Dr. Wan, at my age . . ."

"Shush." Violet spreads her long fingers. "I spoke to him earlier. Dr. Wan says you are in fantastic shape. He says others older than you have been treated and lived active lives. He is a leader in this field."

I shake my head no. But I think, To be wanted now. Yes.

She leans farther in, exposing dark gums. Has she dreaded this day? She must care for me, comfort me. "Papa. Please."

I nod, confused. Her tone has a hunger. Has she told her sister? The boy Wilfred, her son? For a moment it is 1932, and I am working, working. I realize, as I lie here, that the language in the dream had been Turkish.

The doctor moves closer, speaking in low tones, explaining. There are protocols, possibilities. Malignancy, metastasis, radiation, surgery. My eyes water and I fight welling tears; I cry so easily now, whereas earlier in my life I did not cry at all. The treatment he mentions seems so modern, so unappealing. I see myself: "World's Oldest Patient Receives New Procedure." Dr. Wan's face on a journal. I wonder about payments, insurance. Will someone care for Sultan, my cat? But it is all in the distance. In some strange way I am still in the dream, wounded or dying or already dead.

"Okay," I say.

There are smiles, exhaled breaths.

"You had a head injury once, is that right, Mr. Conn?"

"Yes, in the war." Violet must have told him. Nineteen fifteen. World War I, not II. It led to my marriage, to my coming to America. To the things I remember. To my life.

"Do you have records?"

I look at Violet. "Yes."

He looks at me quizzically. "You fought for the U.S.?"

I shake my head. "No." The headache gains force, like a storm's gathered winds.

Dr. Wan looks on, beaming.

"Wonderful!" he announces, and exits the room.

. . .

Dawn approaches in a softening gray. Men mutter, distant, a breeze stifling words and brief bursts of rough laughter. A fire glints and sparks but I am separate, removed. Leaves rustle in trees that shield the starlight spread beyond.

I sit with my back against a trunk's smoothness, watching and listening. Leaves turn and still. Birds twitter, one swooping down to peck in the near darkness. I watch the way its head moves, its tail flicks. It lifts its beak up to gulp food in and swallow. Does it feel pleasure? Know pain? It stares at me one-eyed. Then it flits away.

I turn my head to the campfire, to the dark shapes before it. Beyond lie the others, those permitted no fires, those that sleep on the ground in the cold and dream of home or of death. Some will not wake to this dawn, others may rise but will fall, unable to continue. Some will give up, the older ones or the children, or those who have lost almost everything else. Others will trudge on, stumble to the next campsite, collapse, rise again. At first some cried and complained and begged for water, but most of those are now gone. Only the sturdy remain, and those still with valuables useful for bribes. Maybe seven hundred, from what had once been two thousand. Shuffling, marching, day after day.

I think on how I have come to be here, a tiredness muddling my memory so that bits emerge, almost unwillingly. My name, Ahmet. My father's name, Mehmed. The certainty that the next town is not far. The necessity of reporting to officials in Katma. The days it will take for the return journey home. The fact that my father is dead, that his death sent me here. That I must complete this assignment to gain entry into the army. It all swirls together, then washes away, caught in a blurred exhaustion of dim dream and remembrance. My head nods. I must wake. There are obligations, responsibilities.

I stand, fumbling in my trousers. My urine crackles on dry leaves. Another sound intrudes, or perhaps a smell. I whirl to find a figure standing apart in the gloom. I release myself with one hand, grab my rifle with the other. I adjust my clothing. The figure backs away.

"Who is it?" I ask, pointing the rifle.

The figure continues its retreat.

"Halt!"

The figure stops. I draw closer, the rifle erect in front of me, leaves crunching beneath my feet. I near the edge of the trees.

It is a woman. One of them—the baggy, dark clothes, the braided hair, the large eyes. Out trying to escape, or perhaps murder a guard. I have heard of such things. My charges have been mostly docile, cowed into submission by deprivation and the judicious culling of their men. But I must take care.

I stick the rifle barrel under her chin, lifting her face. I edge her backward, into a plume of glimmering light.

Her face hangs words half formed in my throat. She has mismatched eyes, one dark, the other light, as if neither perfect gene could be denied by her mother. I attribute it at first to the starlight. I even turn her a full rotation to get a better, closer look. The thought strikes that she has been blinded in the light eye, but I know this is not true, as both eyes are alive, reflecting the heavens stretched and glowing above us. I stand silent, struck by this oddity, wondering how I have not seen it before, how she has survived this long march without others taking advantage. She is beautiful beyond the exoticism. She is maybe in her early teens, the small rise of breasts evident beneath the oversized garments.

"What are you doing?" I ask, my voice almost shaky. I could have this girl, now, here on the ground, if I wished.

The eyes stare back, unblinking, as if detached from the body. They resemble, in a way, the blank eyes of a corpse, vacant, almost unseeing. I wonder again if she has suffered some injury.

I finger the rifle. My mouth lathers and dries.

"I was collecting eucalyptus leaves," the girl says quietly. She raises an arm to indicate a bag held in one hand. She does not seem afraid like the others, nor hateful, nor particularly submissive. When I touch my hand to her face, she neither flinches nor cries. Her skin is soft, cooled by the breath of the wind.

I release my hand. We stand for some time, until I step aside to let her pass. I feel confused afterward, as to my actions, as to why I made no move to take her. I convince myself I am merely saving her for later, like a man who saves his sweets for after his meal.

I turn before she vanishes under the trees. "What is your name?" I ask.

She does not respond, or if she does, her name is lost in the leaves.

These things I know: I served in the Ottoman army, I was part of a unit, I fought the British at what they call Gallipoli. I was wounded, my face and head and clothes so battered I was mistaken for a British soldier. I was evacuated to a British hospital ship, then a military facility in London. I have admission slips, dates, facts. I have lost my memory, yes, but these things are documented. And then this dream comes, this fantasy, but I see no soldiers. This could be any place. Any time.

A whistling intrudes, followed by a rub of footsteps and a volcanic "Good morning!" Harry Wan's smooth face appears.

"Hello, Mr. Conn."

"Yes. What is it?" I sound impatient. I see the verdict in Dr. Wan's eyes before he opens his mouth.

"It is a glioma, malignant. A small one, less than one centimeter. We are fortunate to catch it this early. As these tumors grow larger, they infiltrate surrounding tissue like a spider, and as such become hard to remove without damaging the brain."

He continues on, but I am looking at Violet, thinking of when she was young, her hair blond like a duckling's. Her sister, Lissette, was blond, too. Carol's hair was golden-white, like a swan's feathers, before it became thin and dull gray. Even her eyebrows were light-colored. Carol, who brought me to America when I spoke almost no English, who endured years of treatment before her own silent death. I remember her shuffling, her walker with the tennis balls cupped at the ends, her mind opaque and floating. The way her head cocked as if some silent voice spoke to her. And now me. Is surgery not wasted on a man of my age? I stare up at the ceiling, wondering if a question has been asked and not answered. "Okay," I say, when a silence emerges. My voice is faint. I see myself lingering, extending. Clinging. If I were stronger I would turn and demand that they leave me, that nature be left to take its certain course. Even buildings and machines wear down and break. But instead I clear my throat and push my lips to a smile. They look on, expecting me to say something more but I am silent. I find nothing to say.

"We'd like to do the surgery on Wednesday," Dr. Wan says. "You'll be fitted into a frame, similar in some respects to the halo used for the biopsy."

I had dozed through much of the biopsy, awake only to bits of the procedure: the cold, sterile room, the prick of the anesthetic's injection, the brush and crackle of face masks and gowns. I squint now at Harry Wan, noting for the first time the large mole on his face. He is speaking, but the sound seems to come from the mole. "You will experience . . . fatigue," the mole says. "The medication will . . . help you."

I shift position, my arms on my chest. Harry Wan smiles and departs. I have feared hospitals, as far back as the war. For a time I had dreams of lying like a caterpillar in a big white bed, restrained and unable to move. I would wake screaming, my arms waving and circling. Carol would then calm me, hold me, watch as I stood to prove I could walk. Such dreams stopped, long ago. I usually sleep well. But now these dreams come.

I look around. The wall, the ceiling, the curtain are white. A crack runs in the ceiling, disappearing over my head.

"Papa. Does your head still hurt?"

It does not. The pain from before has departed. But I need to tell her. "These . . . these dreams," I whisper. "They come. They are like . . ." I go no further. It is silly now.

"Dreams?" Violet looms above me. "I'll ask Dr. Wan about it. Maybe it's the medication."

I nod. So silly. So *foreign*.

She drives me home. The day is bright, plastic. We pass a child walking, a man bent on a bicycle. I rode a bicycle to work for years, not a fancy one like this man's, but an upright, with fenders and a basket up front for my tools. Gone now, like so much else, though I still feel the pull of the chain, and the rhythm. I remember teaching the girls to ride, the glee on Violet's small face at the moment she balanced, her tricks after that—no hands, standing on the seat, steering backward. The bell on her bike that gave a strange, strident ring. A crow lifts in flight and I think on how odd it is, she and I, this history swerving between us. Can conversation be had without the past so intruding? We do not try now. We do not speak. I stare out at oak trees and moss hanging like beards. I have lived here forty years but it is not so familiar.

A man mows circles with a riding mower, an old woman lifts her paper from her driveway and stares. The car's brakes squeak. The azaleas in my yard need pruning, and trimming.

The house is empty since Carol died. The hospital bed, the linens, the diapers, the medicines—all gone. I cared for her myself until almost the end. It became my routine, my obligation. I grew to accept and abhor it. I envision now a new bed, new medicines, a silver wheelchair. Accidents of the bowel and bladder. Days spent being cleaned, transported to doctors, plied with medication, fed vegetable mush. I cannot bear the thought of these things, or of having them done now for me.

"Let me make you some lunch," Violet says.

"No, I'm all right."

We stare at each other. Violet has Carol's light hair, my dark eyes and skin. She is overweight though still beautiful. She is no longer young. Why are things between us so hard? I place the blame on my working, my absence. She was absent later, with her mother not well. She has been irresponsible. She has a son, Wilfred, who is fifteen and smart but has difficulties. She is protective, keeping Wilfred from me, though I want only to help. This frustrates me so! I remember Wilfred, too, as a baby, a little brown thing so unlike the girls. But like me. I had wished to start over, to be things with Wilfred I had not been before. I still wish this, still try. I had so wanted a son.

"Some tea?"

"No." Her sister, Lissette, is older. She lives in Montreal. She visits once a year, sometimes less often. She calls on the holidays, my birthday. The calls are not long.

"At least let me get you some movies, okay?"

I relent. I have a weakness for movies. After coming to America, frantic in my desire to learn English, Carol and I went to movies. Lots of movies. Sometimes the same four or five times. The first talking pictures, the high-pitched, fast-paced voices Carol claimed she, too, had a hard time understanding. I have loved movies since, perhaps because I think of us there, in those times. I read a lot, too, and in time I enjoyed that as well. Shakespeare, poetry, mysteries. I began to crave books. I found myself thinking in English, forgetting Turkish words. That is the odd thing about the dreams these past days. I have not heard Turkish spoken since before I left New York. I have not spoken it myself since childhood.

Violet returns, with *The Searchers* and *Breakfast at Tiffany's*. I consent to her fixing lunch. I watch the movies—I have seen each dozens of times—trying to lose myself again in these voices and people that are so forceful, so American. Today, though, the dream pulls me. I am distracted. I plow though the chaff of my youth, the bits and pieces that survived war and injury, remembering some things: my father, the veins in his hands, the way he balanced enormous loads on his shoulders. My mother had died much before—her I remember less well. I remember my brother best. Burak was two years older. He went to military school, he wore a little uniform, he wanted always to become a soldier. I trailed behind him like a stray dog, imitating the way he walked, the way he held his head. He was popular with boys and girls, the older people as well. He loved *sucuk*, a type of sausage, and *döner*. He died in the war. This I remember, my father's face at the news of his death. As if the world itself had darkened, as if life had left him, too. He did not live much longer, my father. These things are clear in my mind.

Other things are lost. It is strange, these absences. So much time has gone past. The history I created for myself—a childhood, a hometown—sometimes mixes with the shards of my memory and connects things, confuses them. I have a paper somewhere with things written in the hospital in London, things that came back as I struggled to remember. There is not much there. A few events, a few places, people. Very little of the war. Memories flared sometimes afterward, arriving in bursts of color, but on the whole not much more drifted back than came before I left London: the races we held as boys, the dripping wax of a candle, a group of men bent and kneeling to pray. I remember dreaming as a child of coming to America. Once I arrived, the life I lived before seemed lived by another, someone muted and dreamlike. Someone I remember no longer.

The movies end. There are things to be dealt with—arrangements for my cat, Sultan, letting the relatives know. Violet has taken on most of this effort. Still, it is strange to hear myself say, "I have been diagnosed with a brain tumor," or "They operate on Wednesday." Reactions range from shock ("Oh, my God!") to stoicism ("You'll get through it. My aunt Edith was left for dead six times and still went to Talladega last year") to various religious exhortations ("Pray without ceasing," "God's will be done," or, with repetition, "Repent while there's still time!"). The religious appeals are from Carol's relatives, the flock that surround us in southwestern Georgia, the reason we came here in the first place. Carol grew up in Albany, sixty miles north of Wadesboro. Her people are a religious lot, deniers one and all of the fact that I am not a Christian, or a churchgoer, or anything in between. I left Islam when I came to America, but declined to follow Carol into her church. My daughters were raised as Christians, and I have attended church musicals and weddings and many similar things. I accept all prayers for my soul. But I am too old to start over. Death will be death.

I think of this later in the day as I attend, of all things, a funeral. Carol's nephew Stephen died before I entered the hospital. Stephen was a strange man, loud and boisterous and prosperous. He died on a round-the-world trip. I generally avoid funerals, but Violet asks me to go and I want to be amenable, to prolong our time together. Will Wilfred be there? She says he has "therapy" and will say little more. This shielding is typical. She acts as if others might take him, even me! I resent this. It only strengthens my desire to be with him. I tell myself that she must live her life, that he is her son, not mine, that I should not interfere. But I am drawn to him, this boy. I have much yet to offer him.

Stephen's wife, Mary Beth, meets us in the funeral home foyer. She is a large woman, Mary Beth. White bosoms like watermelons rest in a black dress too small.

"Oh, Uncle Emmett! I'm so sorry to hear about your brain!" She makes it sound as if the thing has run off.

I murmur condolences regarding Stephen. Others stand in the foyer, regarding me slyly through gaps in their eyes. It is always this way—I am the foreigner, the outsider. My children have adapted but I never will. I accept this. I am accustomed to head turns, exclusion. I take in the flowers and ushers and programs, the people. I greet and smile, I am friendly. But my estrangement is magnified. I am a ghost here, a shadow. I am not one of them. I wonder, as I stand nodding—will my funeral be next?

I have not thought much about death, even at Carol's passing, even as at my age it cannot be far. Parts of my body do not work as they did, but my mind is still present. I am not frail. I awake and I think of the day, not the blackness to follow. I do not dwell on sad thoughts. The thing that scares me so is to end up like Carol, alive but not knowing it, saddled not with pain but with nothingness, feeling nothing. I would rather be dead, but is death so much different? I picture the departed as floating and released. Carol was trapped in a shell. To be released seems quite pleasant if I think of things in this way, but what I think doesn't matter. All things must come. Death has always been waiting.

We enter the parlor. The pews have mostly filled. One by one, each row of mourners makes a pilgrimage up front to glance at the casket. I find this custom so strange, even for the South. The viewing, the tears. The rustle of clothing, the gentle coughs. There is a funeral home nearby with a drive-through for viewing—a horn's honk pulls the curtain back. I have driven through once. What is the nursery song I learned with my English? "Life is but a . . ." I force a smile from my lips.

I remember Carol's funeral. So similar—many of those present today were there then. I sat with Violet and Lissette but could not look at my daughters. Their mother who cared for them all the length of their lives, yet at the end they were not there for her. Violet lived in the same town! They offered little assistance. There were a few phone calls, a handful of forced visits. By then Carol did not know them, or anyone—this was long before she passed on. It was difficult to be with her. Still, they owed her respect and failed to give it. I swallow as I think this. I squint back more unformed tears.

We stand and approach Stephen's casket. The odor of flowers

is strong. Stephen's stomach protrudes like a baked cake, visible on a greater level than his face, large and, apparently, bare. At first I think gravity has realigned his shirt, but when I peer inside I discover that he is in fact shirtless, his chest and stomach an odd brownish pink, thin strands of hair erect about his nipples. A pair of shorts peeks below his great belly, tucked into the folds of a sheet. His face is waxen, freshly shaved, his hair combed delicately to one side. He looks better than he did in life.

"He'd always wanted to be buried this way," Violet whispers as we return to our seats. "In his shorts."

I shake my head. I think again about Violet, and Wilfred. Wilfred was born when Violet was forty-five, via a father never identified or acknowledged. He is her second child. Her first was given up for adoption when she was sixteen. Carol and I blamed each other the first time—a child at sixteen, without marriage? Our shameful Violet. The first father a Slavic boy whose parents only shrugged and said in English, "Goddammit." Later I blamed America, its thin roots and permissiveness. One of my few memories from before the war is of American missionaries telling us of skyscrapers, of subways. It sounded so full of possibility then, so modern. And was it not so? Despite the hardships I faced, the difficulties in having skin slightly darker, the need to fall back, to work more. My children have known abundance, though I question how well it has served them. I place Wilfred's troubles here, too, although he also endures the discrimination I suffered. It is the cement that binds us. Wilfred is picked on, ostracized. His unknown father was black.

A woman begins to sing but my mind remains on Wilfred. He and I once met like spies, at the grocer's. Tuesdays and Thursdays.

Violet does not know this. We would talk, he would tell me things. I told him how Turkish sons are so prized because they remain part of their parents' family even as the girls move away. He has not shown up at the store for some time, though. I still go there. I still wait.

I look back at the coffin and think again about death. I have outlived so many. Why am I afraid?

A burst of cold comes from a gusting air conditioner. I smell perfume and sweat. I think about the dreams. *Hatırlamak*—that is the Turkish word. *Remember*. But I do not remember, not much.

The room has stilled now, suits and dresses smoothed, throats cleared, necks bowed. I shut my eyes again, the thump of blood in my jaw. Someone is speaking, but I think only of memory, of what is lost, what never occurred. I open my eyes to Violet, to the imprint of my ancestry, my genes, in her face. I touch her hand, the warmth in it, the slight dampness. And I smile.

That night I sleep soundly, at least for a time. I wake at 2:15 and am pleased, as I have not dreamed. But sleep fails to return. I turn and reposition myself, bunch my pillow, attempt to deaden my thoughts. I count my breaths, slowly, deliberately, until I reach a narrow cliff and fall from it, knowing I am dreaming but unable to stop it. Light shimmers, boards creak. A clock clicks, ticks, and falls quiet.

In the dream morning breaks—a harsh, red morning, raw like a blistering skin. The wind has withered and withdrawn, allowing odors to germinate and swirl. It smells of animals and decay, of death. I walk my horse among shabby tents and patched-together shoes, eyeing the displaced as they struggle to wake. They seem less loathsome as they rouse from sleep, less contemptible. Earlier in the journey some would have scowled, or begged, but their faces now wear only hungry stares, neither hateful nor hopeful, more resigned than resentful. Here and there a corpse lies in stiff coldness, its face clenched in final grimace, its eyes focused away. I stare at one, an old woman with her brown mouth open as if she wants to sing or speak. The deaths are unavoidable, a function of moving thousands of people over hundreds of miles in difficult and primitive conditions. There is little that can be done about them, even if I wish to. They will be left where they lie, for predators, human and otherwise, to plunder.

The deportees have thus far been spared the onset of rampant disease. I have heard rumors of other groups, farther to the south and west, where entire caravans have been struck down by fever and sickness. Cholera. Smallpox. Dysentery. It makes the dirty work of the gendarmes hazardous and even dirtier, exposing us to sicknesses of the herd. At least the soldiers fighting in the north, reinforcements for whom pass periodically in flashes of button and uniform, have opportunities for bravery and valor. Ours is a dull exercise in caretaking, more prison duty than warfare. And how ironic for a shepherd to succumb to a disease of his flock! I would much prefer death in glorious battle, matching my strength against that of my enemy. But I will do as I have been told. I must serve as a gendarme before entering the army. Advancement will present reward, and opportunity. I will be patient.

I know why I stride my horse through the seedy circle of tents this morning—not to check on the group's health, or to kick at new corpses, or to search for hidden contraband. I rarely tread this close to the encampment, in avoidance of disease or attack. Eyeing the squinting faces, I search for the mismatched eyes, remembering and re-remembering so that I begin almost to question whether I saw her in the night. I reach one end of the cloth piles and bodies, turn and pace its edge. I do not find her.

A figure on horseback appears in the distance, swathed in a halo of dust. I watch as a man draws forward to one of my guards, engages, then moves in my direction. He is an officer of some type, either army or police, his back straight under his long gray coat. A bristly mustache the color of iron hides his mouth. His eyes show surprise at my youth.

"Greetings, *ağa*." The man does not dismount.

"Effendi." I motion to the gendarme Tevfik to bring water.

"How many have you here?" The man squeezes his face to glance at the throng behind me.

"Around seven hundred."

The man nods and takes a gulp of the proffered water. "Any trouble?"

I shake my head.

"You will reach Kilis tomorrow," the man continues. "Then another few days to Katma. You will be detained in Katma until further instructions."

I nod, grateful for this information. For many days I have followed a route based solely on that of the caravans before me. Originally I was told that we were headed for the coast, then the border, but further instruction has been scattered and varied. It is all unfamiliar territory, as I have never been south of Malatya. The man's news produces a fluttering beneath my breastbone and a sigh that is almost audible. Relief floods my lungs. This long, dusty trek may soon be concluded.

"Is there any word of the war?" I ask, my voice deep and forceful.

The man squints again. "There is fierce fighting in the Caucasus," he replies. "And at Çanakkale Boğazi." He pauses. "I hear our troops are doing well." His brow collapses in a furry line, as if to inquire why I am not fighting.

"My cousins are in the Eighth Army Corps," I say by way of explanation. "I was instructed to do this before I rejoin them." I fold my arms.

The man grins, exposing brown teeth. "My cousins, too, are in the army. We are from Adana." He pauses, as if this should impress me. "Do you have any young women in your group? I have ridden so far."

A chill creeps up my shoulder blades. "But of course." I whirl and ride back into the encampment.

"You, and you!" I point at two different girls, careful to ensure that neither is she. Tevfik pulls them from their wailing mothers, drags them forward before the visitor. They cower, whimpering, then sobbing, their despairing relatives gathered behind me. I remain at a respectful distance, fearful of having offended with my choices, concerned that he might instead go and find what I have only just sought. But he seems pleased, motioning for the girls to follow, which they do after much looking back and prodding from Tevfik and Mustafa.

I yell to the other gendarmes. "Prepare to move."

. . .

I awake in a panic, wet with perspiration. Sitting up, cold in my dampness, I take in the darkened room, the pleated curtains, the quilt-covered bed. My bedroom. Early morning. America. Home.

"Papa, are you okay?"

I collapse back to wet sheets.

Violet stands before me. "You've been thrashing and moaning all night. Did you dream?"

"Yes." My voice is craggy. If I close my eyes I know I will return, to wind and sadness and hunger and cold.

"Is it the same dream?" Violet doesn't wait for an answer. "I meant to ask Dr. Wan about that. I'm sure it's related to your medication, or to the tumor itself."

The tumor. I struggle out of bed, pulling at my pajamas. Today is what, Tuesday? There are things I must do.

"Are you hungry? I could fix you some breakfast."

"No." I wrap my robe around myself. "I have much to do today, much to do."

"Like what?"

I need to go to the grocery, to see Wilfred. So I lie. "I need to get my hair cut."

Violet shrugs. "I'll take you."

I launch my protest. I do not need her help. I do not need anything. But then I cannot drive, per Dr. Wan. I stand with my head down, my fists clenching, unclenching.

"Do you work today?" My voice is a growl. She had insisted on staying. This pleased me at first.

"I'm taking the day off. We've been through this. Get dressed and I'll make some tea."

She works at an accounting firm. "Wilfred," I say. "Should he not stay here, too?"

"He's got school, Papa. He knows the bus from my place. I had someone stay with him. He'll come see you after your procedure."

I thrash at my clothes. Why must she shield him? Her first pregnancy, the shame she brought then—did it impact this second? Carol and I never considered keeping the first child and raising it as our own. Carol had health issues even then, the beginnings of what would later be diagnosed as Parkinson's disease, which would progress into dementia. It would not have worked out. Still, I look now at Violet, thinking how things might have been different. She would have stayed near us—maybe married?—and been once through child rearing. She might now be a grandmother. I think about this, how experience brings maturity. I consider the possibility that I have made her this way.

A mirror flickers, showing scars on my face. I peer out again, down the hallway at Violet. The odd thing, the thing I cannot say now, is that her presence in the house reminds me of Carol. The illness. The obligation then to my efforts, the duty. Carol was a demanding patient. I owed it to her—she had saved my life—but I grew almost bitter, to the point where I now fear disability the way others fear death. I will not be a burden. And yet here I am, undergoing this treatment, prolonging the inevitable, foisting myself on my daughter. Would my death not release her? I have lived a long time.

"I'm worried about you, Papa." We are at the table now. Violet toys with her teacup. "You've never been sick."

This is true, for the most part. I have been healthy, amazingly so. I cannot explain my physique. I used to swim some, but not anymore. I rode a bike for many years. Even then, people used to comment on my body. "How *old* are you?" they would ask. The doctors are always amazed. I quit smoking when I was fifty. I drink only tea. Perhaps this is why I have gone along with this surgery. I have a few aches and false teeth and sometimes I lose my balance, but for the most part I feel fine.

"Do not worry," I say to her. It is I who worry. I cannot tell her that I have enjoyed my freedom since Carol's death. I have my little routines. My neighbor, Carl Rowe, a fellow widower, is a fine man. We see each other some days. I watch my movies. I have become used to cooking and cleaning, having done it while Carol was sick these past years. I see Violet occasionally, and Wilfred. I talk to Lissette. I am not ready to die.

Violet leans toward me. "Listen, Papa, I know you don't want to hear this, but I think we're going to have to get someone in here to watch you. Either that or move you to a facility where you can be monitored. I can't stay here full-time."

I glance at her. She says this with such compassion, her lips just trembling, that I am unprepared for it, unwilling even to argue about it. Her duty, her responsibility. I have waited for it, wanted it. And yet when it comes, this sadness comes, too.

"Papa."

I shuffle my feet. Her eyes are up now, the brown eyes like mine. "No facility," I say.

"Okay, no facility. I'll see about getting a home health nurse."

I am tired. I look away.

. . .

The home health nurse turns out to be a pudgy, redheaded fellow named Ted. He arrives with amazing swiftness, leaving me to wonder if things had been already arranged. Violet orients him to the house, then stakes him out in the guest room.

"Is he staying the night?" I whisper, when I have her alone.

"Of course. He's monitoring you, remember?"

I grunt. Ted moves to join us. He has dark eyeglasses and a tattoo of a dagger on one arm. He says he's studying to be an emergency medical technician.

I maneuver Violet off to one side. "How much is this costing—all of it?"

She shrugs. "Papa. You have the money. Plus, the insurance covers part of it."

I grind my teeth. One of my failures has been in teaching my children about money. I came to this country with nothing. Money has thus always been so important to me. I worked as a plumber's assistant, a plumber, a plumbing contractor, a general contractor. I made a good salary, at least at the end. I have saved. I have invested, taken risks, but I have always been frugal. My children fling money like rain.

Violet departs to run errands, leaving me alone with this Ted. I find him a talkative sort, carrying on about baseball and popular music and things of which I have little interest. He is, however, a movie fan, and we watch *Doctor Zhivago* together, start to finish. I ask at its end whether he wants me to fix him lunch. He refuses, but I fix him lunch anyway—scrambled eggs and toast—which he eats like a starving man. I ask him about his tattoo, which he says he got in Panama City on a dare. It's a Turkish dagger, he says. I laugh at this.

Something about it makes me think of my brother Burak, rekindling a brief memory, an image of Burak running. Perhaps a dagger was involved? I play this over and over. I see him look back, see his thin-lipped smile. I wonder that these bursts of memory still come, even now. Should I have taken steps to enhance them? Others suggested—even Carol, I recall—that I return to Turkey, travel to my hometown, engage more speakers of Turkish. This never appealed to me. I was busy as a young man. I had no money. Even as I grew older I had no desire to go back. I was living my life, in America. I had a family to support. Everyone in Turkey was dead.

From time to time my children would inquire of their heritage—my heritage. At one point Lissette even took to wearing Turkish clothes and jewelry. I never encouraged it. I wanted them to think of themselves as Americans, not immigrants. In this Carol and I agreed. I spoke no Turkish with them, nor did we associate with Turkish émigrés or their families. We ate American food, watched American TV, celebrated American holidays. I deflected all questions related to my past. I became an American citizen. I never missed my life before, perhaps because I remembered so little of it. The parts I did remember were of family and hardship, conflict and death.

Ted washes the dishes, announces that he needs to take my blood pressure. After that, he assures me, we have time to catch *High Noon* before my appointment at four. He talks as he works, telling me about Macon, his hometown, of how his mother says that eating dill pickles before bed prevents dreams. I nod at this.

The doorbell rings and I answer, thinking perhaps it is Violet. Instead, it is Mrs. Fleming. This is an inconvenience.

Mrs. Fleming is a neighbor, an elderly widow (though perhaps ten years my junior). She has shown unusual attentiveness since Carol died, delivering covered dishes, dropping by unannounced. Carl says she has a thing for me. She is an attractive woman, I suppose, for her age, with an erect carriage and white teeth. Carl, who weighs 270 pounds and has diabetes and heart problems, says he wants to "do" her. She shows no interest in him.

"Hi," she says, showing her teeth. She wants to be invited in.

I pull back, opening the door. We step into the living room, the room that is never used.

"I heard about your sickness." She has a strange way of speaking, where her *s*'s sound like *f*'s.

I nod. Wadesboro is a small town. I assume everyone knows everything. "Please, sit down."

I do not offer her a drink, for I do not wish to prolong things. She takes a seat on the couch. I sit in a chair opposite, not on the couch.

"Are you doing okay?"

I nod. "Yes. Okay."

"When is your surgery?"

"Tomorrow." I hear the man, Ted, in the other room, and hope he will be quiet. I do not want her to know of him.

"Can I get you anything? I'm so worried about you." She shifts her legs, revealing for a moment a white valley of undergarment.

I stare, transfixed by this brief exposure, until a memory springs forth of Burak telling me about women, about life. I had vague notions about sex, notions he solidified in some detail. He told me of his explorations, of a village girl named Sena. I remember being amazed and impressed, enthralled. For a moment I hear his voice, the cadence and crack of his syllables. It is so wonderful. Burak twice in one day! Then it vanishes, leaving behind stirred, empty space.

I find myself wrapped in long arms. Mrs. Fleming is kissing me, her mouth like a bird on my neck. Her body is pressed against mine. I see the down on her cheekbone.

"Oh, excuse me." Ted enters, makes a retreat. "I heard something. I didn't know someone was here."

Mrs. Fleming pulls back, flustered, but not much.

I mutter, "He is staying with me, to . . . monitor." My breath is short.

Mrs. Fleming appears undeterred. I put my hands on her elbows.

"Thank you for your visit," I say. I make my voice strong.

She brushes at her hair, then presents a bright smile. "I'll be praying for you."

"Thank you."

She hesitates still. I close the door. But something shifts in my body, something I have not felt for some time. Desire? I am so old for desire.

I force Ted to take me to the grocery, the Piggly Wiggly, where Wilfred goes. They know me here, the clerks and cashiers, know that I linger, that I never buy much.

Ted comes in also, which I do not like. I do not wish to be rushed. I take the free coffee, even though I do not drink it. We stay, but not as long as I wish. I watch the people, take note of the things they purchase: the boxes of corn flakes, the frozen food in a tray. They push double carts, mounded with pizzas, with dog food, with packaged goods. I stare at the coffee, the purples and grays on its top. The door opens and closes. Wilfred does not come.

In the dream there are colors—so brilliant as to make daylight dull. Sound, too, even smell. I can feel things, feel the cold seep through blankets. Taste? There is halva, *sucuk*, food seared on a flame. I curl my tongue, lick my lips. I am alive here, anticipating.

The last strands of dusk light the sky, coating lean clouds shades of orange and gray. The air hangs smooth and heavy, stirred by the occasional breeze tossed from the plateau below. Gendarmes poke and prod, faces down, eyes intent, separating old women who wail and curse gibberish but do nothing more. One by one the men retrieve what they seek: young, struggling females. Several of the selected weep, one yells and cries, another stands stoic and quiet. Some are barely older than children. The other guards watch from their spots at the camp perimeter, jealous, wanting, coerced by duty to forgo nightly pleasure. One perimeter guard, Izzet, had partaken one night when he believed I was asleep—his back still bears the scars of this past miscalculation.

I find her upon the last guard's selection. The short, heavily bearded gendarme named Mustafa emerges from a scrum of deportees pulling a girl by her hair. She is tall, taller than most, her dark hair cascading from beneath a man's faded cap. She wears men's trousers and a white blouse voluminous enough to hide any evidence of her breasts. Her head twists briefly as they near where

I stand, long enough for me to recognize a jawline, a manner of movement, a hint of defiance even in captivity.

"Let me see this one," I demand. Mustafa hesitates before pushing her forward. She raises her head slowly, almost regally, the hair blocking her face. I reach out a finger to part it, a groom removing a veil. I pause. The mismatched eyes glare back at me, their whites now red and wild as an animal's, large and frightened, bright and translucent. Even in the fading light there is no mistaking them, the lightness of one eye against the other, the petal of a flower against its dark center. She looks past me, as if expecting someone else, fidgeting, breaking free of Mustafa's grasp. The wailing in the background intensifies. The older women trailing catch up.

"I will take her," I say.

Mustafa growls. He is thick and strong, able to lift large loads and tote water barrels with ease. I once saw him lift a recalcitrant camel. He is older than I, maybe mid-twenties, from Pertek, near my village, an acquaintance of my cousins. I have heard he served prison time in Diyarbekır.

"That will be all."

He twists his fingers deep in his beard. The noise around us eases. Heads turn, onlookers retreat. For a while no one moves or says anything. Even the older women quiet. Then he turns and stomps away.

I look at the girl. "Come with me." I motion away from the crowd.

She proceeds. The moon has risen, a quarter globe eaten by darkness. I keep her in front of me, directing her away from the camp with prods of my rifle, down a small ravine and onto a sandy streambed. We march up it some distance, past rocks that take

34

the shape of silent workers—here a gravedigger, there a basket weaver—past a small hill, until no sound from the camp can be heard. The stream sparkles, broadening in spots to a full stride in width, narrowing in others to no more than a trickle. I wonder if she is thirsty. The deportees are permitted water only after the gendarmes, and then sometimes for a price. Often the wells have been polluted by previous encampments. Corpses have been discovered in several. Even the gendarmes sometimes go without.

"Do you want to drink?"

She turns. The cap has been lost now, her hair falling free down her face. She holds my gaze for some time, perhaps not understanding. Then she sinks to her knees and cups her hands, pushing hair behind her ears to sip.

I stare at her, at the lean, stretching figure, the buttocks lifted high in the air. The water splashes and patters, insects motor and hum, a bird calls from somewhere, but all function outside me as if I do not exist, as if I've become paralyzed, encased in a moment to be remembered forever. Some part of me thinks to join her in drinking, but I remain motionless. I wait. She rises, a single, supple movement, brushing hair from her face, wiping her mouth on her forearm. I place my gun on the ground. I will later recall excruciating desire, broad thirst, and certainty. I will remember the feel of the breeze, the position of the moon, the smell of the damp earth. I step toward her.

A painful erectness brings me halfway awake. I twist, the dream slipping from me. Things outside—the great breathing air conditioner, a distant truck's groan—interfere, interrupt. Recognition follows. A clock spins, five a.m. All is dark.

A snoring comes from the other room. Violet? I remember, the home health person. Ted. Violet is to be here at six. I struggle up from the bed.

I am shaken, pulled by the dream. Why must I dream this? I was a soldier, not a gendarme. I scan my memory, coaxing, summoning forth some recollection . . . but there is nothing. No girl. No dusty trek.

I shower. Violet arrives; I am pleased at her attentiveness. We say good-bye to sleepy-eyed Ted and make our way to the hospital. So soon, this procedure! Radiosurgery, beams of focused radiation more precise than a surgeon's knife—I make no claim to understand it. I am a quiet patient. Dr. Wan said the procedure will last several hours, that a preparation is first required, a frame attached. I wonder again why we bother.

An electric door whooshes. I am maneuvered, catalogued. A man tilts his head and its raccoon's-tail hairpiece, steering me down floors shined to slick, sparkling brightness. Others march past, sneaker-clad, holding clipboards. A redheaded man pushes an overflowing cart. All nod. I say hello. I recognize Faye Blanton, whose husband, Bill, is in the Rotary Club. I see Terry Crabtree, Carol's friend. A smiling man reminds me of the gendarme Izzet. I scan patients in a holding area, focusing on ear shapes ranging from rounded to crimped, elongated to flattened, corrugated to bearded to tilted to protruding. Would I know Burak's if I saw it? Wilfred's? I finger my own ear, its thick knobs and hackles.

We wait. I flip through one of the magazines arranged for those waiting, an old news periodical. I have little interest. But it is there that I see it as I turn the last pages, a photo of dark-eyed women and children standing on a dirt roadway, their faces solemn and gray.

I flinch. Air exits my lungs. I recognize these people. In the dream I am driving them to Katma.

I push the magazine from me, then scratch at it, reexamine. I grasp and grab at my chair.

"Papa!"

I breathe, and things still. The article below the picture describes an anniversary, the seventy-fifth anniversary of the Armenian genocide. But it is the picture that holds me. My hands shake and flutter.

"What is it?" Violet cocks her head.

My hands tremble still. My heart is beating, beating. "It is nothing," I say, but my mind is adrift. The dreams, this . . . I know about the Armenians, of course. There were a number in Mezre, the village in which I grew up. They were neighbors, traders, artisans, bakers. Some fought in the war. There was a resistance, of sorts, an alliance with Russia, our enemy. Many had left the country, or been forced to leave. They were different, but I had no quarrels with them. How then to explain this, this recognition? These dreams?

My name is called, the wheelchair spun. We enter a room with yellowish wallpaper. A nurse shaves my scalp, the sound odd and distant like a scratch against cardboard. The metal frame to be affixed to my skull is presented, measured, held aloft, taken away. A technician appears and delivers a shot. Then everything blurs: swarming figures in white, unidentifiable background music, words spoken but not understood, Violet's pink lips. People stand as in the magazine's picture, unsmiling, downcast. I feel the onset of coldness, the brush of fierce wind. Then darkness, like the drawing of a curtain at the end of a play.

The girl speaks to me. We are back at the stream, the moonlight drawing outlines, of lips, hair, eyelashes, shoulders. I am aware, at some level, of confusion, of not expecting to be here, of the sense of a movie interrupted then resumed. I even know, somehow, that a procedure is under way, a mass in my skull is held in mid-eradication. But still I am here, at this stream in the hills with a girl I have pulled away, my desire as pressing as if it never left. Dryness thickens my mouth.

"I have been here before."

The words slow my approach. Did I know she spoke my language? Some of the deportees do, though usually in a languid, marble-mouthed accent.

"I used to travel often with my father. He . . . is a spice merchant. We have visited Adana, Smyrna, even Baghdad."

I have been to none of these places. My father was a knife maker.

"Have you seen the ziggurats? The best is on the road to Baghdad. The hill behind us reminds me of one, overgrown now and forgotten." She turns to examine the small rise, barely visible in the background.

I examine her from behind, the dark, thick hair, the narrow hips tapering up to their zenith. The dark skin. How can she prattle on, knowing the fate that awaits her? She is stalling, she must be, for she would have seen too much on this trek not to recognize the reason for her culling. The memory of her red, wild eyes comes back to me, the disdain I feel for her race. They are all so superior, these Armenians, so prone to condescension, boastful of their education, miserly and clannish, worshipping their God in their little round churches. Better than us—I heard one now-dead deportee proclaim the empire's demise without Armenian bankers, lawyers, merchants, and traders. Yet if the Armenians are so smart and the Turks so stupid, how have we arrived at the current situation? Power will dictate, just as in nature, just as in battle. Just as it will tonight.

"What did you say?"

She turns back to me. "A ziggurat. They were temples of a sort, used in the ancient sects, before Christ or Muhammad, before anything. They were meant to be houses of religion, where the gods could be close to mankind."

I pause, digesting this information, poised between violence and something I cannot identify, curiosity perhaps, even tenderness.

"Shall we climb to the top of the hill?" she asks. Her mouth flattens, the beginnings of a smile. "Bring ourselves closer to God?"

She is off before I can answer, moving laterally, then climbing. I grab my gun and follow. She moves swiftly, at times too swiftly for me to keep pace, such that at one point I conclude she is attempting to elude me, and call out for her to stop. If she hears me she does not show it, but appears moments later, hands on hips, one leg in front of the other, waiting with the air of a governess slowed by a child. She gives such an appearance of innocence, of a girl playing hide-and-seek, that I reconsider my appraisal. I envision the shock she will experience when we reach the top, the change in her demeanor at the onset of adult pursuits. I find the thought invigorating, my efforts redoubling. I see myself from above, a predator fixed on its prey. Gasps follow my exertion, the taste of salt in my mouth, the tantalizing scent of conquest sifting up through my nostrils. I hear myself snorting, feel the tightening in my groin. I reach the hill's crest, and slow.

I cannot find her. I start to shout, then stop, probing instead among the bushes and trees adorning the small plateau. All is silent, even the birds. A knob of larger trees stands in the middle, cathedral-like, branches lifted skyward; I make for this, leading with my rifle, suddenly aware of the possibility of entrapment, of a confederate secreted in murderous ambush. But then laughter echoes, a stirring of leaves, and she appears from behind a tree as if disgorged from its center. I stop. I point the gun at her. Her smile slowly withdraws.

"Take off your clothes."

She stands motionless. Then slowly, ever so slowly, she shakes her head.

I step forward, the gun bobbing in front of me.

"I will shoot you."

She shakes her head again.

I edge closer still, to a point at which the rifle is only a short distance from her chest, to where she could reach and touch its smooth barrel.

"Now." My breathing has shortened.

She does not move.

With one hand I catch hold of her blouse, ripping it down the front in a screeching surrender of fabric. The movement brings me closer to her, the rifle briefly to her side, such that if she wanted she could grab my gun hand and wrestle for the weapon, but she does not. The force of the assault does not pull her toward me. Perhaps she has anticipated the attack and steeled herself against it. She remains still, her arms at her sides, the tattered cloth sliding off her slim torso to heap on the ground below.

The moonlight falls onto her bare shoulders, thin and undeveloped like a boy's, her small breasts with their dark, chocolate-like nipples. The oversized pants seem clownish now. The mismatched eyes shine clearly. From one angle she appears dark and sensuous, from the other cool and aloof. I find it amazing, this effect of looking at two different people. I place the rifle on the ground. I loosen my shirt, pull it over my head, searching her face for the tiniest guilty hunger, but there is nothing, no trembling lip, no piteous pleading. Just those eyes, dissecting, analyzing, as if she has seen all this before. Perhaps she has.

I unbuckle my belt. My pants drop to the ground. I bend and kiss her, my hands on her shoulders, my tongue thrust deep in her mouth. She does not reciprocate, but neither does she clamp her mouth shut or resist. Her eyes remain open, her body taut but not rigid.

I force her into a crouch, then to a prone position on the ground. I reach my fingers under her pants and pull them from her legs, careful for some reason not to rip these, exposing her lower body to the night. I stare at her for a moment, at the smooth skin and long legs, then return my face to hers.

Her mouth has shifted position. Her thin lips move. "Why?" she asks.

I hesitate. Why what? Why this act of congress, handed down from Allah himself? Why the deportation? Why her? Why me? I feel my desire starting to wither, my hesitation forming a course. I grab her breast to right myself, place my mouth back on hers, my other hand between her legs, but all to no appreciable effect. She continues to stare, the eyes now unnerving, as if they have somehow brought this on, have visualized this, have known that this word at this time would trigger this reaction. I grab her hand and direct it to my groin, a final, unsuccessful effort at resurrection. Then I roll off her, shaking, an emasculated fury building within me.

She remains prone. The mismatched eyes, so beguiling before, now gleam with bewitchment and evil, the leer of a venomous changeling. Her mouth is closed. I kick the ground with my boot.

I know then I will have to kill her, that should this episode spread through the caravan it will undermine my authority, perhaps endanger my life. I rise to my knees. Wrapping my hands around her neck, the tremble of her breath runs up through my fingers. She does not move. I press down, into tissue and cartilage. I close my eyes against the mesmerizing gaze. A series of convulsions erupt beneath me, a single, choking gasp, the sound reverberating longer than it should, louder, her voice in it, the voice that only minutes before had asked if I'd seen the ziggurats.

I hesitate. I ease my grip. Then, shaking, I release her, my hands falling free to my sides.

Her eyes widen, tears at their corners, her lungs refilling in small, quivering pants. She makes no other sound. An ember of anger springs up from my chest, a need to rectify, to address the amplifying humiliation I know will rise and suffocate me. I lift my arms back toward her. Her eyes follow the motion. She does not brace against it, or flinch, or tremble, or whimper. It occurs to me suddenly that she wants this somehow, that she knows this will happen, that she is fully and humbly prepared to die. At this place, on this hilltop, closer to the gods.

I pause again. My arms return to my sides. I lower my head to her neck, to where the rhythm of her pulse buzzes up through my nostrils.

· 4 ·

It takes time to focus, to recognize the suite at the oncology center, to pinpoint the music humming somewhere, the people bumping about. I am in the middle of a room yet no one seems to see me. My skin is cold. Could it be I am dead now, a corpse justly ignored? But then a nurse appears above me and asks a soft question. I lift my head.

"What happened?" I ask.

The nurse looks like Violet. She squeezes my hand. "Nothing, yet. The frame was put on, and the imaging—don't you remember? We have to get the automatic positioning set."

Pressure tugs at the corners of my head, coupled with a general numbness and brief, grating pain. A vague recollection sweeps over, of needles and screws, of Dr. Wan yanking my head like a bridle. I stare at a video camera up on a wall, thinking of the camera we once had. A Bell and Howell. We could not afford it. I wanted the girls to have memories, though, to see themselves. I wanted them to be happy.

The grogginess from before beckons. "Is it okay if I sleep?"

"Sure."

I drift toward slumber. Time passes. It is night—no, a gray dawn. I am under a house, planting pipe. It is cold, the soil damp. I blow on my hands. But then I fall back to the dream, the dream that continues; the long, dusty trek. I see her eyes and their burning. I hear her gasping for air. Darkness rushes but my arms are pinned back like a fly with pinched wings. I twist, I elevate my head and its tottering frame. My voice catches.

"What is your name?" I ask.

I drape my shirt over, to cover her. To amend.

She answers in slowness, in syllables. "A-ra-xie."

She looks away, the starlight brightening her light eye.

I stare, and wonder.

We return to the caravan, she and I. She wears my shirt. We do not speak, or if we do it fails to register. I speak her name in my mind. We part as we reach the first tents, their flaps smoky in the gray dawn. I have no explanation, no plan for addressing the situation I have created. I give her a small blanket, to wrap her bruised neck.

No one sees us approach. The forward guard, Ali, sleeps with his head to one side, his mouth open to the cool morning air. The rear guard, Izzet, paces the caravan's other side, barely visible in the dim light. Little else moves within the clumps of cloth and dust, only the rustle of a body turning over, a baby's whimpering. A wolf growls in the distance. We rarely see wolves but often hear them, their feasting evident in the litter of other caravans. Another growls and the two join together. Still, it is surprisingly quiet. Araxie picks her way through the rubble, as nimble and slight as a ghost. She moves quickly, silently, the folds of my shirt lengthening her arms as she walks. Then she is gone, the sun up, the demands of the day back upon me.

The camp stirs to action, prodded by the guards. It is a ritual all have grown accustomed to, this shouting of the gendarmes, the groaning of the deportees, the wailing over deaths that have occurred in the night. Regulated trips to a nearby well follow, the shuffling use of a stinking latrine, the search for swallowed coins now embedded in feces. The gendarmes have begun to demand payment for services, for protection from raiding Kurds or villagers, for permission to access wells. The deportees protest but pay. Most have secreted valuables within the folds of blankets or tents or their own bodies. Usually there is a village to trade with, providing yogurt, milk, and meat for the guards, leftover scraps for the deportees. One day grows into the next, a stirring of dust and rock, sun and air. We seem to plod in an endless circle, our pathway littered with the debris of those traveling before us, the bloated, blackening bodies, the discarded tents and baggage. Heat and boredom make the guards' tempers short. Disagreements end violently.

On average we leave five or six bodies behind each morning. Occasionally someone still alive will refuse to go on. Several days earlier a pregnant woman declined to continue, sitting and not moving, ignoring the pleas of her family. She was left behind in the middle of the road, her skirts gathered around her, eyes closed, belly exposed to the sky. When her small form had vanished behind us, one of the guards rode back. A gunshot followed. The sound sent a tremor through the deportees, an enlarged breath of despondence, such that I eyed the group for signs of trouble, but nothing transpired. It is too bad about the woman, the circumstance, the entire situation. But she is probably better off.

I hear from time to time the whispers of our inhumanity. Even the Germans, our allies, condemn the deportations—I heard one of their engineers say as much before we left from Harput. But what would they have us do? The Armenians are our enemies, allies of the Russians, who have attacked us. They rebelled in Van, attacking a military garrison and declaring independence. A book distributed by the government details anarchist publications and depots of arms and munitions. The fact that we are allowing these groups to leave the country seems more than fair. Would they have done the same for us? The Turkish people are united. Turkey is for Turks. The mixture of different peoples will lead only to strife, like a dog with two masters. Better to eliminate the issue now, avoid the inevitable subversion. Though I have played with Armenian children, worn shoes stitched by an Armenian cobbler, even been treated once by an Armenian doctor, I do not trust their race or kind. They are devious, all of them, sneaky and cunning, as prone to knife or swindle or trick you as not. Painful as it might be, separation is best for them, for us, for all concerned. And in wartime, people, even innocent people, will die.

The girl keeps popping into my mind. Reconsideration of the night's events brings a renewed frustration. She has placed a spell on me, I am sure of it, hypnotized me with an incantation passed down through the dark of Armenian churches. In retrospect, the entire episode has a shadowy, trancelike feel, in which I observed and acted, but not of my own intent. I can see her now, her shirt torn, her small breasts exposed. I feel myself harden in response. I will reverse this humiliation, I vow. I will atone for this failure.

"Mustafa!" I shout, intent on projecting authority. "Go check the back of the line. Find out what is holding us up. Encourage any stragglers."

Mustafa eyes me with something approaching malice, but whirls and does as I order.

I envision the ways I will reestablish myself. Night will fall and I will find her, reengage. I spit, calming as this reverie continues, my thoughts blinded by apparitions of dark hair and mismatched eyes, confusing thoughts that knead my stomach and clutch at my heart. It is as if she stands before me, her voice echoing in my ears, her mouth slurping air from my lungs in great gasps. I shiver, nearly fall from my horse, regain my bearing, straighten my back. I grope for my rifle. I wonder if I've been injured, or poisoned, or taken feverishly ill, but I know I have not, for beneath it all lies desire, a shaking, sentimental hunger that makes me think of the syrupy *pekmez* at the Harput confectioner's shop. I shake my head, unsure of myself. This has not happened before.

Mustafa returns, reporting that the stragglers have been dealt with. Other questions present themselves. Where are we stopping for the night? What wells are nearby? Who will be bartering with the village? Shouldn't those that have skimmed profits be punished, with reduced rations and new cooking duties, or perhaps increased watches? What should be done about the Kurdish women who keep attacking the caravan's rear?

I deal with it all, firmly, tiredly, my thoughts bouncing about like a child's worn string toy, returning in the end always to her.

The afternoon drifts. We stop on a dusty plain near Kilis, in an area where other caravans have previously encamped, even though the nearest well is polluted and the stench of an old latrine smothers the camp no matter which direction the wind. Tents and bedding unfold, some gather wood for a fire. I watch this, distracted. At some point I hike up a small knoll and search for her from above, my gaze left to right and back once again. I assume she is hidden in the caravan's middle, an area marginally safer, perhaps within the small group still harboring a few scraggly oxen and wagons. I contemplate wading in for a closer look, but such action will draw attention, attention it seems best to avoid. From this distance the deportees again appear sheep-like, the gendarmes canine in their nipping and circling. We *are* shepherds, whether they accept it or not, protecting these people, moving them for their own sake. If we were inhumane, we would have simply slaughtered them all—it would have been so much easier. The fact that some of the young and old will expire is true of any long transport.

I consider this as I gaze out over the plain to Katma, now only a few days away. We will all be better off when the journey concludes, the guards and the guarded, the ones who have made it. For me, the possibility of returning to valor is close. I will report back to the army garrison in Harput, my duty as a gendarme concluded. I think of battle and charges, and a uniform—a real uniform—a company eventually to lead. I think of order, and discipline. Eyeing the caravan, I chart its dimples and ridges, its sticks of muted color, its tents that become troops, carts artillery, poles the ends of machine guns, all as I search for a slender, familiar profile. I do not find her. I wonder why this matters so. I arch my shoulders, my chest thrust out as if ribboned. I pick my way back to the camp and its squalor.

That night they bring a man before me. A troublemaker, they say, extorting valuables from his fellow deportees. I suspect he has instead been successful in bribing one group of gendarmes at the expense of others. The fact that he even appears before me seems a testament to this, as typically they would have already shot him. Jafer and Ismail flank him, Tevfik and Mustafa stand to one side. The others look on intently.

The man looks familiar, in a scruffy, indefinable way, but they all look familiar after these weeks of plodding—the same battered fez, the same faded waistcoat. I start to ask if he has anything to say but think better of it, my tongue staying fixed in my mouth. Thankfully, the man is not groveling. His chest heaves in and out, his breath rasps in his throat, but he says nothing. Is he thinking of how he came to be here, dropped into a world of more powerful foes, how his life will be ended with the suddenness with which it began? I half listen as Mustafa speaks, his body tensed, his eyes blinking. I nod. It is as I reach for my gun that I see her, standing behind the other guards, hair under the cap again, my shirt still on her shoulders. I remain calm, not starting at the sight of her, not alerting the others to her presence in an area in which she is not allowed. I continue my motion, raise the weapon. I shoot the man once in the head.

I do not think much about it. It is the only real course, given the circumstances. If I fail to maintain control, my own life is in jeopardy. This is no place for a trial, and it is not as if the man has not probably done what he was accused of, or that he will not die soon, anyway. He is, as I think about it, an anomaly in any respect. Most able-bodied Armenian men were forced into labor or executed before the marches even began. He must have been wealthy or particularly adept at bribery to have survived for this long. By the look on his face he knew this, and was not ungrateful to die.

But she disappears. I hunt for her afterward, as the guards break up into watches, as others pull struggling young women off into the night. I examine each of these, especially that of Mustafa, to forestall her being selected by some other gendarme. I am sure this is noticed, as I have not done this before. My shirt will have been seen on her. And her eyes, how can she hide them? Yet I cannot find her. I work my way once through the caravan, then back. I scour the camp's perimeter. It is as if she has vanished, into the darkness that surrounds us.

White light bites and cuts me. White blanket, white chair, white walls, white ceiling. My head hurts, as if the whiteness has now entered and will not be shut out. A space closed for so long becomes open. Is this London? Then the frame hinders my head, the boxlike apparatus. I peer around, remembering. I am still alive.

The dreams have continued. Despite the radiation, despite everything.

A man approaches. "Well, and how is the patient?" Dr. Wan pulls at his mustache.

I shiver, awake. "I am tired."

"The surgery was quite successful." His mole broadens, flattens. "You felt nothing, I trust?"

"Nothing."

Violet appears behind him, saying something, but I am drifting, my thoughts mixed. My past. The Depression—how I fought for mere pennies! Hungry and cold, only one meal a day. An immigrant, we were all immigrants. Escaping. Harry Wan, too—at what age did he enter? Different, like me, in this rural environment. He has picked up the language, considers himself an American. Does he dream of his old country? I wonder what he regrets.

"Doctor?" I pause. "I still have these dreams."

The mole bunches, like a pencil eraser. "Just now? During the surgery?"

"Yes."

"Hmmm." He glances up. "Let's see if they continue. If so, I will alter your medication. It may be a function of the drugs in your system."

I nod. He bows again.

"Wonderful!"

He exits the room. Violet and I look at each other. I close my eyes.

Katma is a filthy, noxious repository for deportees gathered from the farthest points of Turkey, from Kayseri, Bitlis, Diyarbekır, Erzerum, and even Trebizond, far up on the Black Sea. What was once a quaint market town, with stone buildings, terraced gardens, and a small market, has swollen in size like a blood-gorged tick. People, animals, and insects are everywhere, the smell of defecation hanging low in the air. From a distance the town looks like part of a hill that has been leveled, broken and crumpled into mud-colored clumps. Up close the browns turn to grays, speckled in places with dusty clothing, faded trees, squat and shallow buildings. Black-cloaked townspeople eye us from the outskirts, evaluating, calculating, some with disdain for our group's imposition, others with the greed of the expectant profiteer.

We arrive about noon, guided the last part of the way by a toothless official, an older man named Hassan, who rides out to greet us. The deportees are to be confined in a specific area, a wretched tent city resembling a giant encampment. There look to be several thousand there—the familiar hungry faces, the black clothing, the lethargic-looking children. It could be our caravan, except multiplied tenfold. Hassan has little information about plans going forward, only a vague direction that our group needs to stay together, that plans are changing, that we will move "east" at an unspecified time.

I direct our group to one end of the camp, near large areas of digging I later learn will become burial pits. Flies cover everything, entering our mouths and noses, lodging in our clothing, swirling about our eyes. The earth stinks, as if the bowels of hell have erupted, burrowing into pores even as sweat seeks escape. I cup my hand around my nose and mouth and make everyone file past me, ostensibly to warn them to stay together but in actuality to search for her. I have not seen her since the episode at the campfire three nights previous, despite my periodic forays through the ranks of the deportees. My concern has grown with each search, the possibilities emerging of her having been carried off during one of the nightly attacks by marauding Kurds—although at my insistence the guards had curtailed much of that thievery—of an abduction by Mustafa or one of the other gendarmes, or of her simply having run away. Almost all of the deportees pass by before I recognize her, clad in a black frock that exposes parts of my shirt. She wears the cap again, her face darkened with dirt, hand against her mouth, eyes following the ground. I pull her out of line, make her stand to one side as the remainder of the group files past. Then I take her with me as I deal with the guards.

The gendarmes are a problem, as I had known they would be. Only I had been a prior member of the gendarmerie, the country's paramilitary police. The others had been recruited by the *kaymakam*, a senior official in Harput, from among a group of thugs and other *çeteler* deemed unfit for military service. In addition to Mustafa, I had known several before. Ismail, who has a bad leg, is a friend of a friend. Izzet is the butcher's son. Ali joined us at Gerger when two of the original gendarmes returned to Harput. I remember thinking from the outset what a struggle it would be to keep them under control. After a brief skirmish on the first day out, in which I knifed Tevfik's beard to a wooden wall, they more or less followed my instructions. Still, I watch them, day and night. I recognize them for what they are, more dangerous than any enemy.

Some insist now on leaving, claiming they have not been appropriately paid. Others maintain they are needed back home and never intended to go this far anyway. Still others inquire about lodging. Where are they supposed to stay in this overcrowded shithole? I deal with the money issue first, according little sympathy to these who have profited well from the bribes of the deportees. I dole out a few lira to each, inform Tevfik and Izzet they are free to go if they choose. The others, whom I feel are more loyal in general, I ask to stay on, at least for several more days, until we determine what is requested of us. I can offer them no lodging, provide no guidance as to where to sleep and what to eat. I ask each of those staying to meet me each morning for instruction, knowing it is likely some will soon melt away. I dismiss the group. I wait until they have filed away, till the muttering and questioning looks have evaporated.

"I have been looking for you. Why are you hiding?"

She does not reply. Her head angles down, away from me.

"Look at me." I cup her chin in one hand, pull her face gently upward. The mismatched eyes swing into focus, a hostile gaze now directed upon me.

"I will help you," I say. "For now. At least get you out of this mess." I gesture at the fly-covered encampment.

She shakes her head slowly, her focus back on the ground.

I grit my teeth. "You have no choice. Come with me. Now."

I reach for her. She pulls back. I reach farther, grabbing this time, my fingers on the tendons of her thin upper arm. Her resistance continues, a pull of surprising strength, then as quickly relents. I find myself sweating.

"Please don't touch me."

I stare at her. Does she know what she says? I could kill her if I wanted. I motion with one arm. She trudges in the direction I point, pulling a string bag over one shoulder, her chin puckered and stretched, her gaze held to the ground. I fall in behind her, my head following the swivel of her back, the shift of her hips as she slides through the crowd. We pass a small bazaar catering to deportees still in possession of valuables, the smell of bread and bulgur mingling with the stench of the camp. A cook fire burns somewhere, its smoke in our path. Here and there stand more well-to-do Turks, resplendent in red fezzes, talking and smoking brown cigarettes, entering teahouses, retreating with bottles of raki. People bustle about—soldiers, deportees, merchants, and townspeople—all crammed together in a great ball of dust. Herders tend animals—goats, sheep, and chickens—available for purchase, for slaughter. Babies cry, men shout. Donkeys bray like wounded monsters. Even the women seem loud, chattering as they tote water bottles, shouting after their children. We pass flat-roofed houses constructed of gray stone, broken by layers of wooden beams, fronted by little walled courtyards. Other abodes are simpler, composed of mud brick, with few windows. Dusty trees stand limp and forgotten—an elm, maybe, a walnut. It reminds me of some place I cannot recall.

I had inquired discreetly of Hassan, the man who directed us into the city, of where I might find lodging. Several coins produced the name and address of someone he told me could help. It takes us a while to locate it, a dingy stone building on a narrow side street, but the squat woman who answers the door is more than willing to provide a room at an exorbitant price. Araxie keeps her gaze downward, boyish in her height, her cap and billowy clothing enhancing this ambiguity. The proprietress eyes her quizzically but says nothing. With a flourish of tucked bills and the sweeping gestures of a fighter, she shows us to our "room," a small, curtained-off area in the back of the building. A wooden platform covered by straw and a brownish blanket form one side, leaving what little space remains as stable area for my horse. The curtains bow from the sag of the ropes that hold them aloft, leaving gaps of darkness between stretches of cloth. From beyond unseen feet scuffle, voices hum, animals mutter and grunt. The woman points us down a narrow hallway to a communal bathing area, similarly curtained and evidently utilized by everyone in the building (and perhaps members of the public as well). We are made to believe that a servant named Vahan will provide heated water from the stove at our request. The sound of someone being scolded rises from another part of the building. I conclude—correctly, as it turns out—that this is the unfortunate Vahan.

Other boarders pass as we make our way to our room, soldiers in new olive uniforms, prosperous-looking merchants, and other, dirtier clientele, perhaps gendarmes from other stalled caravans. I draw the curtain behind us, pull my bedding from the horse, eye the blanket provided, then toss it aside. Folding the bedding on the straw, I place the rifle at one edge and sit. My horse, Gece, snorts and paws the mud floor. Araxie remains standing, her head still angled toward the ground. I grab some bread and apricots from my pack and offer them to her, but she ignores me, her jaw set.

She turns after a time. "What do you want with me?" She asks this in Armenian, with which I have only general familiarity, but I understand her nonetheless.

"I want to help you," I say in Turkish. "I think you need it."

"Why?" She also switches to Turkish.

I do not answer. My mouth is dry. I seek to explain, to put words to the things that drive me on, but cannot.

"Why would I accept help from you?" she asks.

I pause, still caught in my efforts. "Because you have no other option."

Silence settles upon us. Someone sneezes in the space beyond. A pot clangs in a distant kitchen. "My option is death," she says, her voice barely a whisper. "Why should I live? My mother died before the start of this journey. The man you shot several nights ago, at the campfire, was my father."

I roll back on the straw pad. Rough sounds like a dog's bark wind their way up my throat. I swallow. "I did not know," I say finally.

"Would it have mattered? We are oxen to you. Why not just shoot us all now?" She pauses, sucking in air. Another sneeze echoes behind her. "What is it about us you hate so?"

I spread my hands before me. I clear my throat. "I am only a small piece in a large puzzle," I begin quietly. "I have a job to do. I did not ask for it, nor have I questioned its rationale. To do otherwise is to invite my own death. I, too, have wondered at these things. But there is a war. Your people have allied themselves with the enemy. Even now, on the northern and western fronts, Turkish soldiers are fighting and dying to preserve our country. What do you expect us to do? The Armenians cannot have it both ways. Perhaps it is a good thing that we should be separated. Perhaps we were never meant to live together."

"The Armenians in my town never allied themselves with anyone," she says flatly, softly. "We do not know any Russians. We are no danger to you, or to any other Turk. Yet we are treated as dogs, or worse. Before we left Harput, I watched a crowd set an old woman on fire. The townspeople laughed and clapped.

Women, men, children—everyone. Our neighbors. What you have done, what you are doing, is murder. It is monstrous. There *is* no rationale."

I do not respond, for there is nothing I can say. I recognize the simplicity of youth in her statements, the naïveté of black and white. If I were in her shoes, would I not feel the same? But the Armenians have brought this on themselves, with their secrecy, their clannishness, their duplicity and trickery. Of course there has been injustice, as there would be in anything. There are undoubtedly honorable Russian people as well. But at some point one has to pick sides, choose his allegiance. The Armenians have made their decision. There is nothing I can do about it.

I lift my head. "Why did you not leave sooner, if your father had the means to do so?"

"We talked about it, but my mother was sick. She died two weeks before we were forced to depart."

I nod. I look away. This young woman has lost so much. How can she bear to be with me, the man who has killed—killed her father? My tongue curls and sticks as I ponder this circumstance. She has little left to fear, this one, not starvation, or pain, or even death. Is she plotting even now to slit my throat as I sleep? I should kill her, I think, before she kills me. I should . . . but I should do many things I will not, I cannot. I regard her again as she stands straight, feet apart. She stares at nothing. I cannot bear to look more.

"Sit. Please."

She starts, as if she has forgotten my presence. She looks at me sideways, the light eye turned to me now, then lowers herself to the straw, tucking one leg beneath her.

"Do you wish to bathe?" I ask. Even the poorest of Turks bathe regularly, usually at the public baths.

She shakes her head with such vehemence the cap falls from her crown.

"Not with me. You may use the bath first if you wish. I will make sure no one enters."

She hesitates, then declines.

"So." I stand, pulling the rifle with me. "I shall bathe. You shall remain here. If you attempt to leave, I will instruct the proprietress to stop you. There are very bad men here, men who will not hesitate to hurt you and use you. You are safer with me."

I part the sagging curtain, close it again, and make my way down the hall.

Time. Time has moved on since the tumor's arrival, spring into summer, blooms into green. I view the drive home from the hospital with new eyes, noting the shapeliness of the trees gracing Miller Street, the shuck and dive of a pair of cardinals, the stare of a wrinkled old man. Roses, Wadesboro's pride, burst from planters and gardens, in reds and purples, oranges and pinks. The last of spent pollen yellows lips around puddles. A train murmurs in the distance, its whistle low like a wind. Life continues, with or without me. I touch my head where the metal frame had been fastened. I am still here. I am still a part of it.

Home feels cool and comfortable, strange. I am tired but afraid to sleep, jumpy but slow, sad and elated at alternating intervals. I have little to do yet time passes swiftly. My daughter Lissette calls. We chat about me, about nothing. A stream of visitors forms—someone over, someone calling, someone delivering something. It reminds me of Carol's last days. Casseroles show up, left by the door like abandoned infants. Flowers arrive, sticky and pungent. I am unable to avoid attention, even as to some degree I feed on it. I brood, I mope, I act like a child. I resent Ted and Violet and the others around me.

I think about the dream. Do I *remember* these things? I search for my records. I even climb into the attic, much to Ted's dismay. But it is in the garage that I find it, the box I remember, its top gray, its edges still sharp. I bring it into the light, and read of myself.

The words are clinical and spare. I was taken from a trench in Çanakkale, the battle of Gallipoli, on 29 August 1915. My clothing had been ripped away, my head completely bloodied. From where I was found I was assumed to be British. I was evacuated through several steps to a hospital ship, where I was diagnosed with shrapnel wounds and brain injury. I was not expected to live.

But I did live, for several weeks more. The ship left for Southampton, carrying me with it. We arrived 23 September 1915. I was taken to a military hospital. A coma, the chart indicates. Damage to the parietal lobe.

The writing changes here, someone new has taken over. Not Carol, yet. Notations are made about my nationality. Perhaps my coloring? I am copper-skinned, though not dark. I awoke from my coma on 10 October 1915. "Turk" is scratched in the margin.

I remained in the hospital for another 217 days. The records show that I spoke no English, that I suffered from amnesia. I spent much time sleeping. I developed a fever, then pneumonia. Again, I was not expected to live. But I did.

Carol entered the picture—I recognize her handwriting on the chart. She must have saved this (what patients get their charts?). Gradually, I recovered some of my memory. But the war dragged on. There is a sheaf of paperwork on the issue of what to do with me. Was I a prisoner of war? Should I be repatriated, or exchanged? Carol was a force by this point, advocating on my behalf, turning back officials who wanted to move me. She claimed later there was immediate physical attraction, but I think she felt pity. She succeeded finally in marrying me, to prevent my deportation. I remember our wedding day, a bleak, cloudy afternoon, a robed and wigged judge. Our wedding night was spent in a freighter line's gritty departure area. Carol had papers, our luggage, and a plan. I have thought many times since of her acts of defiance, first against the authorities, later her own parents. I am still not sure how she did it, or why. But Carol, once determined, was not one to be denied.

I think back on the dream. My injury was early in the war—near its beginning. The deportations must have taken place at about the same time, or after. The records prove what I thought they did, that I was serving in the army then. But Burak, my brother—where was he, and when? Are these his dreams? Does he speak to me now at the end of my life? I grasp at this improbability, I want it to be so. To explain things! But . . . I do not remember. I cannot.

It is difficult, this absence. I think again on the things I created to take the place of lost memories, even war memories. My valor, my medals. My glory. I have harbored these for so long now they become almost real, a convict's belief in the truth of his innocence. What is truth without memory? What is now without then? As an immigrant, though, I found the blanks to be helpful, focusing me then on the present, the future. I was determined to make my way in America. I started with nothing and worked my way up. I am proud of my accomplishments, the solid strength of my efforts. Yet at the end of my life these dreams come, and the ground shifts. I find myself in a dark, tilting house.

Later, I ask Violet to take me to the library. This is a strange request, one Violet raises soft eyebrows to. I have difficulty reading now. I must put on thick glasses, which make my eyes look extra large. But she agrees. We climb into her Explorer. It is a sunny day.

"Do you think about the afterlife?" she asks.

We pass Mrs. Fleming's house. She waves from a window.

"I think of the present," I respond. This is true. I do not wish for a religious discussion, if that is where she is heading.

But she says nothing more. I glance at her. I am ashamed now of my reticence. "Thank you," I say. "For the driving."

She nods.

I want to touch her, to place my hand on the wheel. She will leave soon, once I recuperate. I know this. I accept my abandonment. Still, we have gotten on well, we have not fought. I have tried not to meddle. This procedure—has she not pushed for it? The extension then of my life. I want to stay on this course for the time that is left us, balancing, steering. It could be years! I will be patient.

I look at her closely. She has Carol's jaw. I think of Carol, her parents. Her mother died just after we moved to Wadesboro, but her father lived longer. Carol had left, joined the war effort, and come back to find a home filled with friction: her parents' anger over her leaving, her marrying without their consent. A foreigner? A dark-skinned foreigner who spoke no English? The discord lessened with her mother's rapid death, her father softening, fading, sitting each day in an old, browned recliner watching pastors and football and drinking beer from a can. I thought once to ask him if he knew his eldest daughter. Do I know my own children? Eyes and hair and chins given, accepted, but then differences. Distance. Their lives are not mine. I remind myself so.

We reach the library. I make for the reference section, the encyclopedias. Violet follows at a distance, curious but respectful.

"What are you looking for?" she asks eventually.

I shush her, continue my work. I have my big glasses out.

I am reading about the Armenians, the deportations. There are pictures, similar to the ones in the magazine. I find I must stay away from these, I must concentrate on the text. I am looking for dates, and I find them. The article states that the deportations began in 1915, continuing into 1917, and beyond.

I close the book. There—1915. I was not there. Almost a century has passed. Why must I dream this?

I read some more. I find another encyclopedia, another article that discusses this exodus and its circumstances. It explains that the Russians—Christians, like the Armenians—began driving Muslims from the Caucasus in the middle to late 1800s, and that Armenians living in the Caucasus took an active part in this forced relocation. The northern part of Anatolia became inundated with over one million Muslim refugees. When World War I commenced, the Turks in Anatolia feared a continuation of the Russian march into Turkey, aided by their allies, the Armenians.

I sit back, close my eyes. It is difficult to think of this, to concentrate so. But I continue my search, I find one more article. I must ask the person at the desk for help in using the card catalog—I am not familiar with libraries. Violet has wandered away but is back now, her head twisted as she pretends to read spines of books.

This article is longer, a small book, almost. The author's name is Hollingsworth. It states that near the beginning of World War I, small Armenian bands attacked in Urfa, Bitlis, Musa Daği, Karan Hisan. They targeted the war effort—army recruiters, government buildings. The Turkish authorities were concerned about insurrection, one that, given the size of the Armenian population, could spread throughout Anatolia. So the deportations commenced. The official Ottoman order spelled out compassion for the deportees, instructions for selling property, caring for health and sanitation. Still, by some estimates almost one million perished. The Turkish government eventually charged hundreds for crimes committed against Armenians. Talat Paş a, Enver, Cemal—all were found guilty, and sentenced to death.

"Papa. What is this all about?"

We are back in the Explorer now, the wind in my face. I stare out the window at a boy on a bicycle.

"I am trying to understand," I say slowly. "These dreams have triggered things, things that are not memories, but because I have so few memories of this time, they confuse me." I pause.

"And what is it you are looking for?"

I hesitate. "There was a deportation, of Armenian people from Turkey. During the war. I was not there, but for some reason I keep dreaming of it."

"Do you think it's a past life?"

"How can it be a past life if it occurs during my own?"

She ponders this. "I don't know."

Another thought comes to me, one that has lurked, unexamined. A cross-check. The only tangible link to my childhood.

A man visited me once, while Carol was still alive. In 1974, maybe 1975. His name was Recep Gencay. He claimed to be from my village, in Turkey, to have known me as a child. I do not know how he found me, or why, but he is the only person to claim connection with this life from before.

Recep knew a number of things, including things about my parents, my brother, even our dog. He remembered children I remembered, the streets, the places we would go. But it was an odd and uncomfortable meeting, for I could recall only a few of the things he did. I had no recollection of him, for example. I tried to explain this, that digging back to before was like trying to go back in the womb, that the bed on which I was birthed was in London, not Anatolia. He did not understand. He seemed agitated and regretful, continually asking my pardon. I thought of him for a time as a spirit. I had no wish to see him again. But now . . . He had mentioned Burak specifically. I dig my nails in my palms.

I turn to Violet. "Do you remember the man who came to see me once, who claimed to be from my hometown?"

She shakes her head.

"I think he lived in Jacksonville." Yes, that was it. Jacksonville. "Perhaps we should go there."

"Go . . . to Jacksonville?"

"Yes."

"When?"

I scratch my head. "Perhaps tomorrow."

.   .   .

Araxie is gone. I am alone, except for my horse. I grab my rifle, feel around in the dark. Gone. I peer into the hallway, listen to the snores and stirrings from the curtained-off areas, sniff of the stale, cool air. I creep down to the bath, thinking she might have decided at last to bathe, but the area is dark and silent. The kitchen, the small, dank area where we take our meals, the small vestibule at the entrance, and the corridor are all empty, devoid of any movement.

I slip out into the silky dawn, stifling the need to urinate. If she ran, where would she go? I consider the possibility of abduction but quickly dismiss it. I would have heard any scuffle, and the bulk of the other boarders were so dirty and violent-looking I cannot imagine she would go with someone else on her own.

It seems more likely she has decided to flee, to where, I know not. We have been in Katma for four days, holed up in our room, our *oda*, waiting for word of our movement. Our ultimate destination has never been clear, only the "border," the limits of Turkish-speaking Anatolia. Now rumors abound. Some caravans are apparently pushing on to the Syrian city of Aleppo, several days' journey southeast, others are supposedly being diverted into the desert, for extermination. The ranks of corralled deportees have grown since we arrived, the conditions of the holding area we call the "pit" progressing from squalid to intolerable. Hundreds die each day, the dead hauled out each morning to new burial dumps dug hastily beside ones filled the day before. The ground in the pit has become that of an animal pen, filled with clumps of human excrement, its stench overpowering even at a distance. Military officials fear the onset of disease, less out of concern for the deportees than for the possibility that it might spread to the troops or the town's general population. Deportees with the strength or valuables left to do so hire carts or make out for Aleppo on their own. The rest wait in misery.

Perhaps she has left with the others, although I am relatively certain she has no valuables. She spoke little at the boardinghouse, nodding or shaking her head at questions, eating almost nothing. She went with me to the pit each day, to the stares and knowing looks of my fellow gendarmes (including, one day, a black-faced Mustafa), to the sneers of her fellow deportees. *Boz*, some called out. Whore. *Dönme*. Turncoat. She did not shrink from them, or hang her head, but instead seemed to look through them, as if they no longer existed, as if she, or they, were now dead. After one such visit she spoke to me, one of the few direct exchanges during our days there together.

"Do something," she said.

But I was at a loss as to what to do. I had to wait for orders, which were not quick in coming in the disorganized mess of Katma's command. The *vali* in charge of the region had been away, and the second-in-command was reluctant to make decisions. There was pressure from the Syrians, who wanted no more refugees, and from a handful of British and American missionaries, who wanted alleviation of the deportees' deplorable conditions. One day I saw a bearded, robed man emerge from the command center, the bishop of the Armenian Apostolic Church. German military officials came and went. Still, nothing happened. The temperature rose. Conditions worsened. Food became an issue, the deportees reduced to fighting over scraps, standing in endless lines, picking the seeds from fecal matter. The swarms of flies intensified, if such a thing was possible, heaving about in such densities they resembled shimmering gray and white clouds. Then rain arrived, merciful at first but destructive in time, soaking the shelterless deportees, turning the ground into vile, soupy mud. The heat roared back afterward, moistening and thickening things, a condition more wretched than even before. I loitered near the command center, watching and observing. I annoyed the bey's staff with my questions, my frequent appearances. We sweated, swatting flies. We drank foul-tasting water. We waited.

The cramped confines of the rooming house forced a certain closeness. Araxie and I slept within a few hand lengths of each other, she close to the curtain, her back turned to me. I heard her breathing at night, soft and measured, heard the trickle of her urine in the chamber pot we silently shared. Once in the night I sensed her shaking, her body twitching in soundless sobs. I spoke to her often, even if she would not respond, telling her about myself, about the village in which I'd grown up, my father's trade as a knife maker, my pride for my cousins taking part in the war. I respected her grief and her privacy, averting my gaze, demanding nothing, avoiding physical contact. I offered her food before I ate. I bathed every day, looked at myself in the tiny cracked mirror, made several attempts at combing my hair. I disrobed in front of her only once, proud of my nakedness, ashamed when she looked away.

My money dissipated, drained by the larcenous landlady and the thieving villagers at the bazaar. Only the day before, I had decided we must move out, take shelter in the tent and blankets I had expropriated from a deceased deportee, wait out the orders on the fringe of the dirty town. I spent the last of my *gurûş* on an overpriced haircut. I swung by the command center as I always did, expecting no movement and backpedaling when it came. We were to depart for Aleppo the next day. I did not report this to Araxie, preferring to show her by action how I had made something happen. Perhaps she had sensed it anyway, as this morning when we are to leave, she is gone.

I squint into the morning mist, listening to the creak of wagons and oxen, the snap of the herders' switches, the clang of merchants setting up for the day. The wind shifts, bringing with it a foul plume, the distant stench of the pit. The wail of the muezzin rises, dipping and wavering, bending those standing like wheat blown by a wind. I bow, immersing myself in the rhythm of the prayers, the words repeated to a point past familiarity: "*. . . In the Name of Allah, the Compassionate, the Merciful: Praise be to Allah, Creator of the worlds . . .*" I scratch my head, fingering the shortness of my newly shorn locks.

I stand when the prayers end, stretch, urinate against the side of the building. It is then that I see her. She sits astride the building's roof, one leg hooked over its edge. Her hair glistens with water, as if she has just bathed, and she glances not at me but across the town, across the dust and cook fires and scabs of habitation. Her stillness makes her part of the building, an ornament affixed to its top. I am unsure how she has climbed there, or even how one accesses the building's second story. I see no steps, no doors or ladder.

"We are leaving," she says, part question and statement, her gaze still directed out above the far rooftops.

"Yes."

I wait for her to say more, but she does not.

"What are you doing?" I ask finally. Given that she has spoken perhaps four words in four days, I hardly expect a response.

She glances in my direction. "I had thought to kill myself," she says calmly. She smiles, a sort of sad half-grimace I have not seen since the night at the hilltop. "But I cannot." She twists a strand of hair in her fingers. "The will to live is strong. No matter the pain."

She looks older, thinner, a woman, not a girl. I imagine her scolding a young child, instructing a group of pupils, sweeping the floor of a stone house. So different from my own mother and her crouching presence, but in a way so similar—strong and measured, unafraid. I want to hold her, help her, climb up the side of the building and carry her, smother her, feed her, warm her, comfort her. I want to put my head against her chest and listen to the sound of her breathing. But I watch her instead, watch as she unwinds herself from her perch and slides along the edge of the building, as she drops down its opposite side, her legs dangling and twisting, her arms wide, then thin—a *kelebek* on a branch. A butterfly.

I offer my hand in assistance, but she leaps the last few feet. Her hair *is* wet, her face newly scrubbed, the smell of soap stretched around her. She glances at me, without malice or affection or sorrow or anything, the light eye on me now, then the dark.

I gesture toward the *oda*.

She leads the way.

. . .

Brainsetta drives us to Jacksonville. This is not her true name, of course, but the name by which others refer to her, though not to her face. Her given name is Josephine; she is married to Violet's first cousin, Peter "Brains" Melville. A large, simple-faced woman, she has hair that looks like a wig but is not and breasts that angle forward like the prow of a battleship. She drives a huge Buick with a trunk big enough, she says, to "sleep six." Violet has to work, Ted is not insured for driving, and I am not capable of such, so Josephine (having nothing else to do) has been drafted. She picks Ted and me up at eight.

Josephine talks the way others breathe—without ceasing. She begins with a history of her dog Mule's health issues, followed by her sister Lula's fight with her boss. By the time we reach Monticello she is deep into a description of the unfounded sexual allegations against her uncle Silas, in which a pet pig plays an unclarified part. Ted asks pertinent questions and feigns great interest while I remain silent, thinking I may have to strangle Josephine or myself if this keeps up all the way to Jacksonville. But it continues. The horse that got loose and kicked in her back door. The illness she contracted by eating bad tacos. I stare out the window and pretend to fall asleep. Josephine moves on to baseball, cursing the Braves and the designated hitter, maintaining that the player Dale Murphy has "developed a fat ass."

Her husband, Brains, is himself a strange fellow, having earned his own nickname in legitimate fashion, falling off the roof at the apartments he maintained, ingesting women's birth control pills as a poor man's prophylactic device. I was once told that, due to his southern drawl, the people at his job thought for some time his name was Tater, and still referred to him so. His reputation is as a nice guy, the kind who would give you the shirt off his back. A stupid nice guy. Stupid enough to marry Josephine. Brainsetta.

"Uncle Emmett, how's your headache?"

She motors on before I can answer. More monologue: an incident with a woman at the beauty parlor, a tame squirrel named Mud. But I am thinking of Carol, of how she came from this place, these people. Of how we came to connect. She had trained as a nurse. When the war started she was determined to be involved, even before the United States entered. This led her to London—the British needed nurses—and so to Fulham Military Hospital, second floor, head-injury ward. To the patient deprived of a past.

My earliest memory of Carol is of her hair. She was blond, like the sun, a white angel. She spoke an angel's strange tongue. She was kind to me when others were not. I was there for so long we grew to know each other well, even though we spoke different languages and I remembered so little. Again, perhaps simple pity waylaid her, perhaps my exoticness, my smooth, darker skin. I thought of it then as my destiny, as payment for pain and for service. Only later would I learn of my penance, as her limbs became thin and palsied, her voice stringy with need. She was forced to quit working before we left New York for Georgia. The sudden tremors, the rigidity, the long heartache that is Parkinson's. Her medicines made things almost worse. I do not complain of this now—I have lived the life given. And yet I find it so strange. Seventy years together and she is a ghost to me now.

Josephine has gone silent. We near Jacksonville, the car

slowing in traffic. She shifts position, adjusting her seat belt. Her breasts reach almost to the steering wheel.

"Now where are we going?"

"To the Shady Rest Nursing Home." It is Ted speaking. "I've got the address." Ted has been most helpful in locating Recep. In the end he called every nursing home in Jacksonville until he found him.

"Oh. Is this a relative?"

"No." I clear my throat. "He is someone I knew long ago."

"Where? Back in Eye-stan-bul?"

I shake my head. I was never in Istanbul—Kostantiniyye. At least not that I remember.

"From my childhood." I fold my arms. I do not wish to go further.

She presses on. "I thought you couldn't remember anything from your childhood."

"I remember some things."

I remember snow, and muddy streets. I remember fire in a little hearth. I remember Burak, and a neighbor boy, Emre. But there is more, somewhere. Somewhere just past my reach.

The dream plays back through me. The girl. I think of Burak. I want my dream to be his, to absolve myself. It must be! And yet I think I know it is not. I rub my face, focus again on my purpose here, on what to say to this person, Recep. I try to remember his appearance: a slender man, a small mustache. He has to be in his nineties as well. He is in a nursing facility. Perhaps his mind has gone, too.

I exit the car and ask the others to wait. The building before me is low-slung and gray. Inside, a broad counter stands before a long vestibule, the first of many such gateposts. The floors are shiny-polished, stark, a feel of something once modern. Several residents in wheelchairs perch at odd angles, heads lolling, mouths open. An elderly-looking visitor dips and tugs with metal needles. The receptionist at the desk, a young man with long fingernails, looks up as I approach.

"I am here to see Recep Gencay. I called yesterday."

The attendant grunts as if this is something new. I have no idea why Recep lives in Jacksonville, or what family he has. The man flicks his nails, shifts in a worn chair, reaches to punch an intercom button.

"Bring Recep up front, please."

He motions across the lobby with a slender-fingered wave. "He'll meet you in the visiting room. Over there."

I cross to the room indicated, circling a disheveled man who mutters "Johnny, Johnny" from behind a thick lip. The room is small and stale, with a hard-looking sofa and dirty chairs fronting an ancient TV. A shelf holds collapsed puzzles, a faded board game in a creased cardboard box. Shaded windows emit little light. I am reminded of why I hate these places, why I insisted Carol never be put in one. The floor near the window is stained with bloodlike orange spots. The place smells of urine and sweat, and disuse.

An enormously tall nurse wheels in a gray figure. I stare at the man in the wheelchair, his face slackened with time, his hair matted like cobwebs. His skin bunches and pulls, tight on his cheeks but full at his neckline, like a doll twisted out of its shape. I recognize him from his visit—was it only twelve, fifteen years earlier? But nothing from times before.

"I'm not sure he's gonna know you," the giantess nurse says. "He hasn't said nothing this morning." She shakes her head at Recep, as if scolding a child. "I told him you were coming."

Another man enters behind her, a younger man, dark-complected. He kisses Recep on the cheek, introduces himself as Recep's nephew. I do not catch his name. Perhaps he is a great-nephew, for he looks very young. He shakes my hand. He speaks in Turkish, but I respond only in English. I tell him the language has changed so much that I am more comfortable in English. He smiles and is pleasant. He states that he has been in the United States only a few years. His English is accented. I feel less of an immigrant than he—this is pleasing.

The nurse shifts behind Recep. "I'll be out here at the nurses' station if you need me."

"Thank you."

Recep stares vacantly, in the direction of the blank TV. There is silence, an awkwardness. I wish now that this nephew were not present. I smile, I tell him there are things I do not remember. He says we can be so forgetful.

I knead my hands. "I keep dreaming that I was part of a trek," I explain to Recep's nephew. "In 1915—the Armenians. Do you know of this?"

His neck twists as if I have slapped him. "Yes, of course," he responds. He purses his lips. His eyes flutter. "It was during the war. It was a difficult thing."

I nod my head. "I have read articles. I am trying to know more, to understand this."

The nephew shifts his legs, his mouth open to reveal small, even teeth. "There is so much misinformation about this in the

West," he says suddenly. He leans forward, his hair falling into his eyes. He wipes his face with one hand. "There was a war. There were signs of subversion. The Turks had to react in some fashion, do something. Almost all countries under attack would have done the same, if not something worse. Would those that criticize now prefer a result like the Balkans—a patchwork of tiny countries, divided, always in conflict? I want to tell Americans to look first at themselves—at their Trail of Tears, the march of Native Americans from Florida to Oklahoma, their slavery. Even the internment camps where those were sent who looked Japanese." He grips his elbows with his hands. His face is flushed now. "There is so much hypocrisy."

I start to say something but he waves me to silence. "Please," he says. "I do not wish to berate you." He shrugs. His face takes on a sheepish look, like that of a small boy who has spoken out of turn. His hand flips his hair. "It's just that this issue . . . It is behind us now. The Turks have moved on."

I nod again. I try to make my face look sympathetic, appreciative. I wish once more to be alone with Recep—to remember. To provide form to things. I turn, to see if Recep has been following this exchange, but his gaze still drifts away from us, off toward the window.

"Recep," I say. "It is me, Ahmet. Ahmet Khan. You came to visit me, remember? I am from Mezre."

The cloudy eyes brighten. His mouth forms a word, which seconds later I conclude is my name.

"How are you?" I ask. "Are they treating you well? Are you getting enough to eat?"

He stares at me quizzically, as if I have inquired of odd things.

An arm jerks out, stops. Slowly, painfully, he brings his head forward. "Yes." He smiles. His teeth form a rampart. "Ahmet."

The word is strange in his voice, foreign. Americanized as I have become, my name changed on entry. Emmett Conn. I have become Emmett Conn.

"You remember me, then?"

Softly, "*Evet.*" Yes.

"You may remember—I told you when you visited—I was injured in the war. I lost much of my memory, from before, from my childhood. Lately, I have been . . . these dreams have come to me." I glance at Recep's nephew but then back at Recep, and launch into descriptions, of Burak, the trek, the girl, the deportees. I find it relaxing, even therapeutic, an unburdening of images I have kept to myself. I watch Recep as I speak. His eyes are like apricots, too large for the sockets. He has few lashes. He does not blink.

"These Armenians, Recep, this journey. Do you know anything of this?"

He shakes his head quickly, as if I've said something to offend him. For a time he says nothing, leading me to think that perhaps he has not understood, that he is like Carol, alone in her twilight. His head shifts the way hers did, the eyes never quite aligned.

"I know the Armenians," he says in clear Turkish. His eyes remain trained away. "There were deportations. It was war. It was a bad time."

"Do you remember any girl with mismatched eyes?"

He looks down. The top of his head is scraped like a rock. Then up. "No."

"And Burak, what of him? Do you remember, when he went into the army? I . . . I cannot remember."

I am surprised, suddenly, by the tears in his eyes. He pulls at his face. His eyebrows spring back.

"You do not remember?" he asks in his strangled voice.

I shake my head. "No."

He stares, as if he does not believe me.

"Why?"

"What?"

"Why did you come?"

"To see you! To understand."

"I came to see you, in Georgia."

"Yes. Yes."

"Burak . . ." His voice halts. "Burak was killed before the war. An accident."

"An accident? Before the war?" Something roils in my stomach.

Recep nods. "A rock from a slingshot hit the side of his head."

Something clicks in my mind, to the point of almost hearing it. I remember the wailing, the robes. My father's face. An accident.

"Are you sure?"

Recep's hands cover his face. After a time he lifts them. "*Evet*," he says. He stands, begins a trembling step, falls back in his wheelchair. His face is the texture of paper. "It was my slingshot."

I sit back in my chair.

I do not know what to do, or say. I cannot think. Recep's nephew stares at me.

"Your father died soon after," Recep says again. "And then

you left. You joined . . . the gendarmerie. They would accept you, even if you were not yet of age for the army." He stops, his eyes alight. A guilt shines in his face, and for an instant I see myself in it. "You . . . you do not remember?"

I shake my head. But I know. I know he is right.

· 6 ·

The sand whips and whirls, the sting of thousands of wasps. A *kumaş* clings to my face, leaving a slit for my eyes, but still the tiny grains penetrate, shifting in unpredictable slants, burrowing in crevices, caking my nose and eyelids. I instruct the group to stop, as it makes little sense to advance under such conditions, bent and blinded by clouds of sand. We find a small ravine and bivouac, seeking what shelter the topography affords. We bury ourselves like rodents and wait, the sound of the wind all around.

The original two thousand deportees have dwindled now to three hundred, many of these suffering from dysentery. A number of the guards are gone, too, leaving only three gendarmes, including myself, to prod our group on its way. Our progress has been slow, slower than before, maybe six or seven miles per day. At this pace it will take four or five days to reach our destination. Food is scarce, water even scarcer. The dead and dying increase daily.

At the current rate of loss, only fifty or so of the deportees might actually make it to Aleppo.

I am not sure why I remain with the group—I almost had to beg the area governor, the *vali*, to be allowed to continue. It would have been easy enough to leave the deportees in Katma, to transfer back to fight in the war. Most gendarmes do not complete the entire journey with their original caravan. I tell myself a three-week delay will not hinder my advancement. I rationalize it as a duty, broadened by the abandoned deportees we encounter, the bands of unsupervised, starving packs of women and children that merge with our group, some almost naked, their bodies blackened by the sun. I ponder the need for closure, the delivery of these pathetic, stumbling creatures—her people—to their destination. Neither the war nor their complicity nor the inevitability of this journey has changed. But they are dying—children with tongues swollen large as fists, mothers with dead infants still clutched in their arms. I offer what assistance I can. I call for rest breaks, for water. I urge the group on. I listen to the requests she makes of me. I wonder if I, too, might falter and perish.

The other guards keep their distance. The one, Karim, is as sick as the deportees, necessitating his transport in one of the two ox-drawn carts still accompanying the group. The other, Mustafa, has grown mean and bitter, lashing out at stragglers, railing at small matters. He insisted on continuing to the journey's conclusion, even though I secured specific orders otherwise. In the end I was desperate for any assistance. Now I regret it. His demeanor distracts me, disturbs me. An incident on our second day out exhibited the decline in our relationship.

I had instructed the gendarmes to avoid using their weapons, given our lack of ammunition and the uncertainties ahead. As such, a rifle shot's crack, loud in the clean desert air, sent me galloping in concern to the rear of the caravan. I found Mustafa there, pulling at his beard, his mouth obscured, standing over the body of an elderly deportee.

"What happened?"

He shrugged, looking off in the distance. "She wouldn't move." He kicked at the corpse.

"My instructions were to use your weapon only if attacked."

Another shrug. "You're not growing soft, are you?" He pulled a dirty thumb at a large front tooth. "You and your Armenian whore?"

I eyed his stubby fingers, curled near his rifle's trigger. I fingered my own weapon.

"If you disobey my orders again, I will kill you."

A girl rushed forward, wailing, to drape arms around the dead woman. Mustafa's lips clamped together. He pulled again at his beard. Then he strode away, as if we had not spoken.

I have kept a close eye on him since, positioning him at the caravan's end, taking care that Araxie never comes near him. We sleep under the stars together, she and I, side by side, rarely speaking. She eats my food, the guards no longer dining as a group but scavenging about for themselves. She wears my extra clothes. I want to reach for her, day and night. I crave her breath on my neck, her arm on my shoulders. I dream of the glimpse I had on the hilltop, the small sculpted breasts, the narrow hips. Yet I never consider touching her, for reasons I cannot quite say. Guilt, perhaps, or anxiety. Perhaps something more.

"Did you go to school?" she asks, the third day out from Katma.

"Of course."

"For how long?"

"I completed my seventh year." Burak and my cousins attended military school.

"Do you speak other languages?"

I shake my head. "And you?" She is riding behind me, her hands clasped loosely about my waist, a posture that produces a near-constant erection.

"Yes. French and German. I would like to speak English. I would like to go to America."

"America."

"Yes. You have heard the missionaries, their descriptions of it?"

I have. I was warned away from the missionaries and their strange beliefs, their foreign accents, but I went anyway, to listen. The America they described merged with visions of heaven. Motor cars. Crates that flew through the air. "Things so modern," I say now, "the people so rich. Yes—I, too, would go there." I pause.

"Did you like school?" I ask.

"Oh, yes. I loved it." She pauses, as if considering this statement's finality. "I wanted to be an actress. I was always playacting in school, and for my parents."

We continue in silence. "My father, too, has died," I say eventually. His memory blazes within me, as if I have forgotten and only now remembered. "He died of an illness, almost a year ago now."

She does not respond. I realize my foolish remark has clogged the air between us. I stutter on, unleashing hurried descriptions of youthful achievements, my athletic prowess, my cousins' military advancement, my training at my father's knife-making trade. I explain how blades are forged, cooled, and tempered, how the haft is attached, how the finished product is evaluated. I describe sabers and scimitars, swords and rapiers, knives for pruning and skinning, blades for whittling and killing. I keep to myself my hatred of knife making, the fact that I refuse even to carry a knife. My father's death has freed me from the shower of sparks and the smell of the forge, from the dickering and tedium and pressure to measure up. My life is my own now. I am grateful for this.

"Do you have brothers or sisters?"

I chastise myself immediately for raising this question, for the way it is phrased. If she does have siblings, their fate is likely not pleasant.

"I have a brother," she responds after some time. "He is seven." Her voice catches and trails away. "My father placed him with a Turkish family. He was required to renounce his faith, to become a Muslim. He is in Harput."

"And you—why did you not do the same?"

I feel her hands on my back, pushing, as if attempting to drop off the horse.

"I would not turn my back on my father. Or my God."

I twist and grab her with one arm, my head facing backward. I say nothing, even though I want to argue with her, to point out that her God, their God, has done little to help in their time of need. Her eyes have gone red now, enlarged and tearful, so clouded that the pupils appear almost common and alike. It changes her face in a curious way, accentuating her exoticism, as if she has been revealed only now as a rust-eyed alien, dropped from the open sky into the desert spread below. Her arms fall to her sides as she lifts a leg to escape. Her face tilts near mine. It is in this posture that Mustafa finds us, riding up unnoticed in a curtain of sand.

"We have visitors," he says, pointing to a trio of camels and men in Arab headdress at the other end of the caravan.

I disengage. Araxie slides off the horse.

It is Thursday. I sit in the Piggly Wiggly. Ted accompanies me again, studying the magazines, eyeing me occasionally. We do not speak.

I have browsed the aisles, examined the teas—but there are no good teas here. I have resigned myself to a cup of coffee, testament to my despair. The liquid is vile, like oil. I sip at its bitterness.

Recep's confirmation has shaken me. I have toyed with it, battered it, questioned it anew. Might he be mistaken? He is an old man, confused as I am. But a curtain has parted, a certain door in my mind. I am sure. I remember Burak's death, its aftermath. The timing, the deportations beginning in early 1915, my injury in late August . . .

And then he appears, in front of me. Wilfred. He's grown taller. His face shows the lesions of adolescence. His hair is curlier.

"Hey," he says, looking down at me.

I struggle to stand, to speak. "It is so good to see you," I say when my voice comes.

He nods. He looks so much older, like the young man in *The Searchers*.

"What . . . what have you been doing?" I sound so grasping. So elderly.

"Same stuff." His gaze flits about.

"Are you supposed to be here?"

"Of course not." He sneers, and his face is less pleasing. "I'm never supposed to be here."

"Should you be in school?" He should have a job, but Violet insists on school only.

He opens his eyes but says nothing. I do not mean to frighten him, or condemn him. Just then Ted walks up.

"Hello."

"Who is this?" Wilfred asks.

"This is . . ." I cannot bring forth his name.

"Ted."

"Ted."

Wilfred coughs, grimaces.

I touch his arm. "Wilfred."

He jerks back. "Please don't touch me, okay?"

I leave my hand out. "Okay." I am remembering these swings now, how he switches from sunny to dark, back to sunny in flashes. I had taught him as a young boy to play chess—how it angered him to lose then! Tossed pieces and boards. I let him win some. Chess was something from the hospital in London, something known from before, for I could play even before I could speak again. Matches, even a tournament. I took a third place.

There were rages, too, then, not so unlike Wilfred's. I remember shouting, in Turkish. These lessened with time.

"You look well," I say. "You are taller." He will be tall like me.

Wilfred nods toward Ted. "Why is he with you?"

"He is watching. I have been sick."

"I heard that."

There is a pause. I glance at Ted but he does not leave. "School is okay?"

"No."

"You must work hard."

"I got in a fight."

"A fight?"

I remember a fight once, in New York. A fellow plumber. A Pole. He had loosed a fitting so that sewage rained over me, on my face, in my hair. He had done this deliberately, with malice. Why? I had done nothing to him. I went at him, the shit still in my hair, pounding my fists at his big, gloating face. Another man pulled me off. He continued to laugh, that Pole, the birthmark on his face stretched to form a pink flower. As if the gods had demanded this. As if he had launched a great joke.

"You must . . ." I begin, but Wilfred's voice cuts me off.

"I must do nothing," he says. "Nothing." His eyes are bright like twin stars. "You're just like her, like the rest—don't you see?" He looks from Ted to me. "Everyone telling Wilfred just what he must do."

I want to say no, that I am unlike anyone, except him. That one must fight back, that there is life in the fighting.

He turns and dashes—that is the only word for it, dashes—back to the front of the store. He looks back once, such that I fear he will crash into the electric glass door, but the door opens and he falls through it, as if through a hole. Then it closes, swallowing him. The look on his face stays with me after. It is a look of revulsion, and fear.

Ted and I do not speak on the way home. I am angry, though I try not to show it. There is no need to make things worse. Still, I had wished to be alone with Wilfred. I waited almost a year . . . and then this. I have such little time.

When I get home I call Violet. It is a fight, a brief one. I preach calm to myself. Still, I must press. "I saw Wilfred," I say.

"Where?"

"The store."

"The *store*?"

"He comes there sometimes." I realize, too late, that my call has betrayed him.

"When? Just now?"

"Yes."

"He's supposed to be in school. Why do you encourage this?"

"I do not encourage . . ." My breath shortens.

"Papa, we've been through this. He has enough problems without sneaking off and skipping school. Whenever he sees you he gets all hyped up—you know this. The doctors have him on a regimen. I ask that you honor it."

Honor? How does seeing him show dishonor? He is my grandchild, grandson. The only male left to follow.

"I would like to speak to him."

"Well, he's not here—he's been off with you, when he should be in school." Her breath rattles the phone and there are clicks, the sound of things dropped. "Look," she says, and smoothness enters her voice, "I'll bring him over to visit soon. Okay? With me. The three of us can visit, together."

I chew my lip. "He says he was in a fight."

"Yes. It's a problem, Papa. I'm dealing with it."

"He must fight back!"

"I'm *handling* it, okay?" Her voice is harsh. "If I need . . ." She halts herself.

I ask, "Do you need money, for this treatment?"

"*No*. I don't want your money. Can you understand that?"

"Yes," I say. "I—"

"Papa, I'll talk to you later, okay? I've got to go."

I make popcorn, and Ted and I watch *The Untouchables*. Lissette calls again, this time talking longer. I hear the guilt in her voice and am glad. I drink some tea, the scene playing back. "Please don't touch me," says the voice, his voice again. Hers. I rise and make my way back to my room, to my bed.

The lead Arab is tall, with a single sharpened tooth that peeks between his chapped lips. He speaks no Turkish, relying instead on a smaller, darker man to provide a rough translation. The third man, really just a boy, tends the camels.

They make their intent known immediately. They seek young women, for which they will pay. The smaller man extends a brown palm, shows me six coins. The leader eyes the deportees. I draw back to think.

Mustafa rides up, eyes alight, lips twitching beneath his beard. "How much is he offering?"

I shake my head. The smaller Arab approaches again, assuming my hesitation to be negotiation. His palm now holds eight coins.

I shake my head again. "None are for sale."

The smaller man frowns, not understanding.

Mustafa glances from me to the Arab. He grabs my shirt,

a child pleading with a parent. A twist of his wrist brings me closer.

"What are you doing? This man offers money, and you say no?" A spray of his spittle wets my shirt and neck. He whirls to face the Arab, whose palm remains outstretched. "I will take your offer."

I raise my rifle, pointing it at Mustafa's back. The Arab withdraws. The lead Arab, who has been watching from one side, flashes his solitary tooth and moves to join his comrades. Mustafa turns slowly around.

"Why?" His face is red beneath his beard, his eyes glassy and large. "They will die, anyway. What do you care?" He advances toward me, tendons working his neck. "It is her. I know it."

"No." I back away, arcing the gun to cover both him and the Arabs. The lead Arab has turned to his camel, reaching for what might be a weapon. I have no doubt they will be willing to take what they want if it is not offered for sale. Mustafa turns, sensing this, too. Even Karim pokes his head from his wagon. But the lead Arab merely clambers upon his camel, reaches for the reins, and coaxes the animal into a stiff-legged walk. The smaller man and the boy follow suit.

The taller man says something to the smaller, who shouts to us in his broken Turkish, "We have other opportunities. It is your loss!" The camels pick up speed, stretching their pitching strides. The tall man's dirty kaffiyeh disappears below an outcrop.

Mustafa turns to face me, his skin still inflamed. Karim climbs down from the wagon, holding his weapon, unsteady on his feet. He totters over to stand at our side.

"They will be back," says Mustafa, his voice soft and dead.

"They will take what they want, tonight. And I will give it to them."

Karim looks from him to me.

I pull my gun to my side, my finger still on the trigger, ready to raise it if either shows movement. I clear my throat.

"I have given my order, Mustafa. We will not be selling anyone. As I told you before, if you disobey me, you will pay with your life."

Mustafa's head remains down. Karim sways on his feet, his stomach gurgling, distress audible even at a distance. He skips sideways, pulls at his pants, takes a few steps with his buttocks outstretched before showering the ground in yellow feces. Mustafa, mouth tight, walks away.

I relax my grip on my weapon. I scan the camp, in search of Araxie. I worry anew of Mustafa's revenge. To my right, an old woman's wrinkled bottom lies exposed, her fouled clothing stripped away. Others lie moaning beside meager belongings, too exhausted even to put up ragged tents. A number of the children and some of the adults are naked, their clothes stolen or worn away, their bodies smeared with mud and excrement. Everywhere people hunch, clutching their abdomens—the dysentery has spread so that many even in our group now defecate almost constantly. The flies that plagued Katma have found us, swarming our eyes, nesting in our hair. Lice spread like raindrops. Everything stinks, of defecation and human despair, like the last excretions of a dying body. I consider for a moment whether I have made the right decision, whether life as a slave or concubine might be better than this. Mustafa was right about one thing—many of these people will die.

I stride back through the rubble, searching, eyeing the group. By my calculation at least half are ill, a quarter barely able to walk. We will be forced to slow our pace even further, to leave more behind. I prod prone forms with my rifle, looking for tell-tale clothing, a wisp of familiar hair, a glimpse of an exotic eye. Occasionally I turn over a dead body, its tongue thrust forward, the skin patchy and gray. It is near one such corpse that I find her, huddled against an older, squat woman, her hands gripping her sides. She stares up through lidded eyes, her face marked with pain.

"I have it," she murmurs, as the older woman smoothes her brow. "The illness."

I stand again in my garage. It is hot. I am thinking. It is strange how life works, all one's life looking forward, until at some point a clock shifts and there is more past than future. A long life means death—of companions, compatriots. And the swiftness! Ninety years in an eye-blink, and still things surprise me. These dreams that come late and play out like a movie—*The Big Sleep*, perhaps, *The Best Years of Our Lives*. So *real*, then. I wake and don't know myself. I must think, remember, sort out, catalog. Regain my mental order, after ninety-two years.

I stare about me at boxes. I pull things, unearthing paint cans, old financial matters, things I had been through when Carol passed away. A bicycle rests against one wall, its tire flat; I had ridden it a month ago on a bet then with Carl. Photo albums, furniture. Toys. My old tools. Nothing from the start of my life, nothing hoarded and then forgotten. I examine the gray box again, but find nothing more. I find much that reminds me of Carol.

I had given away most of her things when she died: her jewelry, her pictures and dresses. I offered these up to her sisters, but a few things I kept: a painting she had given me, a stuffed animal I won at a fair. I rearranged the furniture as well. I bought nothing new, only changed things to change them. I did not wish to think of her after her death. The music she liked, the perfume she wore, even things with her handwriting—I scrapped all of these. Her memory comes back now in pieces, like splinters. The day Violet was born. A trip to a park in New York.

And London. The headaches now, the hospital stay bring me back there. Awakening, in a drafty ward where everyone spoke an odd language. The terror in not *remembering*, a void so large as to be wounding itself. Was I sane? I feared I would be killed, by both doctors and patients. At first they thought I was faking, that I was pretending to forget to protect vital secrets. They brought in a Turkish speaker to translate, an old man who reeked of tobacco and regarded me with a certain disdain, as if I had betrayed something or shown weakness. He repeated questions or instructions and reformulated my responses, all without looking at either me or the doctors, as if he had been forced to do this, as perhaps he had been. Was he a prisoner? *I* was a prisoner, an enemy soldier, a fact that made my recovery all the stranger and more difficult. Had I, only weeks before, fired a gun at these men, causing their injury or them mine? I had no recollection of it. Some of the other patients knew of my status, or came to know of it. Some showed friendliness, others hostility, but all in a language I could not comprehend. A guard was posted nearby, for my protection or that of the others, and after one memorable incident when a man screamed and pounded my ribs with his crutch, I was moved to a separate room off one side of the ward. There I met Carol.

I had never before seen such a woman. Her blond hair, yes, but also her skin, her eyes. Her voice was soft. She taught me some English. The room was quiet, away from the bustle and moaning and smells of the ward, and I could hear her, and after some time understand. I learned that as an American she, too, felt a stranger. She would put her hands on me softly, bathing me, checking for fever. Changing the bandage I had worn for so long, smoothing the hair that would never again grow quite right. She smelled of cleanliness, and sweetness. How many soldiers become beguiled by their nurses? She befriended me, took control. She fought for me. She extended me kindness, a kindness worthy of return. She was American—America! She brought a new life.

The doorbell rings, the chime faint in the garage. Is it Wilfred? Please, not Mrs. Fleming.

But it is Carl, my neighbor. I greet him. We retire to our chairs.

"I heard about your tumor," Carl says. He wheezes when he speaks. "It's hell getting old. But you're older than hell."

We laugh at this. I like Carl. He is unpretentious, in the way southerners are. He is also quite prejudiced. The word "nigger" frequently rolls from his lips, along with other expressions of scorn.

Carl is a World War II veteran, of the campaign in the Pacific. Our conversations often turn to war. Carl's ship was sunk and he spent two days in the water. A number of his shipmates were eaten by sharks. He tells this story again and again, but I do not mind. He has not been in the ocean since 1944.

I remember World War II, but as a civilian. I was in my forties then, working two jobs. I was not yet a citizen. After the Depression, after those difficulties, I thought of little but work. Yet the war stirred something in me, some new sense of patriotism. I had begun to think of myself as an American. I wanted to help. Carol wanted to volunteer, as a nurse. But Lissette had been born then, Violet was on the way. So I worked.

Carl is on modern topics today, though. Affirmative action. The Negroes again.

"I tell you, it's nuts," he says. "This country's going to hell. Everything we fought for, the government's pissing away. Giving it to the coloreds, who don't want to work. They don't want to do anything, except breed."

I nod my assent. Carl forgets that my grandson is half black. He does not know, for I do not tell him, of the discrimination I suffered myself, the lost jobs, lower wages. Even now, with my darkened skin, I sometimes feel the sting of disdain, the expressions of false superiority—I, who have worked all my life. I look around at all the things I have purchased, the conveniences, the luxuries. The dishwasher and washing machine. The air-conditioned house. As a child could I have thought of ever having such things? For some reason today they seem dated, though, worn. Am I pleased? I think I would have had more if my skin had been whiter.

I imagine sometimes what life would have been if I had not been injured. If I had not met Carol. I would have remained in Turkey, perhaps become a tradesman. Living in a small house made of stone, making trips to the baths. Drinking tea in a café. A life full of poverty, at least comparatively so. Yet there is an appeal to it. It is silly, I tell myself. But I cannot shake it.

The doorbell rings again. I rise, and answer. A black man stands in the threshold.

"Yes?" I am uncertain. It is as if he has appeared from my conversation with Carl.

"I'm from Allied, the home health agency." The man's voice is low. He is tall. He has a beard. "For monitoring," he says. "Ted has the day off."

Violet appears and welcomes him in. His name is Ethan. I go back to Carl, to explain.

"Because of my headaches, Violet thinks I need to be monitored. A waste of money."

Carl's face is the color of sausage. "In your home?"

I nod. "I suppose it is better than the nursing facility."

Carl shakes his head. "My kids better not try that. I'd rather be shot. I never did that with Gladys, and I damn sure don't want it done for me."

Carl's wife, Gladys, had been an invalid, as well. She died at about the same time as Carol. I notice that Carl speaks now of Gladys in adoring terms, whereas before he complained much about her.

I hear Violet and Ethan from the other room. Carl's eyes move to the sound, as if he can see through the wall. I am reminded that after the war, Carl worked for the Federal Bureau of Investigation.

"Does he stay the night?" he whispers.

I nod.

Carl rolls his eyes.

Our conversation is broken. Carl rises with difficulty, makes for the door.

"God, I'm in pain." He straightens to normal height. "I envy you your health."

"Carl, I have a brain tumor."

"Hey, what year did you become an American citizen?" he asks suddenly.

I think. "Nineteen forty-nine. Why?"

"Just wondering."

I ponder this as he leaves. I have wondered before if Carl remembers whom I fought for, the way he carries on about us veterans and such. Sometimes our conversations bring scraps of memory, battle sounds, the fierce shuddering when mortar shells hit cold mud. People were buried alive then. The steep ditches, the wetness. We were ill equipped. There were rats. We were so hungry.

I go back to Violet and Ethan. He is not talkative, like Ted, only nodding as Violet delivers instructions. I say nothing, either. We stare at each other.

Ethan is not a movie fan. He sleeps through most of *The Lion in Winter*. But my mind is not on the film. I keep thinking of the dream, trying to remember. Did I know girls in my village? Are there Armenians I remember?

I stand. "Are you from Wadesboro?" I ask Ethan, who struggles awake.

"From Tifton," he says. Some fifty miles away.

"Do you like it here?"

"Yeah. It's okay." He stretches his legs. He is a large man, over two hundred pounds. "How 'bout you? Where're you from?"

This question again. "I have lived here forty years," I say. "Before that, New York. I was a builder." I do not go into before. I never do, unless asked.

But Ethan goes no further. He says little the rest of the evening. We have dinner, roasted chicken that Ethan warms in the oven. He speaks in low tones to someone on the phone, laughing occasionally, his voice soft and throaty like a baritone saxophone. Then I go to bed, early. It is only just dark.

That night, Mustafa tries to kill me.

I fell asleep in a sitting position, near Araxie and the old woman called Dodi, beneath a moonless, starry sky made pregnant with clouds. Mustafa kept to the camp's other side after the exchange with the Arabs, but we were small enough now that I saw his glances my way. I prepared my defenses—my back against an outcrop, my rifle loaded and ready. I even secured a new weapon, a blunt, curved *yatağan* hidden since Harput by a now-dead deportee. But my efforts at remaining awake foundered, weakened by fatigue and the stress of Araxie's illness. She had vomited and defecated throughout the day, twisting, feverish. I brought her water and offered her small pieces of bread, both quickly expelled by her body. She gritted her teeth through her misery. At other times she slept. There was little I could do for her except wait, and pray.

Her voice awakens me now, soft and insistent, the words in Armenian but the tone unmistakable. A warning. She is some distance away, in the protective arms of Dodi, but I know she has spoken. I turn, listening, but only the stir of the deportees breaks the silence: the moans, the evacuations of the sick, the sniffles over the dead and dying. What must they dream, these shreds of humanity—of loved ones now gone, banquets once held? I pull at my beard, shift my position. A bat zaps down and away. Insects hum. A wolf howls in the distance. I hear nothing else.

And then it comes, the tremor through the rock at my back, the click above and behind. Movement. I crouch against the rock's base, one hand on the rifle, the other on the large knife. I peer at the top that is tall like a house, note again how it tapers down either side. Anyone coming over the crest will have a large drop and be easily visible, even in the darkness. Approaching from the side will take longer, provide exposure.

I wait. The sound comes again, masked by a spasm of illness in front of me. The movement is careful, timed to blend in, but its tone is different, scampering where the other is forceful, shielded instead of frontal. It lasts a shade longer than the deportee's emission, stops a second later, a hollow-sounding echo left to bounce in its stead. The attacker realizes his error, for he waits some time before moving again, maybe ten minutes. I wonder whether he sees me, conclude he probably does not, yet. I keep still. I rub the haft of the knife, prick my finger on its long, convex blade. A powdery thirst dries my throat.

A loud plop sounds, ahead and to my right. I remain rigid, rotating my gaze to take in the floating blackness. Nothing. I recognize this as the feint, as the hope I will emerge to check the sound's origin. I take several deep breaths. A long stillness follows. Again, I feel more than hear shifting above and behind me. I ponder my strategy. Blood trickles from my finger where it traced the blade's edge.

Araxie has not spoken since the words that awakened me. I wonder if they were even intended for me, whether it bespeaks coincidence or providence that they penetrated my sleep. Her head now rests in a different position, her face angled toward me, her eyes shut. I am reminded of the night we met, under the trees, in the starlight—how things have changed in a few days. As though a river has hit a slope and its water shoots sideways. There is new ground, there are paths unknown. But am I not the same? I am a gendarme. A guide through the wilderness.

The tremors sift through the rock again, higher this time, almost directly above me. A few grains of sand fall and sprinkle the earth below. Releasing the knife, I grab a handful of pebbles and fling them to my left, at the same time pitching myself to the right. A gunshot explodes, kicking sand and debris near my feet. I raise my rifle and fire at a black shape near the top of the outcrop, dust and smoke spewing about me. I fight my way backward, out of this haze, in time to see a dark form drop from the sky and knock my gun from my hands, kick, roll, and re-form into an upright, compact shape: Mustafa. He holds his hands in front of him, like an animal brandishing its claws, shakes sand from his hair, utters a low growl. He starts toward me. His teeth grip a short knife, the effect a malicious grin.

Backing in the direction of my original post, I keep my eyes on his enormous hands, the palms as wide as a goat's head. He advances. He spits the knife into one hand, flinging it with his teeth in an amazing feat that sends a shower of his breath some distance toward me. I backpedal. I reach the spot where I waited, stamp my feet, searching in vain for the *yatag an* I must have dropped there. I look for a weapon, a shield, a diversion— anything. I hesitate.

He charges. I dodge to my left, feel the rush of air, the sour smell of his skin as he thrusts past, the knife arcing. He turns, quicker than I expect, his eyes moist with excitement. Saliva mats his thick beard. I back away again in the direction of the camp, fearful I will trip over something and find him on top of me. Instead, my left foot meets the hardness of my knife.

I look behind him and yell, bending to pick up the weapon as he makes a half-turn at the ruse. He recovers instantly and launches at me again, swinging his blade like a hammer as I roll to my left, my hand on the *yatağan*'s edge. His knife catches the top of my head, shearing hair and skin, releasing a cascade of warm blood that explodes down my face. I flip my blade into the air, catch it at the haft, and thrust at him, all in one movement, blood in my eyes, my vision obscured. His roar and the thunk of resistance indicate contact, but I cannot see it. I yank back the *yatağan*, wipe at the goo on my face. I taste the earth in my blood.

Mustafa grips his right arm, the knife gone from his hand. His hand clenches back and forth like the claw of a crustacean. I expect him to charge again, to take advantage of my impaired vision, but he remains still, perhaps dazed by his injury, a wounded animal now unable to move. I inch closer, the *yatag an* erect, focused now on the rasp of his breathing, the glint of his eyes, until a new pulse of blood finds its way down my face, blinding me, opening me to his lunge, to the oversized pincer of his hand on my throat. I gasp, my weapon dropping, the rattle and glug of my failed breath loud against the camp sounds behind me. I see only his moist lips, the yawn beyond his mouth and the curled hair that surrounds it. I reach my hands upward, intent on his throat, but my strength has ebbed, his one hand more powerful now than my two. His face drops closer, emitting his foul breath, and I wonder if he will not kiss me, suck out the last of my life in a bitter caress. Dark turns to stars, to a strange, blinding light. I flail my hands in desperation, in search of any contact, my one hand finally colliding with liquid, then a rubbery substance, then hardness. I plunge my hand deep into his injured arm, pulling at slippery tendons, wrapping my fingers around ligament and bone. He screams, a hoarse, bleating noise like a camel's whine, his head against the side of my face. His hand loosens, then falls, dribbling down my chest to bounce off my knee. I rise, coughing, feel for the *yatag˘ an*, and find it. I brandish the weapon. Deep gulps of air fill my lungs.

Mustafa runs, his right arm limp and flapping, his body hunched to one side, away from the camp, into darkness. I am too weak to follow. For a time his footsteps sound on gravel and rock. Then all is silent, save for my high-pitched wheezing.

I gather my rifle, seeking other points of protection. I expect Mustafa's return. Finding a small embankment near one end of the camp, I set up beneath it, a position with my back to the deportees, defensible against outside attack. I run my hand through my scalp, dislodge a piece of loose skin, and elicit another stream of warm blood. I finger my swollen neck. The clouds break, the light of the stars becoming stronger and brighter. The camp mutters and drones behind me.

· 8 ·

"Papa! What are you doing?"

I turn. Violet stares from the hallway, her hand on the light switch. I turn back, to the coughing form before me. A black man lies with his back twisted, his head bent close to my chest.

"What happened?" I ask. A coldness enters my stomach.

"You were choking him. I heard him call out."

The man—Ethan—gags, his hands near his throat. He struggles to turn, rises to a near-sitting position, topples and falls. I glance at the clock: 7:27 a.m. I reach around him, to help him sit up.

"My God." Violet's voice is unsteady.

Ethan lifts his head, his eyes red and watery. His neck puffs outward like a lizard's raised frill. He holds his hands near his throat, pulling at nothing, as if their presence might help his breathing, or ward off further assault.

I shiver against a chilled sweat, the growing realization of what must have occurred.

"I . . . was dreaming." My gaze swings to Violet, to Ethan. He struggles to swallow.

"Are you okay?" I bend closer to him. "Violet. Please bring some water."

I turn back.

"I . . . I do not remember." My voice is garbled. The dream plays out before me, the struggle with Mustafa, the hand, the knife. I finger my own neck. My breathing sounds coarse.

Ethan is nodding, attempting to speak. "I'm okay," he whispers, his voice like torn paper.

I shake my head. "Try not to talk."

Violet returns with the water. "Thank God I came by to check on you two." She peers into Ethan's big eyes. "Are you sure you're okay?"

He brings the water up to his lips. "Yes, okay."

She pulls me into the hall.

"I was dreaming," I whisper. "I was in a fight. We had our hands at each other's throats, and then I woke up. I . . ." I go no further. I rub my hands.

"Jesus. You don't remember coming into his room?"

"No."

She shakes her head. "We probably need to call his agency." She stares at a point on the carpet. "Let me talk to him. You go lie down."

Shivers creep up my shoulders. I reach for her, then stop. Dr. Wan changed the medications, but . . .

We stare at each other.

"Do you need anything?"

I shake my head no.

"What can I do?"

"Nothing."

I return to my room, my bed. I try to sleep. I listen, to the murmur of voices.

The shower runs. Someone talks on the phone. Eventually I rise and get dressed. I try to make sense of it all but cannot. Everything has become blurred, my life and the dream and their story and this. The odd feeling that after, I think I remember, far back.

I rub Sultan's ears. His purr is loud, like a motor.

I walk into the kitchen. Violet is puttering about making breakfast. Ethan is nowhere in sight.

"How is he?" I ask.

She cracks an egg. "I think he's okay. The agency wants him to be examined by a doctor." She looks up. "They've also called the police."

I study her expression. Is it accusation? Pity? I nod my head.

I eat. I hear Ethan before I see him. He is carrying his bags down the hall. His neck is swollen, as if stung by bees, ribbons of purple alive in his skin. His eyes are puffy but focused. I start to rise, to express regret. He stops me with the raise of his hand.

"It is not your fault," he says. Something short of a smile cracks his lips. "You are a strong man, for your age."

I look down. Images from the dream stream back: Araxie's neck at the ziggurat, the bloody fight with Mustafa. But this man is a stranger.

"I'm okay now." His voice sounds better, more like wet cardboard. "How are you?"

"I am fine." I bring my head up. "You will see a doctor?"

"Yes."

I nod my head. I want to explain—how do I explain? "It is odd," I say finally, "these dreams that come now. I have not experienced anything like them, not in all the many years of my life. It is not as if I dream the house is on fire—I keep dreaming a certain story, a continuing story. As if I am another person, living a different life."

Violet shifts at the kitchen counter. Ethan stares.

"What happens in your dreams?" Violet's eyes show fatigue.

"Suffering. Cruelty, and bravery. It is a trek. People are dying."

"And fighting, I gather," says Ethan.

"Yes. Fighting." I stare at his hands—so large, like Mustafa's.

The doorbell rings. Violet goes to answer it, leaving Ethan and me to stand, looking at each other and then away. There are voices, a closed door, a starched uniform. The police have arrived.

The officer is a thin, dark-haired man with a bluish face—Officer Hanna. He begins by examining the bedroom, then takes Ethan's statement, then Violet's. This is done in the living room while I wait in the den. I hear little of the conversations other than a few words here and there: "hallucination," "brain tumor." I have the TV on, *The Poseidon Adventure*. I eat but taste nothing.

The doorbell rings again. Another muffled conversation takes place. I assume it is more policemen arriving, but instead the door opens and Mrs. Fleming enters.

"There you are. I saw the police car. I wondered what was going on."

I am surprised but not displeased. She is sympathetic, someone to talk to.

"I assume Violet told you what happened," I say. My voice is low, and distant.

"She said you were dreaming. That you walked in your sleep."

"Yes."

"What were you dreaming?" She takes a seat on the couch, across from me. Her face is pinched in concern.

I stir the remnants of my food. "I dreamed I was in a fight."

"With whom?"

"Someone who wanted to kill me."

"Why?"

Sweat forms at my hairline. "I would not do something he wanted." The dream flashes back, harsh in its detail. I fight it, fight the sense that I'm falling.

"What?"

"I would not sell someone into slavery."

Mrs. Fleming moves closer, her eyes bright with attention. "What kind of slavery?"

"I am unsure—something like a harem." I spread my hands. "I would rather not discuss it."

"Okay." She sits back in her seat. "How fascinating. At one time I kept a dream journal. Do you write your dreams down?"

I consider this. The dreams are clear now in my memory, even from the first cold and wind, but will they remain so? So much time has gone past, now. I have forgotten so much.

Officer Hanna enters with Violet, motions that it is time for us to talk. I follow him into the living room, leaving Violet and Mrs. Fleming behind in the den. Ethan is not in the room when we enter. I assume he has given his statement and left.

I sit down on the couch. The room seems dingy. Dust breaks

and glides through the air. There is the photo Lissette once gave me of the Statue of Liberty, arm raised in greeting.

"Your name, please." The voice is measured, southern.

"Emmett Conn."

"Your age?"

I give it. Certain rights are explained—I do not have to answer. It is not like TV. The questions unfold. Was I angry with Mr. Eppes? Have I dreamed like this before? Ever had a similar altercation?

I am polite in response, cooperative. No, I was not angry. The dreams are elaborate, confusing. I have not fought, not in years. I did not know this man's name.

"What will happen now?" I ask when it is over, when he has closed his slim notebook.

"I don't know," he replies. "We need to talk with the medical people. We need to speak again to Mr. Eppes. We'll have to see. You will stay in the house?" He directs this to Violet, who has entered the room.

We shake hands.

I retire to the den, where Mrs. Fleming still waits. There is silence, an awkwardness.

"Perhaps I'd better be going," Mrs. Fleming says finally.

I smile. "Thank you for coming." I am grateful, truly grateful, but I sound only bored. I wish to be alone now, in the dark of this . . . this . . .

Mrs. Fleming smiles back. "I'll check on you." She swings her hips as she exits.

Violet calls Dr. Wan's office, wades through responses, insists on speaking to the doctor, says she will hang on. My hands still tremble. I think of a job site in New York, a scaffolding failure in which a man broke his leg. I was not at fault, but there was an inquiry . . . Haley—that was the man's name. I felt bad for him afterward. The inspectors questioning, big men with clipboards. I was older then and yet nervous. Could I not still be deported? I remember them talking to my subordinate as if I were not there, as if I were too stupid to bother with, too foreign or dark. I read Shakespeare, Steinbeck! Were my teeth fixed then? Another ground for derision. We spent good money fixing my teeth.

A squawk comes from the phone. "How are you this day!" I hear the voice from where I'm sitting.

Violet explains the situation. The phone whispers. Violet murmurs and clucks. There is a pause, then she holds out the receiver, the phone cord unwinding to become almost straight, like a rope. "He wants to speak to you."

"Mr. Conn! Hello!" Dr. Wan's voice buzzes, a dragonfly caught in a drum. "This is unfortunate. As I think you will agree, it must be treated seriously. You will need to be monitored. Your medication needs to be adjusted. You may need to see a psychiatrist."

A psychiatrist? I am already being monitored. He continues his discourse, but I am thinking again, about history, about genes, how babies' eyes are blue at birth and then brown. About time slipping past like a wind, ninety years, and at the end there is turmoil, as at the beginning. And the middle—the long and dulled middle? Working, providing. Shaping. So much is wasted.

We drive to the medical office, meet with Dr. Wan. Blood is drawn, more questions asked. There is testing to be done, evaluation. And then? I am tired. We sit in the car afterward, the radio on, the melody triggering some memory of music, something—a chord?—from the time long before. I yawn and it fades. I want to ask Violet if she finds it embarrassing, the old man bringing shame, the bitter switch in our postures. Or is it now satisfying, perhaps even pleasurable? I turn but her head is bent as she writes, some note on what to do next or things not to forget. She looks determined. She reminds me of Carol, extracting me from the British. I stare out the window and say nothing more.

We struggle toward Aleppo. The sky becomes the ground, the clouds crags and valleys, turning and shifting and re-forming like sand. Vultures circle, suspended on updrafts, silent, held by a string or a thought from beyond. The sun grows hotter, the terrain drier, water soon becoming our most immediate objective. Our supplies are never enough, particularly for those suffering from dysentery. Many collapse, left behind as we trudge on in the sun. One boy of perhaps nine or ten develops *gurû*-sized lip blisters. The tongues of others turn gray and black. Still others are dragged on thin blankets, pulled by hunched women without shoes, their feet scabbed and bloodied. I allow for multiple breaks and water searches, at the same time insisting on progress. Reality dictates completion of this journey, for any of the group to survive.

We descend on wells like jackals. We buy water (with coins the deportees pull from clothing or orifice) at exorbitant prices. We lick dew from leaves, we beg when trains puff by, we forage in empty fields. We see no sign of the Arabs we encountered earlier, no sign of Mustafa. I place Karim, who has improved to the point that he can now ride a donkey, at the back of our group to guard against attack. He eyes my wound with interest but offers no questions, makes no reference to Mustafa. I keep a close watch on him. I sleep little.

Araxie descends to near delirium. I keep a goatskin of water especially for her. I check on her constantly. The old woman who tended to her when she first became ill grows sick herself and dies and another woman named Ani takes her place, wiping Araxie's forehead, changing her soiled clothing. I offer them various modes of transportation, placing them aboard my horse, pulling them behind in a small cart. Araxie actually feels most comfortable walking, plodding with her head down, her footsteps heavy in the dust. During one such march I thank her, for I am sure she saved my life by alerting me to Mustafa's attack, but she offers no response. During other periods I question myself, wondering why I am here, why I covet her and not others. She is haggard now, the bones visible in her thin shoulders, her arms rigid and stick-like. She smells like rotten meat. The eyes that had so beguiled me before squint now against glare and sand, her lips swollen, her face burned by the sun. Still, I worry, I plot. I dream. I will not let her die.

We follow the railroad tracks, the route I have been told leads to Aleppo and beyond, to Damascus. More trains pass, headed in both directions, their rumble apparent long before any sighting. Several of the northbound trains carry Turkish soldiers in familiar olive-tan uniforms, the soldiers gawking and laughing, shouting derisive epithets. Their jibes make me cognizant of my own appearance, more like that of a deportee now than of a gendarme, my police tunic faded and stained, my head still bandaged from Mustafa's attack. The occasional travelers on foot or horseback avoid us, giving way or making wide circles. One Turkish-looking woman tosses food at my feet, a package of bread, cheese, and halva. Others shout, or sneer, or look on in silence.

The terrain changes as we near Aleppo, desert giving way to tended fields, to farmers working at crops. We pass apricot orchards, fields of wheat and barley, groves of pomegranate trees. Children scurry near a house in a field. A group of adolescents stare from the side of the road. Several peddlers' carts pull around us, knives and cookware jangling. Our pace quickens. Mothers urge their children on, the dying gain new life. It strikes me that I have left my homeland; I have entered a foreign state. For the deportees this will become a way station, a refuge until the end of the war, perhaps a new home. For me, all is less clear.

Farms and fields give way to houses, to people and streets. I stop our group on a boulevard fronted by large white buildings, searching for someone of officialdom, marveling at the sights and colors. Aleppo is large, much larger than Harput, with hordes of exotic-looking women, some covered in black burkas with only slits for their eyes, others with large gold earrings and bracelets stretching from wrist to elbow, still others in colorful clothing and flowery hats. Boys in caftans dart and run, men in suits smoke. Vendors young and old offer walnuts, breads, and candies on tablets hung from their necks. Turkish, Armenian, and Arabic mix in the air, stirred by a flowery language I assume to be French. A number of men in military uniform pass, paying no attention to our filthy band. Finally, an officer in a crisp uniform and tall black boots crosses the street toward us. I move to address him.

The man asks something in Arabic. I bow, exposing the wound

atop my head. I remember again my appearance. I straighten, pressing my heels together in some semblance of military posture.

"Effendi, I have delivered these deportees from Turkey," I say in Turkish, my voice still graveled from Mustafa's grip. "Many are ill."

The man spits, kicks at the ground. "So I see." His Turkish has an Arabic accent. "You Turks send to Syria your lice, your vermin, and your dying, yes?" He looks over the remains of my group, reduced now to maybe sixty-five, then turns back to me. "Most of the gendarmes leave them to find their way here on their own."

He spits again and points to an unfinished two-story structure a block away. "That building is being used as a hospital for refugees," he says. "Take them there." He scratches his head. "Widows will need a permit to stay. Children will be cared for. Others must leave." He shakes his head, eyes the group once more, and departs. His weaponry clinks as he walks.

The hospital is a partially constructed stone building with open holes for windows, but it offers shelter and a measure of cleanliness. For the deportees it provides some sense of finality to the endless journey. A number will find friends or relatives from previous caravans, people who can care for them, help find food, educate them to the rules and customs of a strange and foreign city. The facility is crowded but habitable, the conditions infinitely better than the pit at Katma. The hospital is run by a team of Syrian doctors and nurses who insist on hygiene and provide adequate clothing, food, and water. Medicine is available for the diarrhea that plagues many. Even I receive treatment and a dressing for my injured scalp. Araxie is placed on one of the cots reserved for the sickest patients, her filthy clothing removed, water and medicine forced down her throat. Her eyes are closed. She stirs and coughs and gives signs of appearing more comfortable, but she does not wake.

I stay with her for some time, sitting with the old woman Ani, who has cared for her, watching her chest rise, listening to the thin draft of her breathing. Flies buzz, nurses in stiff white caps come and go. The sun creeps in through a hole in the stones, tossing shadows against blank walls, but neither Ani nor I say anything. The shadows lengthen as the day goes on, plunging the room to dusk, then darkness. The cries of the muezzin come and I prostrate myself, orient myself toward Mecca. The sounds and smells of the hospital creep up through the walls. A small bit of bread and some yogurt are delivered. Finally, a nurse summons me.

"The Syrian official in charge wishes to speak to you," she says in broken Turkish. I follow her downstairs.

A slender young man with a small mustache awaits me. He is about my height, probably only a few years older, dressed in an official-looking smock, his feet in strange-looking sandals. He introduces himself formally in passable Turkish, states his name as Hussein. He does not smile.

"This facility is for refugees only," Hussein says, his fingers tracing the edges of a small clipboard. "You are a gendarme, yes?"

I nod.

"You must leave."

"I . . . I have been injured." My voice sounds foreign in its mangled state.

"You must report to the military garrison, or I will inform

them of your presence." He lowers the clipboard. "I do not expect they will be pleased to hear from me, injury or not."

I study the man, the way his hands move, the thrusting forward of his smallish chest. To explain my status will be futile. I have seen men like this before.

I shift my feet. "What of the deportees?"

"What of them?" His face compresses, the beginnings of a sneer. "You have killed most of them already—are you wishing to finish the job now? You have delivered them, those that have made it. Now leave."

"Will they be allowed to stay?"

"Some will, some will not. The rules change. At present, any woman who can prove she is a widow may stay. Everyone else must go."

"What about the children?"

The man shrugs. "To the extent the orphanages can take them, the young may remain."

"And the others?"

The man's face contorts again. "Many will go to Ras al-Ayn, where there is a refugee camp. But why do you care? Could it be there is a *sevmek* among them?"

He uses the Turkish verb for "love," but I know what he means.

"No. I am merely concerned. I have traveled with this group for many days."

I turn to go, to retrieve my rifle and few belongings.

"Effendi."

I turn again.

"Do not return."

I awake to a gray dawn, to the last vestiges of the closest stars. Moisture dampens my face, courtesy of a wet breeze that fails to quell the suffocating odor of urine, feces, and aged, dampened straw. The stable, if you can call it one, is open to the sky, its roof long since burned or blown away. Its other occupants, a horse and two oxen, shift and doze. Flies buzz. Wooden slats creak softly in the breeze. I brush at my legs, at the vermin crawling upon me. I stand and brush again.

The horse is not Gece. I sold my companion the day before, a parting both necessary and sad. Negotiations began with one merchant, then another, until I had been through six traders and upped the price considerably, though still to an amount only a fraction of his worth. A fine Arabian with all the stamina and intelligence of his breed, he'd been well cared for despite the rigors of our journey. He watched as I accepted the coins from the dour Arab who purchased him, his head cocked, his eyes unblinking. I turned my head as he was led away.

I wandered the streets of Aleppo afterward, past the suq and the spacious courtyard khans, past beggars and peddlers and mosques and graveyards, past stables and markets, soldiers and refugees, on to the ruins of the giant fortress rising up from the city's center. The citadel, stacked layer upon layer over ancient buildings and cultures, was supposedly large enough to house a garrison of ten thousand, supposedly stormed only once, in 1400, by Tamerlane. I walked around it, observing the men and soldiers who marched down ramps worn with centuries of use, staring at its moats and walls, my mind on survival, on a plan (begun with the sale of Gece), of what to do next. My plan of how to stay near her.

Difficulties abound. Despite the sale of my horse, I have little money, no place to stay. I should have reported to the military garrison as I had always intended—I would move from the gendarmerie to the military, receive further instructions. Instead I am a deserter. I have no papers, at least none I want to show anyone, something any respectable employer will almost certainly ask to see. Given the Ottoman army's need for soldiers, a number of Syrians are being conscripted, such that even if I have proper papers or employment I am still subject to being pulled away. I dare not go near the hospital, not after the officious Hussein's warning, though I find myself unconsciously circling back in its direction, hoping for a glimpse of a familiar face: a nurse, a doctor, or someone who might tell me she is better, someone who will know she has been permitted to stay.

I reached the city's outskirts as the sun ebbed away, past the camel and sheep pens, the crumbling edge of the ancient western wall. I inquired about lodging in the seedier-looking khans, my face lowered, my Arabic as short and non-Turkish as possible, determined to sleep outside rather than waste the meager proceeds from Gece's untimely sale. In the end I agreed to stable work in exchange for a bed of hay, a negotiation that required more discussion than I wanted, more interaction with the short, suspicious owner. He checked on me several times, once in the middle of the night, ostensibly to ensure the well-being of his animals, more likely with the intent to rob me if he could. I slept little, given the vermin, the intrusions, and the dreams that blazed about me, the fiery visions of desert and pursuit, illness and squalor, all magnificent, all disturbing. All leading back to a single place. Her.

I squint now at the new dawn, at the flat roofs and domes, the minarets and dark cypresses. The limestone that makes up so much of the city hangs damp and gray in the morning, chiseled into patterns for churches, carved into verses for mosques. Aleppo means "milk" in Arabic, testament to the fabled stopover by Abraham on his way to Canaan, the milking of his cow on the citadel hill—Abraham, father of Isaac, father of Ishmael, grandfather to us all. The muezzin's call, as if on cue, mixes its minor tones with the animals' snorts and shuffles. I fall to my knees, dip my head to the straw. My lips move in rhythm.

The property owner marches in after the prayers, shouting at me in an Arabic so dense I can barely understand it, evidently unhappy I did not awaken earlier and re-clean the stall in the dark. I stare at him, at the tendons at work in his short, thick neck, the mustache that bobs up and down with his wrath. I wait until his breath is spent before stepping toward him, an action that precipitates his scurrying retreat. His mouth opens, quavers an instant, then lets loose another barrage, this time directed behind him. A thin-headed boy emerges, casts a glance my way, and departs. I know it is time to leave.

I gather my belongings, shaking them deliberately, the verbal assault still launched from behind a protective wall's bunker. Doors open, people peer from behind paper windows, the livestock mutter and stomp. I have only a few bits of clothing, a handful of coins, and a short, wicked blade I purchased from Karim (having hidden my aged German rifle the day before), but I take my time nonetheless, making an elaborate show of ridding myself of the fleas I picked up in the barn. Then I steal away, dipping swiftly into the labyrinthine passages that honeycomb the city, the twisted channels beneath arched stone vaults that will not see daylight for hours. The angry voice behind me grows distorted, then muffled, deflected by the passageways that resemble tunnels or caves. I pass few people as I hasten through the darkness, varying my direction, veering into side passages, venturing past half-opened doors that reveal elegant courtyards and fountains, stopping before white mosques and darkened churches, all the while chastising myself for my rashness, for this drawing of unwanted attention. Why am I here? I am risking my life. I buy a fez from a vendor just opening up for the morning, straddle it across my injured head. I spend a few precious coins for some kibbe. After munching my breakfast I wash in a fountain, bathing my flea-bitten legs and darkened arms, dipping my hands and face. I continue on after this, still conscious of the possibility of pursuit, past dense houses and tiny streets, on to the covered bazaar.

The smells of coffee and tobacco mix with food and incense. Peddlers greet one another, unroll rugs, unpack goods. A few early shoppers mill about. Foodstuffs materialize: olives and pistachios, breads and biscuits, walnuts, raisins, dried chickpeas.

Dogs poke in and out of refuse, shooed by one merchant to the domain of another. Bright, colored blankets appear, flapping like flags, hung on invisible lines. Smoke from a cook fire rises and quivers. A large woman with enormous hoop earrings arrives to much fanfare, spreading her wares (evidently jewelry) on the ground in grave fashion. An argument develops between two men in dirty tunics, resolves itself, starts again. People continue to funnel in—a shepherd leading a herd of goats, an elaborate horse-drawn carriage, a small grouping of gray-uniformed police. I move away from the latter, past displays of cotton clothing, colorful divans and hassocks, red and green beeswax candles. The suq has become crowded, as if the whole of Aleppo has now discovered its existence, the sounds of bargaining merging with sharp-tongued women in *çarşaflar*, merchants pleading and cursing, small boys selling or playing. The noise increases to a din, the aromas to overpowering, the crush of population to a thick, brownish tide. I inch back, drop a *guru* in a crippled woman's cup, and observe her toothless smile before leaving, edging through the haze that has settled over the bazaar, a dust seemingly wrung from the gray stone itself.

My wanderings take me down Bab al-Faraj Boulevard to the palace gardens, down wide streets lined with palm trees and handsome white buildings. Wealthy Syrian women walk about, some with jewels in their hair, others in high-button shoes. Businessmen wear odd-looking suits with ties. Fruit and vegetable vendors camp in front of older, more established shops, where tables are set for tea, with white tablecloths fluttering, bound flowers gathered in vases. An air of past glory predominates, oozing from the crumbling buildings, from the pocked wheels of peddlers' carts, from the packs of stray dogs that dig at immense piles of refuse even on the Bab al-Faraj. The odor of elimination abounds, as if the city has been overrun, overcome by a force too great to be accommodated. I stop before a Muslim cemetery, gazing at the rows of graves, the scrawls of Arabic inscriptions. All the world, particularly the Ottoman world, seems swallowed in a sea of disruption. A war is being fought, over what, I am not certain, by combatants I cannot identify, in places I do not know. Lives are affected—mine, my cousins', the deportees', hers. Things will change. At some point this city may become a battlefield, or a fortress, or a mortuary. People will leave and fight, suffer and die. And then what? I squint at the nearest grave and its inscription, trace the familiar words. *Allahu ekber.* God is great. Among other things, a battle cry.

"Ahmet."

I whirl at the unexpected sound of my name, my bag lifted high in alarm. A round, older woman stands before me, her hair under a veil. I stare, my pulse accelerating. Several seconds elapse before recognition comes, relief.

"Ani." It is the Armenian woman who took care of Araxie.

She nods, her body half turned, as if prepared to take flight. "I thought it was you."

"How is she?" I hear the quake in my voice.

"She is better. She sits up now, and can speak."

Allahu ekber. I am unsure whether I say it. "May I see her?"

Ani's thick eyebrows converge. "You are in danger," she says in her languid Armenian. "The man, Hussein, he asks about you, asks if anyone . . . has seen you."

"Is he there much?"

"Yes. He comes to see her often." She glances over her shoulder, as if expecting him to arrive here, too.

"Are we near the hospital?"

"Yes. Behind that building." She points in the direction of a crumbling edifice. "I am going to the market for bulgur. Although they are kind to us and give us food, this *vesika* bread, it is not much. It comes only every few days. Otherwise we have to buy, or beg."

"I can give you some money." I dip into my bag.

"No." She shakes her head.

I pause, my hand still in my bag. "What should I do?" The question sounds desperate, if not ridiculous. Only a few hours before, this woman was my prisoner. Now I ask her advice.

Ani glances around. "Look for me in the big square, by the woman in the center selling jewelry. I will bring you word of her. I am hopeful she will soon come herself."

I nod.

"Now go."

I accompany Violet on a trip to Valdosta, an hour or so away. She has a meeting at the university there, some kind of discussion regarding accounting office practices. I am grateful for a change in routine, a chance to get out of Wadesboro. We have heard nothing more from the police. I have been told by the agency that Ethan is both "fine" and "recovering."

I wait in a small cafeteria while Violet has her meeting. Everyone is so young here, supple and full-cheeked, like children. It is hard to believe many are older than Carol and I were when we married. They nod to me, some of them, or ignore me. I purchase a cup of tea but it is flavored, the way Americans like it. I drink it anyway. I think of going to the library here and continuing my research but what more is there to research? I know the basics. There was war, conflict, insurrection—real or imagined. Deportations. I try not to think about it. Perhaps I have moved on, not unlike Recep's nephew.

I take a seat by a window with a view of a small courtyard. A snatch of music floats in, maybe a band practicing somewhere, but the melody buckles me suddenly down and down, such that I reach to place my hands on my knees but still plummet, the music loud in my ears. I see a band playing, a group of musicians in formal but dated attire. Others stand watching, listening, women in headscarves, men in baggy trousers held firm at the knees. Another sound carries across the music's intervals: piercing, then obliterated, drowned out by brass and strings. At first I cannot identify it, but then it bleeds through, welling up to overwhelm the intertwined melodies I recognize now as Mozart. The sound of human screams.

"Papa, are you okay?"

I sit up. Violet bends above me.

"I am fine," I say. "It is hot here." I search for my cup and find it spilled on the floor.

"Are you sure, Papa?"

"Yes, fine." I am irritable.

We exit the cafeteria to daylight, to jumble. Students trudge on pathways worn in lush grass. A young man attaches flyers to a post with a stapler. Buildings fill and empty, inhaling, expelling.

A group sits at a concrete table with heads bent, as in prayer. It is so ordered, so foreign. In another life I might have learned as they do, but my daughters did, and is that not what I wanted? Violet and her accounting. Lissette studied history. They would have walked on paths like these, bent their heads into books. Yet the thought of captured knowledge serves to feed my discomfort, as if someone will ask me something and then expose my deception. Are there Armenians here, too? A bass thunders close and I hear it, the Mozart. Chills make their way up the edge of my spine.

Violet is speaking, asking me something, but I am dazed and sweating and submerged in the heat, intent on blocking the music's return and, as such, whatever she is saying. What is happening to me? My heart thumps in upbeats, in cadence. The Armenians, these dreams—I did not ask for or want this. Are they glimpses of hell, of some afterlife just beyond? My life spent without God, without religion, and perhaps this is my consequence, to greet suffering with inaction, chained and observant, a man sentenced to watch a child's slow, painful death. Punishing. Equalizing. Such a prideful, vengeful God this would be, a God of retribution, not mercy. Do I think I deserve more? There is innocence, denial, faithlessness, blasphemy. The emptiness of happenstance, nothingness. These seeds I have sown.

"Papa!"

Violet is angry. I have ignored her. I have failed to respond. I think to speak now but would I then tell her, inflict her with the plague of my history, this turmoil that arrives at the dusk of my life? I do not wish to talk or dwell on it. If I talk there will be questions, calls for explanation, and justification. I do not wish to burden her any more than I have.

We enter the car, drive in silence. Signs litter the road, advertisements for mayhaw jelly, for tupelo honey. Church announcements. Remember, Moses Began as a Basket Case. If You Die Today, Where Will You Sleep Tonight? I count the churches, the denominations professing allegiance and yet fragmented, different. I think again about God, Allah, about the words of the prayers—do I remember? I turned my back on it, focused as I was on starting anew, a new life. There is a word for this shunning but I cannot find it. I meant no disrespect in existence, avoidance. My survival. Is it too late now? It is late. I stare out at farm implements. If I were younger I would work that much harder.

We pass green deer stands, the ladders up to short platforms. A dog trots, its head down. A house's gray siding curls like peels from a peach. I am thinking, aware again of my silence. Carol used to do this when angry, growing still and mute, refusing to acknowledge any question or comment. I found it infuriating. I do not wish now to mimic it. I determine to say something, anything, perhaps a new announcement, something clever—like these church messages? I am not clever. Still, I wet my lips. I venture forth.

"Everyone has a map, but most cannot read it."

Violet's gaze remains fixed.

I try again. "Is it better to follow a leader or lead only the followers?"

She crooks her head, puzzling. I indicate a blank sign.

"If God is watching, is he missing something else?"

I am pleased with myself. Again, "One wrenched from his childhood is always a stranger."

I smile, but she turns now, her jaw set. She takes a long breath, as if prolonging some pleasure.

"Everyone is wrenched from their childhood, Papa. You, me, Mother. You know this, don't you? We're all wrenched."

There is savagery in her tone, bitterness. I nod, my satisfaction quickly ebbed. I glance at her. Wrenched, from her childhood—the baby? I consider this. Violet came back but left again. She would have been eighteen then, maybe twenty. We went some time without contact. She was in California, on a land cooperative. Consumed with herself, with discovering "consciousness," she once told me, a rare conversation. She spoke more with Carol. She protested the war, Vietnam, though she would not be a soldier. She did not work. Carol sent her money. Eventually she came back, lived with us again, slept at odd hours. She went to the community college and worked a little, moved out and returned. A series of jobs followed, as bank teller, waitress, salesclerk, secretary. None lasted long. And then a new pregnancy. I think of my life, my obligations and effort. I stare out at new signs. Jesus Saves. Hot Boiled Peanuts.

Peter and Josephine—Brains and Brainsetta—are at the house when we return. This is an annoyance, as I am in no mood for company. I slip around them, hoping to escape to the rear of the house, but Peter catches my arm.

"Listen, I need to ask you something," he whispers, his lips barely moving.

This is a code phrase, for his asking for money. I have invested before, in the failed pest control venture (blasting bugs with sound waves), the failed ostrich ranch (the male and female soon so disliked each other that reproduction became out of the question).

Now that Carol is gone, must I listen? Lissette always thought Peter and Josephine were themselves a bit unsteady when it came to procreation. But perhaps I am the fool, for investing my funds to begin with.

"Listen," Peter continues, his lips still not moving, "I can get you in on a piece of a really great investment, if you're interested."

I open my mouth, unable to speak.

"I've got an exclusive deal on this process to turn cow manure into energy. A guy up in Ohio's done it there. Says it works like you wouldn't believe. And all these dairy farmers, they're facing a big environmental problem with what to do with their manure. This solves their problem. We've got a grant application in to the Department of Agriculture to fund a study."

I try to remember his current place of employment—Ace Hardware? Food Lion? "Peter," I say finally, "I am an old man. I have been ill. I am uninterested in risky investments just now."

"Okay, okay. No, I understand. I was just thinking of Violet, you know, and Lissette. It's up to you."

"Do you still have the ostriches?"

"Oh, yeah. Yeah." He pulls at his chin, twisting his face back to toothsomeness. "I can put a saddle on one of them now, ride her a little ways." He pulls some more, as if he has a goatee, but he does not. "She's a mean cuss, though. Bite the hell out of you if you're not careful. And smart—smart as the devil. Hmmm-hmm. Hmmm-hmm."

I look at my hands and the calluses there. Is life now plans and scheming? I worked twelve hours each day, fifteen hours. In the beginning I spoke little English. I took any job; I worked on tall buildings, underground. I did repair work at night. I studied the language all hours. Men stole from me, cheated me. I plodded on like a beast. My children had it easier, but this is what I intended, that they could further their minds. They could *be*! And yet it has not been, not as much as I hoped. I envisioned them creating, engineering this country, having dark-eyed babies as their husbands charged ahead. Is it discipline, only discipline? Perhaps religion again, if we had started them early—Carol's religion, any religion. I wonder if I have failed them. This bothers me so.

I sit. Peter's voice fades away. I am tired, thinking, other voices blurring, sleep coming quickly as it does at this age. As a young man I slept soundly, the perfect sleep of the dead. Now things are flimsy, shifts of sleeping and waking. And then these dreams, this current that flows through me. Can I not send it past, divert or bury it? I want to wake or sleep and not languish between them. Someone laughs nearby, but still my head falls back, into darkness.

· 10 ·

The tang of dust catches deep in my nose, mixed with dead smoke and a charred metal smell that sneaks under my skin and remains. I pull myself up from the floor. The tools of the knife maker's trade lie about me: the charcoal, wood, and animal dung used as fuel for the fire; the bellows; the vats of water; the hammers; the anvil; the raw pieces of metal; the sharpening stones; the finishing stones. To one side, on a table crowded with pots and urns, lie blocks of wood, knives for whittling and carving, metal screws and fasteners—materials for fashioning hafts. On the opposite side lie the finished products: the small, sturdy blades that gleam and shine in the faint light. I stand, feeling the dim heat from yesterday's coals that have never extinguished, still a dull red under layers of gray.

I have taken a job as a knife maker's assistant, in a shop behind a khan not far from the bazaar. The knife maker, a thin, older man named Abdul with disproportionately sized arms, perhaps owing to his profession, does not say much. He looked at me with long, questioning eyes as I offered my services in halting Arabic and Turkish, asked a few questions about my experience, examined the scars adorning my arms—past contact with hot metal fragments—the pockmarks on my face from the same. He said nothing about a *tezkere* or any other permit. I offered little else.

The work is as physically demanding as I remember it, leaving me exhausted by the end of each day. We arise before dawn, eat a cold breakfast of bulgur, supplemented sometimes by grapes or dates or occasionally a bit of *pastırma* sausage, and begin our work. It is my job to regenerate the fire, to stoke it until the coals glow orange, to tend it throughout the day, to shovel the ash into a small barrel to take to the street. The fire generates a constant plume of black smoke that engulfs us in the small space, burning our eyes, catching in our mouths and noses. Our faces and arms are blackened, marked by patches of white around eyes, nose, and mouth; discharges from blinking and sneezing form tiny paths in the blackness, as if worms have emerged and left trails crawling away. I begin coughing the first day, a cough I remember from my youth, a more or less constant croaking fueled by irritation from the smoke. Abdul exhibits a deeper, less frequent cough, a harsh, wet expulsion that shakes his body and forces him to release hammer or rod in an attempt to rid himself of whatever his body is trying to expunge. I remember this sound, also, a sound my father made in the years before he died.

I participate in almost all facets of the work, banging the raw metal into shape with the hammer, honing and sharpening the blades, cutting and fashioning the hafts, fastening blade to haft, sanding and polishing the final product. The only part Abdul keeps to himself is the sales effort. His trade is mostly wholesale, fueled by a band of swarthy, irregular dealers who arrive from time to time and engage in furious discussion over price, quantity, and quality. We make all manner of knives, but primarily smaller, utilitarian blades used for hunting, skinning, and butchering. On one wall of the tiny shop hang swords, scimitars, and even a stiletto, all strung in a row. Occasionally a dealer will peer through the smoke at these or ask that one be taken down for examination, although I gather from the reaction that the price is high, too high for the certainty of resale.

The work brings back memories, most of them negative. My arms ache from the working of the hammer—I estimate I deliver a thousand blows a day, maybe more—and the pumping of the bellows. Flying metal fragments cut and burn, searing my flesh into a thousand tiny sores that sting as I move. My hands are raw, between the sanding of haft and blade and the operation of the foot-powered grinder, where a slip of concentration can result in serious injury. Working in such tight quarters, Abdul and I bump each other regularly, and it is only the second day when I accidentally touch his arm with an orange-hot strip of metal. He flinches but says nothing, not even a reprimand, moving to a corner of the shop to bathe the wound in a salve taken from a brown jar. I notice afterward that his arms are a mass of scars, like tattoos hidden under layers of smoke. He returns the favor several days later, turning when I do not expect it, stabbing me in the abdomen with the hot tip of a knife just out of the fire. I gasp, trying to mimic his stoicism but failing, clutching at myself, bent double by the pain. He walks calmly to the back of the shop, returning with a dollop of salve and reaching under my shirt to apply it to the angry spot on my belly. It cools the pain, allowing me to return to work, but it will be nearly a week before I feel completely free of the burning sensation, the painful catch every time I twist my body. This, too, I remember from my father's shop, the lightning-like pain of a poke with an ember—sometimes an accident, other times not.

Once a week (for the two weeks I have been there) Abdul permits me to accompany him to the public hammam, or bath. The one near his shop is large, larger than the one in Harput, with spacious separate sections for men and for women. We walk over, our towels and clean clothes slung from our shoulders, to the squat stone building set among rows of fine houses. Abdul's words to the initial attendant bring us to an anteroom, where we disrobe and give our blackened clothing to another attendant. We wait, naked, for yet another attendant to lead us into the bath itself. The place smells of mold, and soap, and some fragrance I know but cannot place. It is warm, to the point that if we wait long in the anteroom I begin to sweat. Sometimes there are other men, sometimes entire families, from withered, white-haired grandfathers to school-aged boys, rich and poor, fat and skinny. Sometimes we are alone. The decades of knife making are evident in Abdul's body, from the definition in his aged shoulders to his darkened, muscular arms, to the scars that show once his skin has been cleaned, markings that make the rest of his body look white and smooth in comparison. I find similar scars across my own skin, blemishes I have not noticed before. Sometimes we hear women through crevices in the walls, snatches of laughter and conversation, exclamations. Other times it is silent. Although I know Abdul has a wife, she never accompanies us to the hammam. In fact, I never see her at all.

Attendants lead us to the main chamber, where heated water

is directed into pools, where other attendants dip the *tas* bowl into water, pouring it over us in dribbles, where we are scrubbed with a *kese*, a rough cloth mitt, to the point that often we bleed from the newly visible cuts on our arms. The attendants seem to anticipate this, as I suppose they have bathed Abdul for years, for they appear with clean cloths and cool salve, dabbing at abrasions, wrapping bleeding flesh. Then they dry us with our towels, smaller and thinner than the *peştemal*-type cloths we used in Turkey, and bring our clean clothes. I always leave the hammam refreshed but tired, a fatigue at once heavy and joyous, like the draw of a blanket on a cold, bitter night.

My work leaves me little free time. For the first few days I go to bed almost immediately after the evening meal, barely finishing the raw onions, bulgur, pistachios, and almonds before sleep overtakes me. After several days, though, I grow in strength, to the point where I clean myself as best I can and venture out before dark, to the bazaar, to hover near the woman selling jewelry, to prowl the curving alleyways, the area around the citadel. I search for her, or for Ani, dodging in and among people and animals, steering near the hospital but never too close. One day I see Hussein, his hands thrust in his pockets, crossing the street some distance away, hurrying, as if on an important mission. I grow bolder. Soon I am loitering across the street from the hospital itself, searching the faces of those entering or exiting. After several days my vigil is rewarded, when Ani's familiar form appears in the doorway, then edges off down the street. I stay on the other side, working my way down in parallel fashion until I judge us a safe distance from the hospital. I cross, catch up, and tap her once on the shoulder.

"How is Araxie?" I ask, my heart thumping in my voice.

Ani starts—my appearance still instills fear in her—but then recovers herself. "She is much better," she says in Armenian. "She is able to work in the hospital and perform some small chores."

A battalion of uniformed schoolchildren pass. I pause. "Will she be able to stay there?"

She frowns. "I do not know. We hear different things. There is a continuous stream of new refugees, many of whom are quite ill. Many that came with our group have been moved out—I do not know where."

I swallow. "Can I see her?"

She looks to either side, as if expecting an observer. "I will ask her. I will see if she is willing."

She turns and goes back to the hospital. I rub dust from my arms, spit in my hands, wipe dirt from my face. I have not had a haircut since Katma, my beard longer now and bushier, to where it enters my vision if I look down my face. I stare at my clothes, at the faded and ripped shirt, the pants with tears at both knees. I dare not wear my old police tunic for fear of being recognized as a Turkish deserter. At one point I considered a robe but decided against it. Abdul pays me only a few lira per week, which I hide in my pile of belongings in the corner of the shop—barely enough to buy food, let alone clothing. I run my hands through my thick hair. I glance at the scars on my arms.

Traffic moves around me. Elderly women and small children, probably Armenian, beg from doorway to doorway. A strange contraption proceeds slowly down the boulevard, metallic and belching fire at one end but operated of its own accord. Its driver, who steers by means of a shiplike wheel in its prow, waves to the gawking crowd. A group of newly arrived refugees pass going the other way, browned and mostly naked, the breasts of the women flat and curling. I look for a gendarme but do not see any.

A tug at my arm sends me whirling around. She stands next to me, dressed in a black veil with orange bands, her hair and skin hidden but her eyes unmistakable, the blue almost turquoise, the brown soft and dark. I find myself unable to say anything, only to take in her face, the wisps of her hair, the faint shape of her body underneath the dark covering. She looks healthier, her face fuller than when I last saw her, the pull of the veil making her seem older and taller, perhaps more exotic. I think of things I might say to her, how I have thought of her every day, almost every minute, through banging anvils and scouring baths and smoky lunches and sleepless nights. I take in a breath. She says nothing. She does not smile.

"You look well," I say haltingly. "I mean, better. I am glad." I am unsure of my wording, or what language I speak.

She nods. "I owe you many thanks," she says softly, almost inaudibly. Her eyes close and reopen.

"How long can you stay there, in the hospital?"

She grimaces, looks away. "Not much longer. There are so many refugees, so many desperately sick. I am nearly recovered."

"What are your options?"

She presses her lips together, whitening them with the pressure. "I am too old for the small children's orphanage, too young to take a trade. The homes for refugees my age are filled, at least the ones I've been able to locate." She pauses. "I hear stories of refugees being shipped back to the desert, to die."

I grasp her arm beneath her *libas*, my face close to hers. "I have a job. I am saving some money—perhaps enough for us to leave. Perhaps we can escape . . ."

Her face lifts upward. "But you will have to save a long time. I am afraid I have little time left." Her hand snakes from beneath the covering. She touches my arm. "The leader of the hospital, this man Hussein—he shows me much attention, too much. He is always asking about me, asking me to accompany him into the garden, bringing me little gifts, little candies. It worries me, his intentions. But I am in no position to refuse."

A dagger pierces my heart. I cough and draw in breath.

"He asks about you," she continues. "He asks your name, whether I have seen you. He asks Ani."

"And?"

"I tell him the truth, that I have not seen you. Ani has told him the same."

"What do you think will happen?"

She shrugs. "I do not think it is for me to know. I wake each day, thank God for my life, look for God's hand wherever I find it." She studies the ground again, then looks in my eyes. "I must go."

"When will I see you again?"

"Look for Ani in the bazaar," she says over her shoulder.

I watch her retreat until her form becomes distant. She crosses the street, to the other side, where the hospital lies, a thin black figure, ghostlike and then gone. A taste forms in my mouth, unimproved by my spitting. I glance down the boulevard, half expecting Hussein's effete form to materialize with an army marshaled against me, but there is nothing—only the crowds, a herd of goats, the beggars, the refugees. With slow steps I make my way back, down the promenade, across the dirty Kwaik River, looking back, waiting for something, for someone, but there is nothing. It is almost dusk when I return, easing my way through the doors of the shop, sliding in darkness to my cloth on the floor. I hear Abdul's cough before I see him, his head bent through the opening that leads to his house.

"Someone was looking for you," he says between gasping eruptions.

"For me?" I have been fogged and numb since seeing Araxie. This news brings me back.

"Yes. A man, asking if I'd had anyone ask me for work."

I nod.

"I did not tell him anything." Another cough comes, deep and coarse-sounding. He raises his head to bring in new air. "Why would he be looking for you?"

I do not answer. I shake my head. "Perhaps he is looking for someone else."

"Perhaps," says Abdul. He reaches for another breath, and pulls his door shut from within.

Rows of pecan trees skip past, their lines rigid like soldiers. Lights fade. The car's wipers whip and slap. We are driving again, this time to Tallahassee, to an appointment for a scan unavailable in Wadesboro. I am calm, my mind on the dream, on her, the way things are released as from a slow, leaking faucet. It was this way in London, the way memory came back, almost sequential then, patterned. First my name, appearing one day after months of not knowing. A few bits of early childhood. People. A trail through some trees. A rug's distinct patterns. Recollections surprising in their hard certainty—once arrived, unassailable, like supports screwed in place, never to be altered again. Yet frustrating, enormously so, in their scarcity, their cold isolation. Why these scraps and no more? I wanted the war, the good and the bad, all of it. I wanted to know. Instead I was teased, my brain and body constrained. Permitted small memory but only singly, in waves.

A young doe feints toward the highway, retreats in a flash of white tail. The rain is spattering, intermittent. Violet keeps both hands on the wheel, skin hanging loose below the knobs of her wrists. She has taken off work on account of the incident, the black man—was that yesterday? Perhaps the day before. No police vans, yet, although Violet holds whispered conversations that speak of some destination, some plotted future placement. I ignore these, or shield my anger when I think of them, for in truth I vacillate between a determination to keep my life as it is and a slumping indifference to whatever might happen. Perhaps the tumor brings this malaise, or perhaps merely time, but the vitality I find now exists in the dream. I think back again, checking my arms for scars, noting the discolored skin, the straps of flesh among moles and black hair. The smells of the hammam wrap around me, the fragrance that is like sandalwood but is not, the odors of soap and wet hair. It is a new life, almost, a younger life. I sigh and stare at yellow paint stripes, the curled lengths of wet asphalt.

We stop at a gas station near the state line, Violet gripping the pump as I stand watching, half wet. I want to be helpful. I trudge inside to the "Food Store," to the glare of advertisement and sourish smell, where two overweight clerks, one white and one black, mutter hellos and look back out at the rain. I gaze at the assembled goods, the double-aisled row of candies, the triple cooler filled with soft drinks and beer, the potato chips and cheese swirls. Locating the tiny grocery area, I examine a can of baked beans priced at three times its value. I wonder if there is halva. Kibbe? *Sucuk kebab*? I move back to the snack section and select a package of peanuts, bring this to the counter. The black clerk greets me with a star-emblazoned gold tooth.

"Will that be all?" She tugs a chain at her neck.

"Some gas also, please." I gesture toward Violet, who puts the hose back in place.

"Okay."

Her register whirs. I glance at the jar of pickled pigs' feet behind the counter, the flesh pink and humanlike, the juice murky and stained. A wall of chewing tobacco stands behind it. Levi Garrett, Trophy, Morgan's, Taylor's Pride.

"You're not from around here, are you?"

I look up, surprised but then not. "I am from Wadesboro."

"Oh." The gold sparkles. "You been there long?"

Memories flash past of the years in New York, of jabs and taunts, fights. An immigrant. Then Georgia. Wadesboro during the Iranian hostage crisis, when America's attention (even Wadesboro's) turned to the Middle East, the heritage of any darker-skinned person new grounds for derision. The jeers, "A-rab," "sand nigger." Some from neighbors Carol had known all her life. I withdrew from it. The kids were older, they were both blond— they were shielded. For this I was glad.

"Yes, I have been there some time." I hear the silence

surrounding my answer. The other clerk raises her head. "And you?"

The black clerk scratches her head. I hold her gaze. "Yeah," she says. "I'm from Pelham. Been here all my life."

I think about this as we continue our journey, past the brick and hedges of Deerfield Plantation, the blue-and-orange "Welcome to Florida" sign, the liquor store perched at the invisible state line. Six or seven generations now since the clerk's ancestors arrived—she probably thinks of herself first as American, only second as black. I know the looks she receives, the constant striving to be something else. Does she think of her forebears? I wonder whether their lives interest or plague her, whether she secretly wishes to examine slave logs in Africa or whether, like me, she has blocked it all out, relegated it to an element of the past, as nothing that could ever be changed or would be. I wonder if she hates herself, or white people, or the whole of the oppressive South. I wonder if she dreams of restraint.

I feel myself slipping at the first Tallahassee traffic light, at an intersection fronted by a cleaners, a convenience store, a bank under construction. A clinking noise enters the car, perhaps from the job site nearby, like the sound of machinery but softer, more striking, until I am falling, slumped in my seat, sinking as I had in the university cafeteria, my hands to my lap to my knees. I hear Violet's voice, fading, calling me, and then no more, only the clinking, rhythmic, repetitive, continuous. Monstrous.

It is dark. The light of stars shines down on a pathway, on a group, moving. Prisoners. They are tied together, their wrists bound behind them, connected by rope at their hands and their waists. They do not struggle or crane their necks, their shoulders bowed, the light glinting and shifting against the dark sweep of their hair. At one point one of them stumbles and pulls half the line with him. Men emerge then from the shadows, prodding them upward, with grunts and curses and pokes of long knives. The clinking starts again, having stopped with the man's fall. The men march now with the prisoners, exhorting, demanding. There are many knives, sometimes two or three in one hand, in my hand. They clink together as we walk.

We reach a clearing, lit only by the stars. The prisoners stop. Some raise their heads, some kneel and collapse others to the ground alongside them. The clinking stops, replaced by the sound of sobbing, by pleas for deliverance, by bitter and sorrowful prayers. And then it begins, the rush and thrust of weapons, the screams and grunts as metal meets flesh meets bone. I lie back, unsure, taking care not to be cut in the frenzy, even as something stirs within me, an excitement, a rage that expands like a great bubble and bursts. I lift my weapon. I am an attacker, one with the attack. I am a man. A thing like a wave grips my shoulders and pulls. Gasps come, escapes of air and fluid, moans as my knife make its punctures and exits. I strike again. And again. Their liquids splatter, wetting my face, down my neck.

"Papa!"

I awake slowly. My hands tremble. The car is not moving—we perch in a driveway. I am wet, my chest and hands. I look down at my body as if from a cliff. Blood seeps from my chin, staining my shirt a burnt red. Violet thrusts something toward me.

"Here, take this. Are you awake? You've got a nosebleed."

I accept a tissue, tilt my head back. The warm slide of blood continues, now down my throat.

"What happened?" I ask. My voice echoes and hums.

"You had one of those spells. Your hands started shaking, then your body. This time your nose bled, too."

I shiver, the drying blood slick and rubbery. The clinking has vanished, though its imprint remains.

"I fear I am losing my mind," I say to . . . whom? To my daughter.

"No, you're okay. You're going to be okay." A trickle of a smile breaks and falls down her face. "Let's get you cleaned up."

We drive to a McDonald's. I wait in the car. Violet returns to swab at my face, the blood turning the napkins a dirty mud brown. The rain starts again, spitting, then strengthening, wetting her back as she bends to her work. She finishes, closes the passenger door, rushes around to the other side.

"Jeez." Her hands pull hair back in place. "It's okay," she says, turning to me. "It's not your fault." She examines her face in the rearview mirror. "Not your fault."

She pauses, her gaze forward. She turns again. "I don't know about today, Papa. I'm thinking we should go back, check in with Dr. Wan. I'm worried you'll have a big one of these and I . . ."

I protest, but weakly. I lift my head . . . If I could only lift my head higher my life might come back then. There are matters still to prepare, analyze. There are things I must do. I examine Violet and wonder what I have passed to her, what weakness. Cruelty? An orange light burns and I slump back in my seat.

11

I sneeze. It is dusty amid the rubble of the knife maker's shop: the chisels on their racks, the unfinished product from the day before, the bucket of water, the anvil, the dulled fire. I stretch, rubbing my stomach, scratching my head. I remember the conversation with Abdul the night before, about the man looking for someone like me. The plan.

The door to the shop creaks open. A woman's head appears, covered in a black scarf. She lingers in the doorway a moment, her eyes adjusting. Then she focuses on me.

"Abdul is dead."

"What?" I take a step toward her. "What happened?"

"He died in his sleep. He coughed and coughed, and then he was still."

She glances around the shop, as if she has never seen it. She is a short woman, her head barely rising to the level of my chest, her eyes far apart and set deep in her face, like a bird's.

I look down, unsure of what to say. I have grown to like Abdul and his quiet, competent ways. He has treated me fairly, even covered for me. Now he is gone.

"You must leave," the woman says, without a trace of emotion.

I nod, set about gathering my extra shirt, my tunic, my meager coins. I place my knife in my pants, the knife I bought from Karim. I straighten the bedding I had only just risen from. It all takes longer than it should because my hands are stiff and trembling, my vision watery. I want to look at her but do not. I finish gathering my things and stumble to the back door, conscious of her gaze still fixed on my back. "Good-bye," I whisper, as the door closes behind me. I hear the latch fasten shut.

The smells of early-morning Aleppo rise, odors made sharper by my numbed, shaken state. I slip past a flock of bleating sheep, past men on camels who look like they've ridden all night, past corpses facedown in the street. I have no idea where I am going, no plan of what to do next. I stick to alleys and side streets, to the dark of Aleppo's passageways. I find myself near the hospital, and then backtrack, through a wealthier section comprised of courtyards and chiseled stone, past the missionary-run Armenian orphanage and its crocheted socks and blankets arranged hopefully and pitiably for sale. I walk for what seems like hours but may be only minutes. I count the minarets near the citadel, one to twenty-nine.

I stop at the first cries of the muezzin, there before a white-domed church. I kneel, orienting myself toward Mecca, my lips forming the familiar words, my forehead bent low to the ground. Each time I raise my head I see the cross at the church's top, odd and blasphemous but at the same time familiar, as if I have been here before, knelt in this spot, bowed before both of these things all my life. I continue, prostrated, the prayers spraying from my lips and merging with others as my mind bends to my need. I ask Allah for help. I ask the Christian God for help. I ask for strength, for sustenance. I pray for deliverance, from a something I cannot name.

The prayers end. I stand for a moment, counting my coins. I have only eight lira, a handful of *gurûs*. Glancing up at the church spire, at the sun's first foray into crevice and shadow, I deposit a coin in the alms box before continuing down the walkway, my remaining wealth in my hand, glancing in doorways, slowing at the sound of voices. I ask for work at khans, at cafés, at almost every open establishment, but each time there are only blank stares, disdainful looks, quick and forceful rejections. I backtrack, searching for businesses I might have missed, trudging through passages and corridors until finally I arrive in a sunny little courtyard, an opening of a stone street and shops in which several corridors converge.

A young woman with unusual red-colored hair sweeps dust from a stoop. She smiles as I approach.

"I am looking for work," I say in halting Arabic. "Do you have anything?"

She wrinkles her nose, two moles equidistant across its top. I realize as I grow closer that they are tiny tattoos. "Perhaps." She shrugs. "I will ask Sasha."

She calls back through the doorway. "Sasha! Sasha!"

I wait, my stomach growling, wondering what kind of person this Sasha is—businessman? Teacher?

A broad-shouldered woman makes her way through the doorway, squinting in dismay at the late-morning light. Her uncovered hair is askew, as if she has just awakened, her mannish-looking face thick and blotched like a curd.

"What is it?" she asks in Arabic.

The redheaded woman points her broom at me. "This boy is looking for work."

I flinch but say nothing. Sasha looks me over, as if appraising a goat at the bazaar.

"Perhaps," she says, flipping hair from her eyes in an exaggerated way. She wears a strange-looking dress that reveals her broad shoulders, then drapes shapelessly below. Her large feet are bare.

She glances at the younger woman, then back at me. "Come inside," she says, with a corresponding pull of her neck. "Be quiet. The others are sleeping."

I follow her through the doorway into a surprisingly large room. At the back several rows of mats and low divans have been arranged, all facing an elevated area beyond. Separate doorways lead in opposite directions from the room's sides, another, attached to the elevated area, from its back. The smell of stale incense mingles with tobacco and perfume, spices and sweat. The room is dark, with no window or exterior light. A single candle burns near the back doorway.

Sasha reaches under her robes and, to my astonishment, emerges with a cigarette. She strides to the candle and bends, cupping her hand. She rises in a bright cloud of smoke.

"What is this place?" I ask, almost without thinking.

Sasha smiles, draws a deep breath, exhales. "You have not been here before?"

I shake my head.

"You are new to Aleppo?"

"Yes." I do not elaborate. She does not press.

"This, my boy, we call the *klimbim*. A dance hall." She smiles, waving her cigarette at the area through which we entered. "We entertain."

I look around again, realization slowly dawning. I stare at her, then back to the doorway, where the red-haired woman has now disappeared. I sputter, in search of my voice. "What would you like me to do?"

She shrugs. "We need help cleaning. We had someone, but he left. When the girls awaken, I can show you more."

"How much?"

She shrugs again. "You are a bargainer, eh? A few lira a week, maybe more if business is good. You will eat with us." She pauses. "Can you cook?"

I nod. Can I?

Her head rocks forward and back. "You help us cook. In the meantime, help Isis sweep." She indicates the red-haired woman, who has reappeared behind me.

I nod. I reach for her broom.

I adapt to the ways of the *klimbim*. The dancing begins at dusk and continues, in one fashion or another, until almost dawn. As such, my sleep pattern changes, most of my work now done after midnight and in the afternoons. Often I see the sun rise. I sleep in the mornings.

My jobs at the dance hall vary. I sweep the stone floor and straighten the mats, I clean the elevated area they call the stage, and, most important, I change the cotton sheets in the back rooms in which the girls retire after their dances to consort with the highest-paying clientele. This requires adroit maneuvering and timing in dimly lit spaces, as there are only three such rooms and five girls (six, if you count Sasha). I am to retrieve the often-wet bedding immediately after one session but before the next, avoiding embarrassing contact with either group in the narrow corridor behind the stage. On the first night Sasha accompanied me on my duties, instructing me in the subtleties of determining when a coupling had concluded, of arranging the sheets on freshened piles of straw, of checking the candle to make sure it had not burned low. The rooms are small, almost cell-like affairs, with a large area of bedding, a small divan, and not much else. They smell of the same tobacco, perfume, and sweat as the larger room. Each has a small window opened to the alley outside. In the middle is a fire, sometimes lit, more often not.

I grow to know the five dancers: Isis, the redheaded woman I met the first day, funny and likable, originally from Egypt; Avi, the dark and solemn Armenian who never smiles but whose emissions during her back room sessions shake the building, it seems; Bibi, a woman with tattoos across her forehead who lived with the Bedouins for a number of years; Rasha, a crowd favorite, with very large breasts; and a stunningly beautiful Turkish woman called Sala, who is always in great demand. The girls sleep together in a small separate building behind the dance hall that also houses a cookstove, a small communal area, and Sasha's quarters. I sleep on one of the pads in the rooms behind the stage.

Activities at the *klimbim* begin in the late afternoon, with the girls stirring as the first patrons arrive. A certain stealth about the operation makes me question its legality, although soldiers and government personnel are by far its largest clientele. I have been told that even Cemal Paşa, the military governor of Syria, once visited. Several large, stained narghiles are provided for the benefit of the customers, one of my duties being to provide tobacco (if needed) from a small pouch Sasha entrusts to me, and to periodically replace the stinking water in the pipe's bulb-shaped bottom. Alcohol is served—again, somewhat surreptitiously—by means of goatskins and goblets produced from beneath Sasha's robes. Sasha is everywhere, urging the dancers on from the back corridor, attending the front door, pouring glasses of rakı or wine, negotiating various payments. On my first night, and, as I soon discover, on many nights after, a patron would become intoxicated and abusive, whereupon I would be called to assist Sasha in escorting the individual out the front door. Sasha is large and deceptively strong, to the point where inebriated men often underestimate her willingness to provide a knee to the groin or an elbow to the face to help them on their way out. More than once a man has been left outside, doubled over and bleeding, to shout threats of reprisal as he limps off down the alleyway. I suspect the police are in some state of collusion, as we are never troubled with raids or with miscreants. The only time I ever see an official during the daytime is when a fat captain circles back to ensure that news of his collapse in a back room is not reported to his superiors.

After several days the girls take to me, treating me as an insider, sharing jokes, regaling me with descriptions of their customers. There are a number of regular patrons: one man they call "Long," another the "Thirty-Second Man," each for obvious reasons; the mustachioed senior military official who demands that his consort stand at attention while he undresses; the wealthy local merchant who pays for two girls but is unable to perform with either; the slender man the girls call "Dena" who weeps profusely at his climax; and any number of "first-timers," men or boys out to prove their masculinity, usually exhibiting stage fright or performance anxiety that results in a quick and thereby more profitable session. I learn to anticipate the length of time a group will be in a room, to unobtrusively glide by parties I pass in the corridor, to sense when a patron is becoming unruly, to know when trouble is about to begin. I keep my head down, given the preponderance of military personnel, concerned that someone might ask for my papers or inquire as to my nationality. No one does. Their attention is focused on tobacco and wine, hips and flesh. Their thoughts are of backstage.

Although I witness the girls in various stages of undress, from the bared bellies and exposed breasts on the dance floor to the more revealing glimpses I catch shuttling among the back rooms, I come to think of them more as sisters than as objects of desire. They tease me unmercifully, demanding I drop my trousers to exhibit my manhood, pinching my bottom as I walk past, deliberately exposing themselves as I enter a room, questioning my heterosexuality. The redheaded girl, Isis (which, I presume, is not her given name), takes a particular fancy to me, rubbing my arm as she asks pointless questions, insisting I accompany her on her walks to the hammam. Perhaps it evidences the degree of my obsession, but I offer her little interest. I think of Araxie constantly, dream of her, picture her face above the other girls' bodies.

I worry in equal amounts, of the imminence of her deportation, of my helplessness to stop it. I daydream so frequently the girls take to calling me Gharîb, Rîb for short. Different. Strange.

I see Hussein my third night at the *klimbim*. He enters late, well after midnight, and makes his way up to the front row of mats. I recognize him immediately, his strutting little chest, the way his head cocks, the pull of his neck as he slips around Sasha. They nod to each other, evidencing familiarity. He gives the impression of being a regular customer. My heart beats double time at the thought that I might have to serve him, but Sasha reaches him first, motioning me to my duties in the back. I pass within a few feet of him, my head down, my face pulled away. I calculate that I could spring at him, snap his flimsy neck before he knew what had happened, but what good would that do? I would be jailed, or shot, or hunted down with a vengeance. Araxie would still hang in limbo. And so I stay in the shadows, observing as he watches Bibi dance, cleaning the room the two of them will occupy, lingering long enough—too long—to see them through the large crack in the room's door, the unwrapping of his robes, the twitch of his buttocks as she sinks and kneels before him. I busy myself elsewhere, careful to observe from afar when he emerges some time later, bids his muted good-bye to Sasha, and exits as the last patron of the night. I perform my end-of-evening tasks in a murderous frenzy, attacking floors and sheets as if they were enemies, shrugging off questions and teasing. By the time I am finished I am panting, black cauldrons of breath steaming up in the cool dawn. It takes hours to fall asleep. I do not speak to Bibi for days.

I see Araxie the following day, having arranged with Ani to meet her at the bazaar. I am vague about my new employment, telling her only that I have procured a job that keeps me up late at night. I do not mention seeing Hussein. Araxie looks better, even from the last time I had seen her, the color back in her cheeks, the added weight evident in her face and carriage. People stare as we work our way through the suq, craning their necks, caught by the oddity, the unsettling beauty of her eyes. She guards against this, or seems to, her gaze down, her focus kept to the ground. She keeps the scarf pulled around her. Her pace is measured and poised. If she notices the attention shown her she fails to mark or evidence it.

"What is the situation at the hospital?" I ask as a herd of goats pass.

She waits for the noise and stench to clear before answering. "I must leave soon," she says tonelessly. "There are rumors that Talat Paşa has called for the extermination of the deportees, even here in Aleppo. The doctors say I am nearly cured, and there are many, many sick. More deportees arrive daily. People are lying on blankets in the halls."

I nod. It is this way throughout the city. Refugees huddle in clumps between buildings, beg in doorways, sit vacant-eyed in the middle of walkways.

"Where will you go?"

"One of the doctors has made inquiries for me at an orphanage. Although they are filled, and I am older, he thinks he may get me in. In the meantime, he would like to train me as a nurse's assistant. He believes my chances are better if there is a service I can perform. But it is frightening. Yesterday they came and removed a number of people, including several who had traveled with us from Harput."

"And Hussein?"

She grimaces. "He is still there. He offered me employment with his sister, some kind of factory job—I do not really know what it is. I told him I was pursuing other things, that I was grateful, that I would let him know. This did not make him happy. I try to avoid him, but it is difficult."

The image of Hussein in the *klimbim*'s back room flashes past me.

"I have something to give you," I say, reaching under my shirt. I pull out a small package. Beneath its wrapping lies a necklace I purchased the previous day, a purchase I agonized over afterward, second-guessing myself for spending that which should have been saved for escape. I have thought much of this moment, envisioning in alternate scenarios her pleasure, affront, or indifference upon receipt of the gift. My hand shakes as I hand it to her. Will she refuse it? I find I cannot watch as she spreads the paper and opens it.

A sound emerges from her lips. She holds the necklace aloft, to where the light plays on it, sparkling the polished blue stones that fall together to form a pendant. Though irregularly shaped, the stones, when grouped together, look as one, perhaps cut from the same parent; I imagine an artisan working a lathe as I had with the knives. I watch as she fingers the stones, separating, letting them fall back together like a puzzle re-formed. I do not know the rock from which they derive, or the necklace's true value, although I bargained the jewelry dealer down to almost half her original price. After contemplating asking one of the *klimbim* girls for advice, in the end I decided against it—I did not wish to associate them with her. I decided I simply liked this piece. I could imagine her wearing it.

"It is . . . wonderful," she whispers. To my surprise, her eyes are murky with tears. "This is the first gift I have received . . . in such a long time." She lifts the necklace over her head, draping it around her neck, then tucks it under her robes. She lifts her gaze to meet mine. "Thank you." She wipes her eyes with her middle fingers.

The crowd presses closer around us, voices raised, then lowered. Two merchants make accusations in loud tones, a knife is pulled, light flashes on metal. I edge Araxie away from the commotion, my fingers on the crook of her hip, my mind on the certainty that the knife I saw briefly was one I had made. We stop in the shadow of a row of buildings, the air cooler here. A smell of sawdust rises, the charred scent of cut wood.

"I must go soon," Araxie says. "I begin training this evening."

We watch a pair of gendarmes escort a group of ragged deportees down the road past the bazaar. "I will protect you," I say without thinking, without knowing what even I mean.

"Thank you." She tilts her head toward mine. The odor of soap clings and perfumes the air.

I want to say more, to prolong things, but do not. We linger a moment, her light eye upon me. Then she turns and walks on, through candle vendors and shepherds, baubles and bread on a stick. I watch her go, awash in the bittersweet charm of surrender. The fear of what lies ahead.

. . .

Violet and I drive back to Wadesboro. I am silent, thinking. I am remembering, for some reason, the birth of Violet's first child, the strangeness of it, the uncertainty. Violet had been sent to a home for unwed mothers, in New York—this would have been 1955, maybe 1956. I was working the day she left. Carol told me about it, how Violet had stood by the door and proclaimed she would never be back. But then one day she returned, only smaller, and older. I never saw the child. She did not speak of it. As I think of this now, I do not remember if she bore a boy or a girl.

It is strange how these thoughts come, a boy or a girl. Does she think on this now and shake her head in slow wonder? For me the past is so dominant. Memory receding, obscuring—discovering something new is like finding hidden treasure. Or an unmarked grave. I look out from the car as the sky clears, the sun shining cleanly through pine needles made golden. The taller trees bend and sway, their lower branches like hands on thin hips. Will I see this again or must I only remember it? A hawk passes above, its wings beating downward in broad, slow, smooth strokes.

I lower my window to let in fresh air. The sweet smell of smoke enters from a planned burn up ahead, a fire in imitation of nature set to clear underbrush. The aroma brings memories—of cook fires, the little hearth of my parents—and I am remembering, almost touching, when something else enters, some darker connection that grasps and takes hold. I pitch forward, my hands on my knees, and I am shaking. Lights flash. Darkness follows, then deadening silence.

Daylight returns, a grimier light like that at a cloudy day's end.

A group of women gather around a fire, dancing or, as becomes apparent, being made to dance, onlookers pushing or prodding them on, men with knives, with long-barreled guns. One man urges them to sing, then demands that they do so, such that soon high-pitched wails merge with the crackle of flame, the shouts of derision. The dancing women are of varied ages, some old and shuffling, some merely girls, thrashing all apace in a terrified rhythm. I watch as a man reaches in with a sword and stabs a young woman, slicing her breasts off with quick, violent strokes. She bleeds, great buckets of blood, her screams mixed with the thin trill of the others. The crowd grows larger, more demanding, edging the dancers closer to the fire. Soon the wails are all screams. The sour odor of burning flesh mixes with the smell of wood smoke. I turn, toward others standing off from the onslaught, women with arms folded across their chests, looks of indifference or satisfaction splashed on their thick faces. I open my mouth but nothing comes from it, no sound. The smoke becomes thicker and I cough silent coughs.

We sit before Dr. Wan, a truant child with his mother. I am the center of attention, the patient. The problem. Am I thus so like Wilfred? I picture Violet before principals and guidance counselors, her eyes reddened, the same crease corrugating her brow. I have been in her position with Carol, seeking answers that provide direction, attempting to decide between options, each unappealing. It is lonely and frustrating. Carol could be as mean as a chained dog, exacting and obstinate, then gleeful and bubbly as if hosting a ball. I am unlike her in this. I have these episodes, but my mind is still here. I am not so needy, so selfish. Would it not be much better to drop everything now, to let things play out? I have tried to tell Violet this, that I am fine without treatment. That rest and resignation and natural course might be best. She only listens and shakes her head, as if my preference is irrelevant or my thinking merely childish, my passivity the simple product of a closed, too-damaged mind.

Dr. Wan is both comforting and apologetic. "The spells you describe sound like complex partial seizures," he says, "not uncommon. The dream states, though, are unusual. We will adjust your medication, but I think it is best that you be monitored. I have suggested to Violet that you see Dr. Mellon. He will arrange for your placement."

My placement? I know Dr. Mellon. He is a psychiatrist, a Rotarian. I am already being monitored. I do not understand this.

Dr. Wan looks genuinely sorry, as if he has forced me down a far plank. "How are you feeling? Any headaches?"

I shake my head. I want to ask questions but it seems best not to do so. Violet examines her nails, looks away, examines again. A nurse arrives and administers an injection.

The day stretches on. We leave Dr. Wan's office, drive to radiology for my treatment, drive on to Dr. Mellon's, fill out more paperwork, sit in yet another waiting room. It is again as with Carol, the parade of offices, the personnel in white coats. I glance at Violet and feel pity and pride. There were scattered illnesses in her childhood, a broken arm once. Did I not wait on her so, trusting in gloved professionals? Hazy memories stream back. The day

I obtained my citizenship we waited in a room much like this. They gave the girls little flags—Lissette was young then, maybe eight? We had ice cream after. We had a dog at that time, a boxer mix we called Jowls who let the girls ride his back. They placed the flags in his collar and made him march in a parade. I followed, strutting around the living room, Carol clapping, the "Stars and Stripes Forever" crackling forth from the radio. Did we make movies of this? I should find them and watch them.

Dr. Mellon is loud. I remember he likes to slap people's backs. He is a black man from the islands, his teeth large and white. The reason for Dr. Wan's hesitance quickly becomes apparent.

"Look," the big doctor says, spreading fingers like daggers, "this is going to sound worse than it is. From your descriptions, you're having delusions or hallucinations, maybe hypnagogic in nature. I'm going to place you in SGPC for a few days, at least until a bed clears in Eastside. You'll be fine—it's not a bad facility. You can be monitored there, your medication checked. I think it's the best thing right now. I'm on the staff, but because of protocols, you'll first see another physician, probably Dr. Wellman. He's a good man. I think you'll like him."

My stomach drops, as if a stone has crashed through it. SGPC. South Georgia Psychiatric Center is the state mental hospital, the place crazy people are sent. I glance accusingly at Violet, who stares at a far wall. "The institution?"

"I know. Relax. It won't be that bad. I'm going to prescribe a psychotropic drug to try to cut down on these episodes. Given the medication you're already taking, you really need to be monitored."

"Can Violet not monitor me at home?"

He smiles, his lips stretched. "I don't think so."

The rest of the conversation is lost. I am stricken, observing as if through thick glass. The oddness of this room, the lilt in Dr. Mellon's voice, the interracial aspect of his practice (so odd for Wadesboro), the people I recognized also waiting to see him. An institution. A *hastane*. Anger cuts through me in a spasm. I quell it. How could . . .? This cannot be. I am a victim, of incompetence, injustice. I am okay! And yet these images, this smell— I erect a large wall but they seep through, relentless. The fire, the women. I rub my nose with both hands. I grip my chair to touch something, to stay aligned with things present, but still the room starts in motion, textbooks mixed with potted palms, with hooked lamps and rifled papers. I lean forward to ground myself against dizziness, determined not to dream or collapse as the blood shakes within me. I think of Carol and rows of white cots, and for a moment I am back there, wrapped in bedsheets in London, someone asking me something using bright, foreign words. Why would I speak this language? "Sir," they say. "Sir." The hospital dark and smelling, the echo of footfalls. The excitement the day the queen visited and spoke to other patients. Then things shift and I am working in darkness, fumbling with pipe fittings and cold earth like a mole, but providing. Working. If I work and do well there may be a promotion. Promotion? A man laughs and others join him. My name is spoken. A hand grasps my shoulder and pulls me upright.

"Papa!"

"Yes."

"Look at me!"

Violet's face fills my vision, an object too close to a camera.

"The sheriff's office is sending someone to pick you up. I know this sounds horrible, but they have to handcuff you to provide transport to the facility—it's state law for anyone being . . . placed there. We have to wait in the adjacent room until they arrive."

I stumble next door, wishing to let all things pass. White sheets. Nurses. The hospital, again. I am in a faded chair, a dozing semi-sleep. Intrusions knife through: Violet's movements in and out, the arrival of someone new, the opening and shutting of doors, Dr. Mellon's voice through the wall. I think of Araxie. How could all be so lost? Then I am moving, down a hallway and out through the vestibule, past the stares of others still queued and waiting, a woman sobbing, her face deep in a handkerchief. I stumble out into sunshine, to a day left earlier than I remembered it to be.

"You'll be okay?" This from Dr. Mellon, to Violet.

Doors shut, a motor revs. Hands grasp my wrist, binding. My head tilts back. Violet is speaking, but to someone beyond. "They're sending him now." Her voice cracks. She says nothing more.

12

I awake to someone's touch, to a fluttering against my neck, a brushing of my chest, a teasing manipulation of my groin. I sit, staring into the gloom around me, trying to orient to person and place, time. I smell incense and wax. The woman in front of me withdraws, smiling, chirps of laughter escaping lips curled like a flower. She perches at the end of the bed. I shift, feeling straw beneath the thin sheets. Recognition comes slowly.

"Were you dreaming of her?" Isis asks, fingering my big toe. "You certainly seem . . . aroused." She laughs again, a high-pitched, reedlike sound.

"What time is it?"

She shrugs, shifting her body in a practiced way. "Morning." Beads of sunlight enter through cracks in the walls and the window in the back. "I could not sleep."

I pull my knees to my chest, wipe my hands down my face. "So you came to bother me."

She smiles, exposing blackened bottom teeth. "Yes."

"Tell me," I say, sharpening, remembering. "How did you come to be here?"

She laughs her magpie laugh. "Oh, it was quite a journey. I was born in Egypt, hence my name." She smiles again, offering a small bow. "My father was in the army. He was killed in a fight in a café, in Alexandria, when I was eight. My mother was forced to find work, but she had no skills. She did whatever she could, poor woman, cleaning people's homes, selling firewood, even growing her own vegetables. After a time I noticed a number of men visiting our house. I didn't understand what they wanted, why they disappeared into the back room with my mother, what the moans and curses and movement were all about. But soon I learned. My mother became pregnant from her efforts. She didn't want this baby. She already had me, and my sister, Hami. Plus, the pregnancy would hinder her business. So she visited a doctor, not a regular doctor who had attended university, but one who lived in the poor part of town, like us. He gave her some medicine—I don't know what it was. She became sick, and the baby died. Three days later, so did she. I was eleven.

"I tried to provide for Hami, who was only nine, but I was even more inept than my mother. We ended up begging at the side of roadways, the entrance to mosques. Men from the government tried to capture us but could not. We lived like this for almost a year. Then one day when I was nearly faint with hunger, a man offered me money for . . . service. I didn't know what to do, exactly, but I had an idea. I didn't particularly like it, but I liked the money. It bought food, and clothing. It altered my life."

"How did you get to Aleppo?"

She grins again, shifts her position. "Through Sasha. Sasha is, as you know . . . unusual. She was once one of my customers."

She lifts her gaze. I swallow. I did not know this about Sasha.

"At that time," Isis continues, "we had lost our house—some men moved in and then refused to leave. We could do nothing about it. In this trade, if you have no place to go, no bed or room or refuge, it throttles your business. Sasha suggested I accompany her to Aleppo. She offered to make arrangements for Hami to be placed with a family. It was difficult for the two of us to part." She gives another breast-bouncing shrug. "But it was probably for the best."

I nod, chew my lip. "Do you like what you do?"

Another laugh, another shrug. "Most of the time. Compared to the situation I was in, this is much better."

"Do you have boyfriends?"

"Too many!" Her laugh broadens her face. "That part is hard. I would like to be married someday. But I don't know that I will be." She pauses, glancing across at the light dancing up the far wall. "Sasha is good to us. She understands that sometimes you hate yourself, that you need time to recover. She knows men can be violent. There was one man, a few months ago, who nearly strangled Bibi. Sasha heard, entered the room, pulled him off, and tied him up. She then permitted each of the girls to terrorize him. Some slapped him, others peed on him. Bibi and Sasha rammed a candle up his bottom—it was like a party. We never saw him again." She pauses. "Sasha also helps with disease and pregnancy. There have been other girls here . . . Sometimes they have to go away."

I shift on the bed. "There was a man here the other night,

with Bibi. His name is Hussein. Thin man, young—maybe my age. Do you know him?"

She nods slowly. "Yes, I know him."

"Does he come here often?"

"Sometimes. Why?"

"I just wondered. I recognized him from somewhere."

She scratches her leg. "He was here the night of the raid."

"The raid?"

"Yes. It happened several months ago. We were in the midst of a normal evening—a girl who used to be with us, Luki, was onstage—when the door burst open and ten policemen entered. They stormed into the back, interrupting sessions. The customers, cowards that they are, ran off without robes or trousers, dangling and flapping. It was the funniest thing. Then the police captain, who I guess had a sense of humor, rounded up the girls and told us we would not be charged if we put on an adequate show. My, you have never seen such a show! It ended with Sasha seducing the captain onstage. Everyone clapped and cheered! But this Hussein, he was one of the runners."

Voices resound in the hall. I stretch and stand. Sasha's oblong head pokes through the adjacent doorway.

"Isis! Are you delaying our employee from his duties? We girls are hungry."

"I am only telling him the ways of the world," Isis counters. "Stories of the *harim*." She stands and exits, offering a final waggle.

"You are quite the popular one, Ahmet," Sasha says. She spreads her robes, seats herself on the end of the bed. "The girls talk about you constantly. Who is this young woman you meet in the bazaar?"

I hesitate, studying Sasha's face, trying to guess her age. Thirty-five? Forty? Traces of mustache are visible in the dim light. I sit down beside her. "She is an *arkadaş*," I say, using the Turkish word. A friend.

"She is Armenian, yes?"

I nod. Are my movements so well known, so obvious?

"And you are a Turk."

I nod again. "What are you?"

Sasha laughs, a low, guttural sound that rises from deep in her chest. "Oh, I am many things, my dear. I am a Syrian, and I am an Ottoman. I am a Muslim, and I am a Christian. I am a believer, and I am a skeptic. I am a woman, and"—she lifts her robe, exposing a miniature, fully formed penis—"I am a man."

"H-h-h . . . how?"

"An accident of nature." She (or he) waves a bejeweled hand. "Sometimes Allah overwhelms with his gifts. There are similar examples throughout the world; I have met five like myself. One, who considered himself a man, was for a time my husband. I decided some time ago I was more comfortable as a woman." She reaches over to touch my leg, bracelets jangling. I recoil in response, but her hand stays on my knee. "I am more concerned about you."

I do not respond, caught between discomfort and a desire to unburden myself, to share secrets, seek guidance. My lips move but only air emerges. Tendons twitch in my thigh.

"I always ask the girls what they're looking for," she continues, "where they want to go. Some have unrealistic dreams of becoming princesses, of employing many servants. Others have no dreams at all—they want only to eat. I try to help each of them, to fashion their goals into those that are achievable, to make them think about what will come next. For no one can do this forever." She sits straighter, releasing my leg. "I would like to help you as well. I like you. I like the way you work, the interaction you have with the girls. I like your devotion to your Armenian friend." She pauses again. "How can I help you?"

"I . . . I want to go to America."

She smiles and leans back. "As do we all. Do you want to take your friend with you?"

"Yes."

She nods. A bead of light catches her face, making her look older, almost haggard. Wisps of gray cling at her temples.

"Do you know anyone in America? You need a job to get in. It is expensive." She turns to me, her square jaw thrust forward. I can picture her now as a man, the rounded shoulders, the light beard. "Do you have any money?"

I shake my head.

She nods again. "It is a difficult dream, my son. How long do you think you have?"

I place my face in my hands. "Not long."

She stands, her fingers brushing the top of my head. "We shall work on it, then. But I can promise you nothing. It is, as I said, a most difficult thing."

I nod, grateful but fearful, of unstated quid pro quos, of the mutations seen lurking beneath Sasha's robes. Are the girls some-how indebted? I look at things in a new light.

My day proceeds in the usual fashion, cooking, refurbishing mattresses, replacing spent candles. I accompany Sasha to the bazaar to buy food, I accompany Bibi and Isis to the hammam. I unload casks of wine from the cart of a man with no teeth. I bring candies to Avi, who is not feeling well. At dusk I sneak away to see Araxie at the citadel, concerned that so many are aware of our meeting, a concern only heightened when I cannot find her there. I pace about, staring with disinterest at peddlers picking up their wares, at camel drivers and rope makers, at the loading of donkeys and carts. I examine the iron-plated citadel doors, decorated with carvings of intertwined serpents. I waste money on a Turkish cigarette, filling my lungs with the harsh, tarry smoke that chafes my throat and makes my eyes tear. I search faces and profiles. I recognize no one.

I interrupt my pacing to examine a bed of flowers growing in a courtyard nearby—roses, in different shades, buttery yellow and sunset orange. I stoop close to one, a red so deep as to be almost lavender, sniff and think of picking it for Araxie as I look about, trying to remember why I have not seen these before. Has this courtyard been open? I imagine my future, sniffing a rose some decades hence, setting sail, weathering, nailing crossbeams, growing old, being reborn. And yet the past crouches, the clink as men march roped together, the blood of the woman's sliced breasts. I think about the start of this journey, the knifing of the men, the forcing of the women into sick-smelling flames. How my arm ached from the thrusting, the blood bathing my face! The sound of air gushing from punctured lungs, the stench of perforated bowels, the final expulsions of the dead and the dying. The wails and sorrow, like song, feeding my energy. The camaraderie. The ecstasy. I must push it all back.

"Ahmet!"

I rise, squinting. It is almost dark. Ani is difficult to recognize in the shadows.

"I have been looking for you everywhere! Araxie is sick. She has the stomach illness. She sent me to tell you."

I stiffen at the sound of her name. "She is sick?"

"Yes. I am hoping it is not the sickness from before, a relapse. She will try to meet you tomorrow, but at a different place—in front of the Khan al-Wazir. Do you know it?"

I do. The so-called minister's khan, with its black-and-white marble façade. I have grown to know Aleppo well, to learn the distinctions between the labyrinthine streets and the various covered bazaars, to differentiate the spice suq from the one selling women's clothes, the Khan al-Gumruk from the Khan al-Sabun. I stare up at the citadel above us, caught like a fist in the dying residue of the sun.

"I will be there." I return my gaze to Ani, who has partly turned to go. Candles flicker in yellowing windows, the streets and passageways now shrouded in darkness.

"Ani," I say. I want to say more, to address what has happened, to explain—how to explain things? I can see now through her dulled, gloomy eyes. I should ask . . .

"Yes?"

I pause, the apology I intended suddenly caught and contained. "Tell her I will be there."

She nods, her quizzical expression turned solemn. "I will do so."

I wander back to the *klimbim*, down sweet-smelling corridors with blurred faces and murmuring voices, through the smoke of cook fires, the drifts of spice and incense, the odor of burning hashish. A woman calls out to me, reaching from the shadows to pull at my arm as I pass, dancing, evading. Laughter and chanting merge and fade, replaced by a strange, atonal music, a shuffling of drumbeats, a patter of wind or of rain. From somewhere a bell rings clear like a knife. I experience all of this and none of it, my mind locked into sickening remembrance, this searing time past I cannot now seem to shake. It is done, I say. Done. I walk for miles, maybe for hours, for it is late by the time I return to the *klimbim*, the first show having started, the mats already filled with squatting male forms.

Thus begins a strange night, even by *klimbim* standards. One of the first customers backstage is an elderly man I have seen before, a man named al-Wati, whose unsteadiness requires support on either side from sheepish sons or associates, until he nears his destination and gains a new life. He parts the swinging door at almost a trot, paired with his consort, Avi, at which point I pay them no further notice, busy as I am with other customers and the orders of a petulant Sasha, still unhappy with my tardiness. Moments later, however, a low scream pierces the thin walls, different in tenor from Avi's usual eruptions. I rise up in the darkness of an adjacent room. Sasha hurries forth in the corridor outside. Avi emerges, going the other way, precipitating a near collision in the narrow, dim hallway. Edging along the damp wall, I sidestep the still-muttering Avi and follow Sasha into the vacated room.

Al-Wati lies prostrate on the bed, naked, his body even thinner than I might have imagined, his ribs exposed and brittle-looking, his silver-enshrouded tool still semi-erect. His chest does not rise and fall. He makes no movement. I listen to the sounds of the *klimbim*—the muted applause, the rise and fall of the old man

Omar's lute, the sniffles and moans and sighs—as Sasha brings the candle over to examine al-Wati's head.

"He is dead," she says, after the briefest of looks. She turns to me. "Go find the young men who assisted him in."

I stare for a moment, at her, at the shuttered, smelly room, then do as she orders, easing back through the darkened hallway out into the more lighted expanse of the big room. I do not see the men she has referred to, or if I do, I fail to recognize them. I linger a moment, trying not to appear obtrusive, averting my gaze against those heading my way. I scan the crowd once, again, then return to the back hallway, to a scene of renewed commotion.

Now it is Bibi who streams past, her voice in high-pitched alarm, her head thrust away from Sasha's entreating, accompanying form. Heads poke from other rooms, the sounds of activity slowing, diminishing.

"What is it?" Isis whispers in the darkness.

I shrug my shoulders, return to al-Wati's room. He has fallen from the straw bed to the floor, his one arm now forward as if caressing the ground, his rigidity further reduced to only a hint beyond normal torpor.

"Did you find them?" Sasha returns, breathing hard at my shoulder.

I shake my head. "What happened?"

She groans. "Bibi entered this room by mistake. I think she mounted him, without realizing he was dead." She bends double to the floor and places her hands beneath al-Wati's armpits. "Help me lift him."

He is heavier than I expect, and difficult to maneuver, his bent body sagging like a bushel of flour. We bang him into the door frame as we exit the room, into the wall in the hallway, and into the door providing passage to the alleyway outside. Isis and a customer pass us in the corridor, flattening themselves against the wall to allow us space, eyes wide in the dim light. We prop al-Wati into a sitting position by the outside door. I drape a sheet over his naked body.

"Get back to work," Sasha orders. I resume my duties, shuffling sheets, wielding the wineskin. I keep a lookout for the young men who were with al-Wati, but do not see them. More customers arrive, more wine fills thin glasses, water bubbles in the long-stemmed narghiles, smoke and chatter hang in the air—the usual course of another full night. Currency shifts from pouch to pouch, dancers emerge and retreat, patrons rotate from front to back. Only a few minutes later, the next disturbance begins.

An enormously fat man, his skin stretched to great lengths, appears in the doorway. Only with considerable assistance, a twisting to one side, and a certain amount of intense grunting does he make it through the entrance. When he rights himself it is clear he is as large as three men, his girth cascading down the sides of his body, his neck so large as to have melted into the rest of him, such that his head seems to sit directly atop his torso. Two young men appear beside him (the same that assisted al-Wati? Some kind of social service?), offering hands to push him forward. He totters at the back of the room, scattering those seated beneath him. The young men bring him forward, to plop on the ground, which he does with a resounding *oof* that causes Omar to stop his lute playing, and Rasha to quit gyrating onstage. For an instant all eyes are focused, as if a bomb has exploded in the back of the room. Then things return, smoke rising, cups tilting, music winding, hips circling. Eyes retrain. Lips are licked, opened.

The fat man, whom Sasha calls Ebbe, is evidently quite wealthy, for he immediately sets about consuming rakı in large quantities. After four trips I begin pouring him two cups at a time, which he picks up with miniature, hooflike hands and drinks in almost single gulps, to no apparent effect. During my trips backstage I become aware of a certain discord among the girls—first Sala and Sasha, whispering in bursts that sound like train pistons, then Bibi (recovered now, and back in action), shaking her head so emphatically it appears her neck might snap off. Heads peek from behind curtains, eyeing the immense form in the back of the room. Sasha makes another trip back to Ebbe, offering information that clearly does not satisfy him, for he scowls monstrously before slipping Sasha more cash from a cupped, almost fingerless hand. Sasha disappears backstage, to the muffled sounds of continued disagreement; I watch with incredulity as Rasha, barely clothed, her big breasts swirling, stomps the length of the big room and out the front door, to the accompanying cheers of the crowd. Sasha reappears, sweating and flustered, providing much-gesticulated explanations to the still-scowling Ebbe. Those seated nearby look on in amusement. Finally, after much back-and-forth, in which an animated Sasha cajoles and grovels, Ebbe is hoisted to his feet. The two young men who had helped him earlier materialize from somewhere, and like merchants directing a load, maneuver his bulk the length of the room and through the tiny back door. The crowd cheers again.

A sense of normalcy returns, at least for a moment. Omar plays, the wine flows, Isis dances onstage. My mind, left undisturbed, races back to my memories, fueling guilt that still sways and burns through me. I pour wine and spread sheets. I think about the night at the ziggurat. I look at these men who are no worse than I am. I think, Should I . . .? What could . . .? But events soon intervene. Sala rushes through the back door and grabs at my arm.

"Hurry, you must come quick!"

"What is it?"

"Sasha needs your help."

I put down the wineskin and make my way to the back. It takes several seconds to adjust to the darkness. I hear the rustle of bodies, muted whisperings, shouted threats. I edge past Sala and Avi to the last room off the hall, where Ebbe's corpulent frame is caught in the doorway. Sasha's deep voice echoes from inside, all but drowned out by Ebbe's shrill swearing.

"Ahmet! Is Ahmet here yet?"

"I am here."

"Ahmet, crawl under him and come inside. Then you can help me push."

I duck below the trembling mass and emerge with some difficulty into the near darkness of the small room. Sasha's robe hangs open, exposing her squarish breasts; she closes it with a diffident wave. Ebbe's bulk is squirming, like a gargantuan fish on a hook, his voice raised an octave, threatening now to shut the place down. At Sasha's direction, I place my shoulder against Ebbe's side, which collapses in a good way, but then goes no farther. The door frame trembles, as does the building itself. We push again, without result. Sasha shouts for more help. Other voices echo. Finally, with a great creaking of lumber and a dust-scattering vibration, Ebbe squeezes through the door frame into the dimly lit corridor. Sasha and I pause, panting. Others in the hallway give way. Ebbe shouts some more. The young assistants materialize again, lifting his arms, prodding his huge buttocks with the studied movements of animal handlers. The maneuvering continues, along with calls back and forth, the bumping and shuddering of door frames, the high-pitched, tremulous cursing. As the movers and their freight clear the last doorway, as Sasha, Bibi, and I stand watching, a swaddled form shuffles past, his arms outstretched like a man expecting a gift—al-Wati, either risen or never quite dead. He wanders into the main room, sits, glances around, motions for wine. Sasha mutters something, Bibi looks as if she might faint, but at my instigation we are consumed with a breath-throttling laughter, a convulsion that recurs periodically over the course of the night.

The evening wears down. The crowd in the antechamber thins. At perhaps two in the morning, just as the last song is launched, Hussein strides through the doorway. Our gazes meet as I serve wine to a pair of Bedouins near the back of the room, long enough for there to be a flicker of recognition in his dark eyes, a narrowing of his brows. I look away, edging into the shadows to observe without being observed, my heart thrashing, the blood driving fast through my limbs and my chest. He does not look for me, as he might have done if he had truly recognized me, nor does he dawdle in his intentions. He flashes money to Sasha, engages in muted discourse, tilts his head, accepts a cup of wine. At Sasha's departure his focus returns to the stage, to Rasha (evidently returned, in good graces), to bouncing tissue and smiles. At the end of the song he is up, following Sasha into the back, his narrow hips swinging, his neck thrust back in the proud, familiar posture. The fear I felt at his entrance dissipates, replaced by the anger I had known from before. Again I think of how easy it would be to break his thin neck. Again I feel resentment at the object of his manipulations (this time, Avi). The thought of him with Araxie drives me to new levels of fury, pulsing blood in my fingers as spots break in my eyes. I keep away from him, away from the room he occupies with Avi, busying myself in a frenzy of cleanup, wrapping mats, removing sheets, fiercely sweeping the hard, sandy floors. Even after he has gone, after Avi has retired to the house to giggle with the other girls, after the rooms and the stage have gone dark and quiet, I smolder, working with an energy that leaves me soaking with sweat. Only at the end of the night, as the first pink of dawn enters the sky, do I achieve some measure of peace, a tranquillity brought on by a resolution for change. I have no plan, no definite idea of what I will do next, but I know I cannot continue this way. I climb into one of the newly changed beds, and sleep a restless sleep.

13

The entrance to South Georgia Psychiatric Center is a well-worn state park, with groves of mature trees, redbrick posts with pyramid-shaped tops, a guardhouse, a ranger. An abandoned community pool sits in blue across the street. On closer inspection, however, the grounds start to look sinister, with sentrylike entrance posts, guards packing guns, and trees like the hair on a giant's large head. The car motors to the circle next to the guard post, to the right of the flagpole and its limp printed cotton. I stare out, the image shifting from park to reform school, from summer camp to work camp. Detention area, hospital, cell block. Prison.

The she-deputy driving me rolls down her window and waits for the guard. She hums softly. She coughs before addressing him.

"I have Emmett Conn."

It sounds possessive, as if others might claim me. She disembarks, opens the vehicle's trunk, waits a moment, slams it shut.

The guard eyes her, nodding, as if she has performed some ritual. She says nothing more.

We drive and stop, buzz a buzzer, enter a building. Inside is drabness, like flesh hung on a carcass, with white walls and few furnishings. A table displays magazines that appear to have been never opened. *Modern Maturity, Business Week, Forbes.* There are questions, more forms. Violet is here, answering, her voice soft. We sit before a glass cubicle, facing a clerk with a shiny V from what was once a widow's peak. Some questions come to me but I nod, uninterested. I search for other prisoners—patients? keening lunatics?—but there is no one, only the aged plant in the corner, the rows of cupped chairs. A faded spot where a TV once sat. No sounds, no soothing music.

The clerk shuffles papers, rises, pushes glasses back up his nose. I am taken into a room, stripped, and examined. Such a strong man, they say. Are you really ninety-two? I urinate into a cup. I shower in an adjacent bathroom, remembering the hammam, the smell of patchouli, the soft, curling steam. I part my lips and taste bitter rakı. I close my eyes against sound and image, but still they follow. A dirty child laps at water. Soldiers march past swinging chains. A woman's bracelets jangle. A man smokes a cigarette and disappears, and only then is there silence. I put on my clothes, thinking of the knife maker Abdul, dead now. They are all dead.

A black man stands waiting in the corridor, arms folded across a womanish chest. "Mr. Conn, I'm Andre. I'm going to take you into the unit. You'll need to say good-bye here."

Violet steps down the hall. We had parted during my examination but she is back now, her face mottled, her mouth drawn firm but pulled down at the corners. Her eyes are warm, sympathetic, guilt-heavy. She looks away.

"I'll visit tomorrow," she says.

I stare at her. I am confused but grateful, agitated. I am a child left alone.

We embrace, our faces together, her skin warm against mine.

"Please don't leave." I get these words out, these words that show weakness. My hands shake in a slow dance.

"Papa." She pulls away. "We've been through this. The doctors think it's best."

"But *you* . . . agree." Resentment flares. "You have not fought it."

"They're professionals." Her eyes are red but dry. Her lip trembles slightly and she makes it stay firm. "Look, Papa, I'm sorry, but I think we have to do this. It's for the best, best for you."

"Best for me."

She smiles, her neck bent. Have I ever needed anything, wanted anything more? Her devotion, protection. To not be left behind.

"I have to go now. Take care, okay?"

I do not look at her. I listen to the sound of her footsteps, her hand turning the knob.

Andre picks up my bag. I follow to a metal door, a key pressed in a lock. I am shuffling, thinking, but it is so hard to think here. Alone again, a stranger. Must things always circle back? We proceed down a new corridor, a longer hallway with glassed cubicles. A woman sits at an oblong table, another woman slumps with her head in her hands. A locked glass door, then another. Andre points out the dining area and its weather-beaten piano and hard plastic tables, the women's area visible through yet another glass door, an exterior door that leads to a patio outside. In between is something he calls the "secure area," a place reserved for the violent. A young black man sits here at a table. He smiles as we pass, a tooth-filled, too-wide smile.

"Do you smoke?"

The question is puzzling. I had smoked in Aleppo.

"No," I say, after much hesitation.

He nods. "Smokers are permitted two cigarettes each break—every two hours."

He backtracks, unlocks another door, motions me inside. "This is the men's dayroom." We enter a stark, open area, devoid of any pictures, peppered with bits of furniture. A vinyl-covered couch occupies the middle of the room, in front of a TV draped in plastic. A handful of other chairs are scattered about, some facing the TV, others turned away. Several drugged-looking men glance up at our entrance. An older man stands, winds up his arm, and hurls something in our direction. I duck in response but he has thrown only air.

"That's Elmo. Elmo, this is Emmett."

Elmo gazes with disinterest. He is bald and rather short, with a yellow oxford shirt and a pallor mixed with pink at his temples.

"He doesn't say much," Andre continues. "But he tends to pitch a lot. He told me once he was better than Ferguson Jenkins."

"Was he a ballplayer?"

Andre shakes his head. "Nah. I think he was a stockbroker."

He extends his arm. "That's Alfonso, and Leo." He indicates two men. "We call Alfonso 'Puff.' Gentlemen, this is Emmett." He pauses. "The fellow over there"—he indicates a sullen man slumped in a corner—"is William."

It is a hospital for the infirm, like Recep's—shiny polished floors, nurses in rubber shoes, the smell of urine and disinfectant. The patients slow and shuffling, medicated. Puff, a black man with tufts of hair in each ear, seeks to shake my hand as we pass. Leo, a stringy-haired white man, bows prayerfully toward me.

Andre takes a few more steps. "This is your room." He points to an open doorway, through which two metal beds can be seen. "The bathroom's over there." He points across the large room, behind the TV.

I enter the small room and sit on one of the beds. Andre drops my bag on the floor. I've been allowed to keep my wallet, my keys and watch.

"Dinner's at five-thirty, breakfast at eight, lunch at noon. Lights out at ten. They'll have a program set up for you: medication, treatment, all that. Dr. Mahoney will be by to talk to you about it." He pauses, glancing about the room, as if he has not seen it before. "Your roommate is John Paul. He's around here somewhere." He turns back to me. "You got any questions?"

I shake my head.

"Okay, then." He shows a gap between broad teeth. "Cheer up, Mr. Conn. You'll be all right."

All right. I remain sitting. I count the ceiling tiles (twelve, with parts of four others). I examine the walls. I glance at my watch. Thoughts of the dream come, but in a muffled sort of way, as if the building itself blocks them out. My limbs are sluggish, the result of the deadening drugs, but we are all dead here. My stomach protests. Life beyond seems so far, like faint dots on the moon, fleeting and graying, then gone. I think of Wilfred, and Violet. I think of her.

"Hey. What's your name?"

A serpentlike head pokes its way into view, dark hair mixed with oversized glasses, brown stubble spread across a powdery face. The voice is deep and almost breathless, the voice of a much larger man.

"Emmett Conn."

"I'm John Paul." He slithers into the room. He is young, maybe thirty, the first flecks of gray at the base of his temples. His hair is short but swept in different directions, his face thin, blue veins stretched in hollowed eye sockets. His arms have bright scars crosshatched at the wrists. He holds out a pale, slender hand, and I shake it. He keeps his head turned away.

"Welcome. What are you in for?" He has a rushed way of speaking, such that his words run together to form strange constructions: "I'mJohnPaul"; "youinfor."

I run my hand through my hair. "I had a brain tumor," I say slowly. "It has caused these . . . visions." I pause. "My daughter had me committed."

He glances at me briefly before turning away. "Acute schizophrenia, for me," he says in his rapid form. It takes me several seconds to understand him. His head bobs and shifts like a bird's. "Did your daughter want you out of the way?"

"I . . . do not know." Did she?

He shrugs, as if it is of no interest. "My mother commits me when she's tired of me—there's not much you can do about it. Are you coming to dinner?"

"Perhaps. I am hungry." I lift up from the bed. "How is the food?"

"Okay, I guess. The beef stroganoff on Mondays is deadly. The fried chicken and hamburgers are edible, if you like that sort of thing. The only thing that's really good are the desserts. They have excellent pecan pie." He swings into step beside me, his bony arms extending and collapsing, his scars lengthening with movement.

I recall Ted's formula for preventing bad dreams. "Do they have dill pickles?" I ask.

His face folds. "Dill pickles. No, I don't think so. There's a set meal, depending on the diet you're on." His back hunches over. "Have you met the other patients? It's quite a crew—we take clients from a twenty-four-county region. Some have been here for years. Others are back for return visits. Most stay only a week or two." His head rotates swiftly toward me. "What do you do?"

"I . . . I was a builder." A plumber, then a builder.

"A builder. Oh, okay, that's good. A builder. I don't think we have one of those. We have a lawyer, a stockbroker, a whole flock of teachers, several maintenance men, a banker, a newspaper reporter, but no, no builders."

I cough. "And you? What . . . do you do?"

"I'm a student. A graduate student. I'm working on my doctorate, in instructional design."

We walk to the dayroom, the jumble of chairs and couch. Someone has turned on the TV at low volume. Baseball images make shadows on the screen. Puff, Leo, and several others stand in a semicircle, staring, not commenting. Elmo totters over to join them, winds up and throws a pitch, but stops in his follow-through to peer closely at the screen. He looks around at the others.

"Dale Murphy's getting damned fat."

I stare at the TV. The group queues for dinner and I fall

in line, following the others to the dining room. The food is surprisingly good: roast beef and potatoes, spinach salad, green beans and cornbread. John Paul is right, the pecan pie is outstanding. He stays at my side, John Paul does, acting as my interpreter despite my difficulty in understanding him, explaining, introducing. There are probably forty people in all, including a dozen or so staff. Maybe one-third are women, most appear over fifty. I meet the HSTs (health service technicians), Ralph, John, Stephen, Melissa. I know Andre. I meet Carla, a pleasant-looking lady with wide-set eyes; Esteban, a young, dark-skinned man with a sunken forehead; Max, an old man with a cough and a yellow-stained beard; a pair of twins; a man with one eye. There are others John Paul motors past in his machine-gun manner, names I cannot catch, faces he does not mention. One man, long-haired, with bushy eyebrows, snarls as we pass. They form an odd group, but no odder than forty people found in a bus station, a Chinese restaurant, or for that matter a church. My sluggishness lessens. I chew my cornbread and drink my fruit punch. I think of times past.

John Paul accompanies me back to our room after dinner. His patter continues.

"You know, they normally lock up the rooms during the day, except for nap time after lunch. They don't want anyone hiding in there. If you're suicidal, they put you in the secure area—you passed it on the way in. Trust me, it's much better here. Medications are given at nine, one, six, and nine. Do they have you on psychotropics? Everybody's on psychotropics. Maybe you're on something else for your tumor, maybe Dilantin?"

The sound of splashing water bleeds through his

questioning—perhaps from the bathroom across the way or a sink or washroom somewhere—the sound growing, overwhelming in its approach, until it washes through my skull like a tidal wave's lunge. Blood rushes and circles, recedes. A light flashes on as if beamed underwater. I gasp, a liquid formed in my throat, my eyes shut against it. I need to cough or take in air but cannot seem to do either.

I know where I am before I open my eyes, from the dread lurking in the pit of my stomach, the sound of the water still coursing in my ears. The sun beats on my forehead, warm but not comforting, the first drops of moisture amassed at my temples. The air is thick with humidity, with the pungent stench of decay. Shrieks resound over the rush of the water, gasps and wails, protests, directives, commands. I open my eyes to a blade of light. I see it all, clearly. And I remember.

The River Euphrates is thinner at this point, brown and unappealingly muddy, with an island in its middle providing respite for fording. Other caravans have come before us, their debris evident on the riverbank and beyond, abandoned carts melded with blankets, with tents and rope, clothing, cookware, bedding. And bodies. Huge masses of vultures pick at remains so bloated as to be unrecognizable. Strands of hair stream from pecked-out faces, scattered among severed limbs, open skulls, disembodied hands and feet. At least twice during our passing the vultures' digging punctures a swollen corpse, releasing internal gases in loud pops that send the birds skittering. The stench grows as we reach the water, as the bodies multiply, as the air becomes thick with the brazen vultures and their huge, hand-shaped wings. Farther downstream, black clumps of yet more bodies lie exposed, death birds gathered around. There must be hundreds, thousands. Maybe more.

We force the deportees into the water. Those protesting receive a swift bayonet. Others throw themselves at the water in deliberate efforts to drown. The current is not swift here, but swift enough—it carries a number of our party away, including one pregnant woman, her belly raised like a turtle. Women carry children upon their shoulders, across their backs, in uplifted arms. Those still with carts force them through, oxen bellowing, wheels churning and sticking. The deportees on the opposite side shake like rats seeking shelter, gathering what is left of their scattered belongings. I remain to the end on the eastern shore, pushing the stragglers. All must move on.

It is there that I feel the woman's pull at my leg, hear her anguished voice, see the plea in her big, gloomy eyes. She holds an infant in one arm, wordlessly offering it up to me—a request, evidently, to ferry the child across the water. I refuse. She says something, something I do not understand, then places the infant on the ground, rips off her clothing, and stands naked before me, her long hair flung back across her shoulders, her breasts full with milk. Again, she says something. I dismount. She prostrates herself in the dust, her white legs parting, revealing. I kneel and enter, heedless of the shouts from afar, the vultures circling and flapping, the splash of the dirty water, the gendarmes picking through trash and bodies, but at the same time aware of it all, as if I or everything else has been stilled. The world rotates around me, spinning so that I see from above the last of our deportees crossing, the bloated bodies, our group on the opposite side, the next wave behind us. And then comes the horseman, his face obscured, approaching, pawing the ground nearby, directing his steed's hoof squarely onto the infant's skull, crushing it in a tiny burst of liquid, a smallish squish of sound. I feel myself scream—feel the burn in my throat, the compression of my lungs—but I do not hear it, for the sound has become lost, swept up in an explosion of wind and feather, hoofbeat and wave, all overridden by the writhing, abject agony of the woman beneath me. I gulp for air, my hands at my eyes. My voice becomes audible, my scream deep and raw. And then John Paul's pocked face and thick glasses are before me, his hands on my shoulders, his rapid voice cracking.

"Hey! Hey! Hey!"

I fight to control my hands, to stop the twisting and burning. My voice continues, muted for now. I gasp for air. My muscles stretch and contract.

"Wow. That was something. Was that a grand mal? Your eyes rolled back in your head, your body was shaking, and you were yelling like you'd seen a monster. You almost levitated off the ground."

The sound of lapping water becomes the thud of running footsteps, the wordless murmur of voices. A male attendant I have not seen before, a redheaded man with a small goatee, enters the room and rushes to me. A metallic sound comes from an intercom: "Code blue. Code blue." Another man, a doctor, arrives seconds later.

"What happened?"

"I think he had a seizure." John Paul's voice is full of importance.

The doctor edges him out of the way. "How do you feel?" he asks me.

I struggle to speak. My muscles are clenched, as taut now as bowstrings, my lips thick and sealed. A dampness moistens my crotch but I cannot bend to examine it. At least part of my mind remains suspended, reeling from horror and shame, from atrocities perpetrated, abominations allowed. How could I have done this? I know she must have been there, wading through mud and current, watching as friends took their lives and were swept away, dodging swollen corpses, listening to the shriek of the overstuffed vultures. Did she notice me then, as the woman offered her infant, as I dismounted to engage in my pleasure? Did she look on in shock and in hatred, watching as the hoof rose and fell, as life was extinguished, as flesh became sand, as unknowing man ripped out his own heart? Did she cry out to her God, damning his indifference, pleading for justification, asking why why why why WHY?!

My voice finally sounds, a gurgle of gibberish like a car trying to start. A hand grasps my wrist. Others press on my shoulders.

"Just lie down now, okay?"

John Paul's voice leaps from somewhere, the words unintelligible.

"John Paul, why don't you go back to the dayroom? We're going to get Mr. Conn stabilized, maybe take him down to the exam room. I think he's okay."

John Paul's feet tap, slide, tap again. The hands remain on my wrists and shoulders, the voices still in my ears. My muscles begin to slacken, sore now from the strain. I taste blood in my mouth.

"Let's get a chair over for him."

The goateed man departs, returns moments later with a wheelchair.

"Do you feel you can sit up?"

Movement is jerky, difficult. A muscle burns in my side. I collapse into a sitting position, aware of the faces peering in from the dayroom. The doctor pushes the chair through the crowd, acknowledging voices, shushing questions, speeding past the fuzzy, unheeded TV, fumbling with keys at the door lock, out into the hall. It is cooler here, quieter. The chair's wheels squish as they roll. My mind goes back again, even as I try to steer elsewhere—the Euphrates crossing would have been earlier, closer to Harput, where the river was smaller and easier to ford. The deportee group was much larger then, perhaps a thousand strong or more. From there we would travel to Gerger, to Behesni, to Kilis and Katma, through boulder and outcrop, foothill and desert. The ziggurat would have been later, closer to Aintab. Nearer the end.

"Let's get you up on the table."

We are back in an examining room. I move again, with difficulty, my side stiff and painful, to where the doctor and the other man he calls Roger can hold me under the arms and lift me onto the table. Lights flash in my eyes, hands grasp my wrist, a wooden stick enters my mouth. Blood is drawn, charts consulted.

"How are you feeling?"

I am tired.

"What day is it?"

I struggle to respond. Thursday? Saturday?

"Is it day or night?"

Another hesitation. My voice rumbles deep in my chest. "I think it is night."

"Where are you?"

"The hospital." The sights and sounds of Aleppo creep back,

the smell of sweat and sulfur, the stream of stick-thin deportees. The doctor bandaging my head.

"What is your name?"

I take a deep breath. How best to protect her?

"Ahmet. Ahmet Khan."

The doctor jots this down. He looks at the other man, the man with the goatee, and I realize I have given the wrong answer, the wrong language, that I am in the United States, not Syria, that my constant back-and-forth has confused things. Do I know who I am, or where? Where is she?

"Doctor. Can you help me?" My voice is thick and strange. "I did not mean to do this. I cannot . . . keep things straight."

"It's okay. You had a seizure. Many people experience confusion afterward."

"Will this stop?"

He frowns. "I don't know."

Other conversations follow, discussions on whether I should be sent to the emergency room, the fact that my chart shows evidence of prior seizures. The voices recede, then return. I am asked how I feel, asked to move my arms and legs. A light shines again in my eyes.

Eventually I am raised, placed back in the chair, and returned to the unit. The others stare as I enter the dayroom, as I attempt to right myself, to flex sore muscles, to lift my battered body from the confines of the chair. The doctor and the HST help position me on the bed, remove my clothes, find the pajamas Violet packed for me. John Paul's voice drones somewhere, a few of his sentences thrusting like swords. "In a petit mal seizure, don't they often bite their tongues?" "Of course I'll keep an eye on him." The rat-a-tat of his chuckle after. The small, rapid shifts of his head.

14

Araxie laughs and wrinkles her nose. We sit under a bridge, in the cool shade of a hot afternoon. She looks better, healthier, the lines of worry and illness erased from her forehead.

"I saw a man in the market today—I've never seen anyone like him. His hair was cut short, and the back of his head was wrinkled and curved, as if the contours of his brain were exposed there. I wanted to touch him. Then I laughed—why should I touch him? As if I would touch someone's brain."

I laugh with her. When she dips her head or moves her shoulders, the rope holding the necklace becomes visible under the edge of her *libas*.

"Do you like Aleppo?" she asks. She tosses her head back, despite her hair being covered.

"I think so. Do you?"

"Yes. I am glad to be out of Turkey." She averts her gaze, as if remembering leaving. "I like my new job."

I study the palms of my hands. My mind flits unbidden to the Euphrates, to the incident at the brown waters' edge.

"Tell me about your job," I say, squinting. I fold my fingers together.

"I work for Dr. Ghavani. He is of Persian descent, a nice man, decent. He and his wife and daughter live in a house behind the hospital. They allow me to sleep on the floor. I work with the nurses, clean up after the surgeries, help transport patients."

"The sight of blood does not bother you?"

She pauses. "I've grown accustomed to blood."

"And Hussein?"

"He remains a problem. Dr. Ghavani has asked him to take his leave of me, but he refuses. He brings me candies and gifts, then pouts if I'm not appreciative. I angered him when I was sick, because I refused to see him then. He yelled that he could have me deported, that I must show proper respect. I try to be courteous, but it is always so difficult."

"Does he," I hesitate, "attempt to touch you?"

She shakes her head. "Only once. When I was first resident in the hospital and still quite ill, I awoke to find him standing over me, his hand on my belly. I thought at first he was a doctor, but then I recognized him. I screamed, and he pulled away. He told the doctors I was delirious."

She shakes her head again. Bile forms in my throat, merging with shifting memories, of my thirst at the stream at the ziggurat, the tear of the fabric as I ripped off her clothes. I fidget. My nails cut grooves in my palms.

"If you could be anything you wish," I ask, seeking to start anew, to turn all things forward, "what would you be?"

She glances into the distance, at the sounds of transport and barter. "I always thought I would be a merchant, like my father, trading goods, traveling to exotic places. Now I am less sure. I am happy helping people, doing what I do now. Perhaps I will become a nurse, or a doctor." She spreads her hands across her lap. "And you?"

I swallow, the reference to her father unsettling. "I always thought I would be in the military," I say quickly. "Work my way up the ladder."

"And now?"

I smile. "And now I am less certain." I glance at her hands, at the bend and curve of her fingers. "I want to go to America."

I raise my head to find her staring at me, her eyes narrowed in concentration. "And how will you get there?" she asks.

"By boat," I say, as if I have worked it all out.

"How?"

"Either pay or steal my way on board. Or get hired as a ship's mate."

She nods, glancing again at the bustle of the suq. "I would like to go to America."

"Would you go with me?" I ask quickly, impetuously.

She does not respond, at least for a time. Saliva moistens my mouth.

"I think so," she says finally. She smiles, her fingers on the necklace curled beneath her loose clothing.

My doubt flips to exultation. Suddenly all things are possible. "Do you want to have children?"

"With you?"

Blood rises to my face. "I mean . . . in general."

She laughs, her face broadening, then thinning, returning now to its prior concentration, her eyes up and alive. "I think I would like to have a family someday. I have lost almost all the family I had. Sometimes I question this, though. The thought of losing someone else, someone I love, is almost too much to bear. I wonder if survival has changed me, perhaps damaged me in ways I can't see."

I look down again. "How do you imagine it? America, I mean. What do you think it is like?"

She pauses. "I hear there are streetcars, and subways—trains that run under the ground! It is big, with large cities that make Aleppo look tiny, and vast spaces it takes trains days to cross. I have cousins in New York, the largest city. I would love to see them.

"Do you dream?" she asks.

The question prickles my scalp. "Do I *what*?"

"Dream. Do you?"

I pause. "Yes. I dream of the past, of my home, and the future." I glance away. "Do you?"

"Yes, every night. Colorful dreams, of my home, my family, the journey here, the death along the way. Some of the dreams are frightening, some joyous, others disheartening. In one a dog chased me down a valley, through a thicket of thorns, into a river and beyond. He kept after me, swimming so close I could feel the heat of his breath through the water, feel the scratch of his paws as he brushed up against me. Then, back on land, he caught up with me, tackled me, sank his teeth into my leg, shook me with such a vengeance that the bones clicked in my face. And then he let go. Why would he give such pursuit only to release me once he had me? I thought about that dream for days after. I could not get it out of my mind.

"I had another dream that haunted me even longer. I was very young, maybe three or four, out for a walk with my mother. We stopped and spoke to a Turkish woman, a squat, older woman with eyes that rolled back in her head. In the dream my mother said something I did not hear or understand, something that made the old woman angry. She cried out, this loud, contemptible wail that carried through my dream, such that I could hear it for days. I saw the woman's blind eyes and cruel mouth in the sun and the sky, even the stars. I still wonder what my mother said to her—did she insult her? Offend her? But I tell myself it was only a dream."

She smiles. I say nothing.

"Do you believe in God?" she asks, her thumbs placed together.

"Yes. Of course." I finger my beard. God. Allah. "God is life."

She stares at her palms. "Life. I've seen so much suffering and death. Despite my prayers, the prayers that the missionaries taught us, the prayers that the will of God would be done. And yet he who is so all-powerful—will not his will be done whether I pray for it or not?" She shakes her head, strands of hair falling loose down her face. "God, my God . . ." She extends her arms, as if taking in Anatolia. "How could it happen?"

I shake my head. How to explain the unexplainable, the things meant to be mystery? Birds fly. People eat. Allah gives all, demands all. Has he not given us this, each other? We must look forward, not back.

"In America," I start again, "all things are possible."

She nods, pitting her chin. "In America."

Again, silence roams. My thoughts split and carom. How best to assure her? I picture her thinking, jumbled in fear and spent logic. How can she trust this man who has killed—killed her father? The man who tried to rape her. Differing options unfold, paths to outcomes, an array of doors with dim passageways beyond. Practicalities. Youth and its blindness. Race and division and circumstance—these surmountable, all! My gaze strays to the necklace. I should speak, I should offer support for rebirth, transformation, but instead I am frozen, my tongue stilled and thick. What is my direction? My offer? She has made no accusation, assigned no blame to anyone except God—her God. This is her right. Should I not agree? I could blame the heavens, blame fate or luck or inheritance, but it is all to no gain. My shame is boundless, my guilt so heavy it outweighs even truth.

The silence lingers. Her eyes glisten, the light eye appraising, the dark eye reproving. I imagine competing armies warring in great, speechless battle. I will her to speak again, to release me! But she is silent. The shadows grow thicker, the day stumbling on. Bits of the world intrude and withdraw. I stand at one point, try to force the words from me—we can go forward, an ocean's distance behind us! But nothing comes then, no words. No vessel by which to make good our escape.

The cries of the muezzin bring the sunset prayers. I stir, less from mental instruction than from some deeper impulse. I raise my hands to my ears, fold them right over left on my breast, bow, and place my hands on my knees, stand, dip my forehead low to the ground. I think, This will please her, ease things. Allah has offered us peace. I am joyous. But then a panic seeps in, a cold rain on my heart. Is this not the divider? Allah. The Christian God. The war, the deportations—they are birthed by this cleaving. And then us. Muslims do not marry others unless they convert—I know this. She knows it. We have spoken of togetherness, not marriage, and yet this wedge strikes, guilt-hardened. Her brother, staying behind and renouncing his faith. She would not do this. I want to cry out. Could I not have foreseen it? The words of the sura drone through me, the buzz of bees trapped in a hive—*Guide us in the straight path / The path on whom thou hast poured forth thy grace . . .*— but I am conscious only of her, waiting, the light eye questioning, the dark eye confirming. What was it the imam told me as a child?—we pray to keep life in perspective, to remind ourselves that we are poor worldly creatures, to submit our will to Allah's. Submit. Have we all not submitted? I could . . . She . . . I arise to find her standing.

"I must go," she says, her tone final, and sad.

Again I am mute. Her voice lingers, soft after the prayers. I am reminded of the night we first met, of the encounter under the eucalyptus trees, the way I brought her out into the moonlight to examine her eyes, my first thought that her one eye had been blinded. I remember her traveling on Gece, barely hanging on, her face shrunken, her hair matted, her eyes hooded and closed. I recall her smile when I handed her the necklace, the smell of her skin near my face, the gleam of her right eye, her left. But still I say nothing, as if my tongue has been cut.

She hesitates, as if she, too, has much to say but no means to say it. A dog barks in the distance. A door or windows bang shut. She steps toward me, her hand on my arm, but then pulls away, pivoting, looking back once and then gone, vanished through gloom into shadow. I stay for some time, faint, then nauseated, then exhausted, then inflamed. I walk to the *klimbim* later, my anguish buried inside.

15

A hospital room. Two beds, a sleeping figure. For a moment I assume I am with her, feigning illness, hoping for intercession. Then it is London, and darkness, the piercing rays of the sun. But no—the form moves, a sharp nose pokes beneath bedcovers, a bird whistles, recognition dawns. John Paul shifts in his sleep, his face twitching slightly, his body in motion even in repose. He snorts, flips onto his side, and resumes a measured droning that sounds oddly of the Qur'an's opening sura. I place my pillow over my head, the odor of my own hair and skin in my face. For the first time in my life, I am ready to die.

Lights flip on mechanically, or perhaps by an unseen hand. John Paul rises in a rush. His feet pad the floor. His breath is musky as he leans in toward me.

"Hey, wake up! It's rise and shine. Did you sleep okay? Did you dream?"

"I am okay," I say from the pillow.

"Good morning, gentlemen. Time to wake up." A tenor voice enters—southern, effeminate. Hands grasp the pillow and remove it from my head, leaving me staring into the face of a reed-faced man, his head and neck dotted with the pits of once-ravaging acne.

"I'm Lawrence. You must be Mr. Conn."

He extends an orange hand. I shake it without thinking.

"Come on. We have breakfast, we have medicine, we have lots of fun in store. If you want to use the bathroom or take a shower, you have time."

I rub my face. "Is there tea?"

He glances at a chart, smiles. "There is. Once we get to breakfast. For now, we need to get moving."

Movement strains sore muscles. My head knocks and throbs. I grope my way to the bathroom, to the open shower, strip off my clothes, and turn on water that becomes only slightly warm. Others enter—the black man they call Puff, the stringy-haired Leo. They turn on other nozzles, standing bashfully to one side as the water heats up. I avoid looking at them, at their sagging rumps and distended organs, but both of them stare at me as if I have sprouted a new neck. I turn off my nozzle, exit past turned heads and wordless stares, dry myself as best I can with the thin towel Lawrence distributes, climb back into my clothing. I glance at myself in the mirror, noting the slackness, the eyes that look aged and different. I decline Lawrence's offer of a disposable razor. My face is numb.

Breakfast is a replay of dinner, complete with eggs and sausage, toast, and weak coffee. There is no tea. I have gained a certain familiarity with the other patients, or at least I think so—I recognize people, we nod greetings, some hold out hands and say, "What's your name?" or "Who's this?" Many appear drugged, or severely ill, gripping their plates in hunched-over fashion, glancing neither left nor right. I sit at a table with John Paul and another man, a scowling giant with red-rimmed eyes and a forelock of blond hair that falls into his face. John Paul introduces him as Sydney.

The meal is, as expected, accompanied by a John Paul mono-logue. Sydney says nothing. I tug at my eggs, the wooliness from before back upon me, my mind stumbling in different directions. The dream, Carol, Violet. Death. I remember the closed wing of the hospital in London, the psych wing, the howls and sob-bing that wafted from behind large wooden doors. The man—an escapee?—who appeared periodically and came up to each patient to ask, "What time is the lorry? Where's the lorry?" before others arrived to hustle him away. I had no idea then what this meant, but others taught me. It became almost the first English I learned. I rarely saw other patients from behind the big doors, never knew what criteria caused one to be placed there. A rumor abounded that those in the head-injury ward who never improved would go in. As such I gave myself headaches trying to bring forth scraps of memory. But then I was moved to my room, I met Carol. The threat of confinement eased. If I think hard enough I can still hear the wails, though, still summon the same anxiousness.

Something clatters, interrupting John Paul. Heads turn to take in the dropped tray and the source of its fumbling, then turn back. I take advantage of the momentary lull, the silent instant before John Paul resumes speaking.

"Tell me, John Paul—what are you researching?"

He looks puzzled, like an actor thrown off his script.

"Did you not tell me you were working on your degree?"

"Yes, yes, yes. I'm studying the mechanics of instructional design in several disciplines, how different management structures affect capabilities . . ."

But my mind is spinning off again, sailing its way back to her, to my shame and frustration at the way we had parted, my clumsiness and inadequacy at the Khan al-Wazir. I want to go back to her, rush to her, try once again; in America, anything is possible. *Anything.* But I recognize, on some level, the nature of my quest, the finality inherent in the path I have taken. I look back on life now, in America. Where all things are possible, but not guaranteed.

"Medicine!" Lawrence the orange-skinned HST pops into view. We are back in the dayroom, the other patients shifting, queuing up before a Dutch door–like window attached to a wall. There, a nurse consults charts and asks questions, dispenses water and hands out pills. I wait, watching her face as it rises and falls, rises and falls, as those in front of me extend hands and tilt necks. What are they saying? I have been placed here, held here. I have come here to die.

The nurse grasps my arm, examines the wristband I have no memory of receiving, glances from chart to band, lifts her face to expose an expanse of gapped teeth.

"What is your birth date?"

Again, to remember. "The year 1898."

"Very good, Mr. Conn." She hands me a small cup containing five pills, another small cup of water, then watches as I gulp them down.

"What happens if you don't take your medicine?" I ask John Paul as I pass through the line.

He grimaces. "By law they can't force you, unless you're classified as violent or a danger to yourself. If that's the case, they give you an altered form that dissolves on your tongue. Or, failing that, an injection. After one or two experiences with either, most people take the pills."

I nod. My stomach rumbles. We stand for a while. The drugs slow my heartbeat, then lengthen my tongue. The lights of the room dim and yellow.

"Mr. Conn." Lawrence, again. "May I call you Emmett?"

I make the slowest of movements.

"We have you set for treatment team at eleven. Right now, you get to go outside." He pauses, consulting a chart before him. "Let's see . . . you're not a smoker, are you?"

The others are queuing again, like schoolchildren bound for recess. HSTs and nurses nudge them along, buzzing and clucking, and suddenly I am back, the association so clear I can almost see it, back on the hilltop overlooking the deportees, examining the sheep and the canines. I search from left to right and back again, across the plain in the direction of our journey, then to the rear, the way we had come. The same sense of disappointment follows, the same loss, before I find myself standing in line again like a tottering old tree, wiping my forehead against the south Georgia heat.

"Hey! Are you all right?" An HST peers back my way.

I nod my head. The line ahead shifts, the tail of a fish held at the mouth. I search for someone I recognize. Violet? Do I know anyone here? I am cantilevered, defined now by absence—Burak's,

Carol's, Araxie's, my own. But I am alive still. Breathing and spitting. Like a camel in sand.

The exercise area consists of a concrete pad perhaps one hundred feet long and sixty feet wide. A ten-foot brick wall, angled to create more room at the back, forms the perimeter of the area, with a volleyball net at its midsection and a basketball goal at one end. An overhang closest to the building shields a Ping-Pong table and metal picnic furniture. The patients hobbling before me break off into groups, some taking seats at the picnic tables, others standing together in the sun's sharpened light. The women join us, HSTs dispense cigarettes, and one by one heads bend toward devices built into the wall that look like braziers, and return in puffs of smoke.

"See those black boxes?" John Paul points to a series of small rectangles at the top of the wall. "They're motion detectors. The ground is sloped on the other side, so it's only three or four feet from the top. If you were to climb over the top, they'd detect it." He steps farther down the wall. "See this?" He points to a recessed light. "They put the plastic covering over so you can't use it as a foothold."

I glance up at the wall. "Have many tried to escape?"

"Not that I know of. One guy got up on top of the walkway running between our unit and the open unit and ran around for a while before they pulled him off."

"The open unit?"

"It's for more permanent residents. They have their own cafeteria where the food is made, not brought in, like it is here."

We stand silent a few minutes. The day has begun to heat up; most in the sun edge into the shade.

"Mr. Conn!"

I turn.

"You have a visitor."

I follow Lawrence back into the building, through the locked doors, into a glass-paneled cubicle off one side of a hall. I am confused again by this place. Am I dreaming? I have no visitors, no one here knows me. I am a foreigner. An *enemy*. But then a woman turns. Gray-haired, erect, she is familiar, so . . .

"Hello, dear." Mrs. Fleming rises and offers a perfumed hug. I remain standing, despite my body's lingering soreness. Dizziness fades her image, shifting her face in and out.

"Violet will be here in a little while. She's getting her hair done this morning."

Mrs. Fleming. Violet. I do not know of a relationship between them. She returns to her seat. The magnification of her glasses makes her eyes soft, like a cow's.

"How are you doing?"

I slide into a seat near the door. I am imprisoned, time draining, while Violet has her hair done.

I look up. Mrs. Fleming's hair is the scruff of a lioness. I say, "I am surprised you have come to see me."

She gives a little snort, exposing capped teeth. "Just because you're in here? I've come here before." She pauses, shifts in her chair. "My Cecil was here once."

She looks as if she might cry, then crosses her legs, the flap of fabric parted, returned. "I told them I was your sister." She smiles. She nods her head. "You don't know what to think of me, do you?"

"I am unsure of most things." The wall behind her is changing, now speckled, now swathed in black stripes.

"Part of what I do is visit people, when they're sick, when they're in the hospital. I know what it's like there. I've had cancer twice, been written off for dead at least once. There's power in grouping. Some people think it gives me a rush, and maybe it does, but it's more than that. My mother always says that indifference is the greatest cruelty. I try not to be indifferent."

I nod again, my mind fluttering to brief images of what Mrs. Fleming's ancient mother might look like before returning, slack, to its languor. Warm tears come, unbidden and unexpected, leaking as if from an old faucet, the seals dry and worn. What brings this now—compassion? My own pity? The tears slide into crevices, through wrinkled skin, pooling, dripping. They are *water*, I tell myself, but what of water? My life spent providing it, diverting it. The stream where, at my offer, she first bent to drink. The water I bartered for, rationed. The goatskin I provided when her body expelled everything. The fountain I bathed in as I tried to stay near her. Indifference? I wipe my face and my nose.

"Emmett."

I jump.

"Are you all right?"

"Yes." I have been left behind. "I am sorry. What did you say?"

"I was asking about you. I don't know that much about you."

I tell her, or at least I try to. I am from Turkey. I fought in the war. I was injured, then rescued. An immigrant. A father. I cannot tell her, though, of before, of what I know now, of what

I remember. That I was a gendarme, a . . . murderer. That this is my shame.

My voice trails away. She is saying something, asking something else. She likes that I still want to live. Others my age want to die. She says something about the future.

But there is no future. I am ninety-two years old. I have a tumor.

I am a monster.

Our eyes lock. No one knows of this past. I hang on a precipice, reaching out for a rope, Mrs. Fleming laughing as if she now holds it. Did I tell her? This must remain covered. Her head bends back in a new baring of teeth.

"What?" I ask.

"Peter Melville, Violet's cousin. He was awarded that grant from the U.S. Department of Agriculture. Five million dollars—can you believe it?"

I struggle. Peter. Brains. The ostrich farm, sound-wave pest control. Five million dollars? But I am weighted, deadened. Money is of no use to me now.

A knock sounds at the glass door. Hinges swivel. Dr. Mellon enters, his big frame filling the room and changing the atmosphere, the colors. I glance at the wall behind Mrs. Fleming, returned now to its institutional white.

"It's time for Mr. Conn's treatment team," he says, his voice measured and deep.

Mrs. Fleming rises and picks up her purse. "I need to go." She pauses at the door and looks back. "Take care," she says. Her glasses flash. She is strong, her back arched like a dancer's. "You'll be okay. Violet will come see you soon."

The door swings shut. Dr. Mellon helps me to my feet, the smell of cologne on his hands. I am shaky and slow. I follow him from the room like a dim-witted child, a thin, older woman behind us. We enter another cubicle, stand awkwardly, take seats around a similar table.

"How do you feel?" Dr. Mellon folds his large hands. The thin woman produces a tape recorder and notepad, arranges them like homework before her. She leans forward, exposing dark rings that make her eyes seem much larger.

"I am okay."

The questions follow, the same questions, the questions I answered before. Do I dream? Are these dreams frightening? Are there things I have done in these dreams? What things are these?

I respond, at least to most of them. I want to be respectful, to authority and to Dr. Mellon. My fellow Rotarian. Is it true? Is it fair to all concerned? This is the Rotary motto, or part of it. But the questions become repetitious, so tedious that I soon grow distracted, staring at Dr. Mellon's smooth skin, which stretches up like a black chess piece. A rook, perhaps? Bishop? I remember how I played chess in London, how the others were amazed, patient and doctor alike, that I could remember how to play but remember nothing about myself. Three of us there had lost memory, head injuries grouped together before the guard came, and I was moved. The man next to me was Harold—a boy, really—with yellowish hair and a caul-like red scar that crossed his face and one eye, leaving that eye puffed and large, as though he only squinted through the other. He was fascinated by the chess games, periodically shouting out "I remember now!" but quickly growing despondent when it became clear he remembered little, about anything. He would then shake his head, lifting the heavy metal bed with creaking springs and great thumps until the nurses came, the interrupted game could be resumed. I did not see him again after they moved me, but I wonder now: Did memory return for him? Did he regain some former life? Perhaps he was placed somewhere, housed forever in an institution like this. His mind darkened and aged and bent beyond all recovery.

"Do you know your name?"

I sigh. "Emmett Conn."

"Do you know why you're here?"

"You put me here, you and Violet. I have a brain tumor. It has produced vivid dreams."

Dr. Mellon leans back in his chair, a hint of a smile on his face. I gaze at the thin woman, noting how her left biceps resembles a chicken's wing.

"Do you know who I am?"

"You are Dr. Mellon. The Rotarian."

He laughs, the big, booming laugh. He looks around, as if searching for someone to backslap.

"You seem to be doing okay." He pulls out half-glasses, adjusts them on the bridge of his nose. "I'm going to ask you a few more questions, okay?"

"Okay." But my mind swoops away again, a bee buzzing off to a flower. Great rows of pumpkins line the far wall, their stems twisted to arm shapes, to hands and black feet. Flies swarm. And then the vultures, pecking and pulling. I hear Dr. Mellon's voice, see the thin woman's eyes, take in the room, the table, the chairs, but other sharp things as well: oxen bellowing, rats shedding water, soldiers beckoning, a dark man on horseback. Hands reach out for me. Voices sigh. I come back for a moment, thinking that I deserve this, to die alone as their prisoner . . . then dance away, a dog dodging a stick, listening but not hearing, watching but not seeing. Wind whistles somewhere, its sound in my ears. The impact, when it comes, knocks me off my feet, slamming my head to the ground as I fall.

"Hey!"

I fight to get clear. Breath hisses as my foot meets a groin. I bend back fingers from a strange, prying hand. Only the voice pulls me out of it, the booming, non-laughing utterance that sounds oddly familiar, that makes itself clear across a roomful of people. The cadence of a distant island. Dr. Mellon's voice.

"Emmett! What are you doing?"

I find myself on the floor, Lawrence's acne-scarred face near mine. Dr. Mellon stands behind him. The thin woman peers from the wall like a raccoon.

I release Lawrence's fingers. He retreats, rubbing his hand.

There are questions, but my answers seem muddled. I am confused. Time again has been lost. My release . . .

I am returned to the dayroom. John Paul hovers near.

"How did it go?"

I shake my head. "I began seeing things. Then I found myself on the floor, with Lawrence trying to pin my arms." I glance over at Lawrence, busy adjusting an ice pack.

"I hope you bit him." John Paul scratches the tip of his nose. "You know, it's all about dopamine," he continues, "dopamine and receptors. Some of us have too much, some not enough. In diseases like—"

"Lunchtime!" a voice proclaims. Andre appears, arms about

his head. John Paul rises. I follow, fighting light-headedness, the dots and curlicues that form and dissolve. I merge into line behind John Paul and his pink nose, the stooped black man Puff, Leo and his steepled hands, and then a new figure, broad-shouldered, close-cropped, a head with ridges so prominent as to be lobes of his brain. I stare, remembering Araxie's description, chills at work on my spine, chills that strengthen to near-paralysis as the figure turns and exhibits his face, his familiar masculine jaw, his wide-set eyes and protruding lips. It is Sasha's face. I reel, grasping the couch for support, staring at this intrusion from another time and place, shorn and re-clothed and perhaps re-gendered, but otherwise one and the same. His gaze meets mine as he passes, a glazed and medicated glance that bespeaks no recognition but collapses me nonetheless, and then I am fine, stolid and resolute and surprisingly hungry. I straighten my shoulders and pull at my trousers. I follow the others on the slow march to the dining area. Lawrence stands at the doorway, still kneading his hand.

I sit at a table with Elmo and this new person, the man Lawrence introduces as Victor. My questions as to his background produce no response, save for the dull smacks of his eating, his swallows of sweetened iced tea. I content myself with just looking at him, remembering my conversations with Sasha, his double, calculating the improbability of this strength of resemblance. Perhaps we have met elsewhere, perhaps as client or employee or friend, but I can visualize him only in a tentlike *jilbab*, cutting his deals with his customers, haranguing or praising or pleading or sweeping, anger or avarice at play on his face.

"Medicine!" The queue forms. Heads bend to charts, necks tilt, practiced hands toss tablets down throats. I eye my pills, the two yellow tablets and three red-and-white capsules. I empty the cup into my mouth, add water, swish it down, open my mouth to meet Andre's inspection. We disperse afterward. Lawrence strides ahead, unlocking doors to the rooms along the dayroom's one side. Some of the group shuffle inside, yawning and stretching, while others stare at the doors or the TV. Elmo hurls a pitch at a far wall, Leo bows in prayer. Puff speaks to Lawrence, laughing, rubbing his hands along the sides of his face. I stop near the couch, dry-mouthed now and weary. John Paul pulls up alongside me.

"They let us nap if we want to." He dabs a napkin at his nose, which is bleeding. "Are you tired?"

I silence a yawn. "Yes. And you?"

"I usually don't nap. You can lie down if you want to."

John Paul continues talking, about steroids, transfiguration. He will not quiet. I envision my hands on his head, shaking. Finally, he leaves.

I enter the bare room, sit on the bed, remove my shoes, stare at my feet. Glancing out the doorway, to where a baseball announcer's voice echoes from the dayroom, I look for him, for Victor/Sasha, but he is not there. I close my eyes, searching again for patterns in nothingness, noting the shapes floating past, the mutant half-bodies, the dragons that become griffins that become vultures that become—what? Jesus? The Prophet? I am renewed. *Canh.* And then I sleep.

16

I awake to darkness, to the pressure of a hand at my throat. I struggle, but the hand holds me back. I kick. I flail my arms at the body beyond but strike nothing, as if the hand is a ghost's yet retains all its power. My breathing grows short. Lights glow in the darkness. And then, just as my abdomen convulses and my hands make contact with the assailant's thick arm, his voice appears in my ear, instantly recognizable.

"I want you to see something." The hand releases its pressure, the figure backing away. I sit up, coughing, as a candle springs to light.

"Do you see this?" Mustafa points to his right arm, or where his arm should have been. It is gone, sheared off at the shoulder, leaving his torso strangely oblong, like a chicken cut for the market. "It became infected, after our battle. The doctors cut it off."

I cough some more, to recover my breath. A knife gleams now in Mustafa's one hand.

"It is difficult with one arm. Everything in life becomes harder. Every time I eat, or piss, or button my shirt, I think of you, of this moment." He pauses, lifts something off the divan with the blade of his knife, holds it up in the air. "I have followed you, my friend. I lost you, but with the help of a kind man, I found you again. I know what you do each day, where you go. Even when you were at the knife maker's shop, I was there. I was recovering, regaining my strength. And now I am strong again. If not whole."

He tosses the object to where it lands in my lap. Even in flight I know it, know its outline and texture before my hand brushes against it, before I touch the familiar stones. The necklace is cold, oily with sweat or blood or some other substance. I trace its edges and ridges and the smoothness of its pendant, just as I did on the day I bought it, the day I gave it to her. My heartbeat pulses in my jaw, in my face, down the contours of my injured throat. I eye the knife in front of me, the dark stripes on its end.

"You recognize it, yes? A little bloody, perhaps, but still there. I wanted you to see it. I wanted you to know this, to share a little of my pain. It is so hard. Do you see? It has all been so hard."

I nod, wheezing, my breath in ragged draws. I dig my hands in the sheet on the bed.

"What do you have to say, my friend? I do not hate you, for you cannot help yourself. A part of me says I should not even kill you. Perhaps I should only cut you, remove a piece of you—perhaps your arm? Then we would be alike, chopped by life and left to go on." He smiles. "I must know, though, Ahmet. Do you feel it? The fear in the back of your throat, the certainty that all is now lost? The girl, your arm, even your life—do you not wish to fight for them? Let's see who is stronger. After all, I have only one arm." He raises his eyebrows, as if inviting me to join him. The candlelight gleams on his blade. "Only one arm."

I fling my sheet at the candle as I dive in the opposite direction. The light flickers but holds. Mustafa seems to have expected my action, as he takes only a half-step in the sheet's path before reversing his course and lunging toward me. I scramble to my feet, roaring, an outburst at once loud and unintelligible, dodging as he hooks the knife forward in a fierce left-handed thrust. The blade catches the edge of my forearm, turning me sideways and down, tearing skin and muscle before lodging in the wooden pallet's base. For an instant we hang there, the knife embedded, Mustafa nearly on top of me, my arm free of the knife but afire with bright pain. I smell his foulness, his animal-like sweat. The bristles of his beard scratch my neck. He thrashes upon me, as if he seeks to punch me while I'm pinned down but has forgotten he has no right fist. His body rocks. He pulls at the knife, his teeth snapping, catching some part of my ear and sparking new pain to life.

He releases the knife and grabs for my throat. I twist sideways, my one arm caught beneath me, attempting to throw him off with my legs and free arm, but he is heavy, too heavy. His weight pins me down. I buck like an animal under a rider but succeed only in shifting his bulk, my back now more fully against him. I shake my head. He knees me, stomping with his feet, trying to gain any purchase. His fingers dig deep in my neck.

My breath contorts. Light dims. I try to roll but cannot. I jerk my knees up but fall back. With my one hand I gain small movement, enough to grasp the knife's haft. I pull against it but have no leverage. My arm is weakened by pain. I rock the knife, bruising my palm against its tempered hardness, thinking of all the knives I have forged, formed, and sharpened—I need only this one, now! But I cannot free it. I rotate it like a pestle, concentrating my hatred of all knives upon it, but it only quivers and holds fast. My arm throbs in defeat. I cannot breathe now, I must release this and try something else, and I *do* feel the panic, and push one last time with the flat of my palm. The wood cracks then and splinters. The knife frees. I pick it up, reverse my grip. Mustafa must feel this, for he lifts up slightly, his hand still on my throat. I am thinking, absurdly, of what he must think now—is it anger, or doubt, or only murderous instinct? I shift beneath him. My eyes cloud without air. With a pain that spears my arm like a poker, I drive the knife backward, deep into his chest.

Mustafa stands, the knife like a rib pulled apart from its brethren. His face shows surprise, a mask nearly of pleasure. He starts to say something but blood garbles his words. Staggering, his hand out and grasping, he reaches his full length until his palm strikes the candle and the room falls into darkness. I turn but lie paralyzed, wanting to scramble to my feet, to run—is he not dead? He does not topple. I smell him, hear his shuffling feet, picture him swaying and squinting. I should scream but cannot. Something clatters, and a fresh terror seizes me. Has he *pulled out* the knife? His moans are almost deafening. I reach my knees but he lurches toward me, his body corkscrewing, weighted perhaps by his single arm, a force that pitches him back down on me. The knife, still embedded, strikes me full in the face, breaking my nose and front teeth as if they were sticks. Pain explodes, blinding me for some seconds. I swallow pieces of tooth. Choking, my arm almost useless, my face crushed and leaking, I push his body from mine. I struggle to stand upright.

A light flares. Sasha stands before me, grabbing Mustafa's hair with both hands, pulling his body onto the floor as something—I think his neck—snaps in the process. She brings a small candle closer.

"You have enemies, I see." She explores my wounds with her fingers, rotating the light with her hand. Blood seeps over my clothing, the exposed straw of the bed, my bare feet. I take in great gulps of air. I feel faint.

"We must hurry," Sasha says. "Others will come." She sets the candle on the floor, turns her attention back to me. With a deft movement she grabs hold of my shirt and rips it down its front. "Ah, your arm." She presses the ripped cloth on the wound.

"I must go," I say. My throat burns from the effort. I lift my legs, attempting to stand.

"Where will you go? Can you walk?"

"Yes. To her. She is . . . in danger. Araxie." If she is even alive. I look about wildly, digging my fingers through straw.

"Wait here." Sasha leaves the room. I continue my search, on the bedding, across the floor. The pain climbs up my injured arm, rendering it limp and useless, such that I must use my right arm, my fingers as rakes, the straw slicing under my nails. I find it half buried beneath the thick body, requiring both arms to remove it, an action producing such pain that I cry out in anguish. The room darkens, encased in a whispering black before brightening again. I hold the necklace before me.

Sasha returns. "Do you have any other clothing?"

I nod helplessly at the foot of the bed. She grabs my *gömlek* and swiftly undresses me, practiced hands slipping bloody pants over one foot, then the other, until I stand naked, looking down at her, any thought of embarrassment washed clean by my anguish. Sasha pulls up the *pantolon*, rewraps my arm, places a compress around my bloody ear, fits the *gömlek* over my injured head and arm. She stands before me when she has finished. Her breath brushes my face.

"Take this," she says quietly. She places a small pouch in my hand.

I bend to examine it. A sheaf of bills juts from its top.

She smiles, a smile made sad by the candle's dim light. The wrinkles are thick at her eyes. "I hope it takes you far."

I search for something to say.

Sasha reaches over onto Mustafa, grunts, returns with his knife. "You might also want this."

"Thank you," I whisper. "Thank you so much."

She kisses me on my cheek, the hard, forward kiss of a man. "Go, before someone comes." She glances at the prostate body. *"Twaqqa!"*

I tumble out of the room, into the hallway, out the side door to the alley beyond. The sound of footsteps carries from somewhere. Voices dim and vanish. The first pink of dawn shows to the east, the sky above still purpled and black. The street is dark, the familiar landmarks hidden, such that I bump into a trash pile and a water barrel before I right myself, reestablish my direction. I hurry on, more by feel than by sight, my left arm dangling like a crippled dog's leg. The arm's limpness alters my gait, my shoulder slumped to the injury, to the point where I imagine myself a mirror image of the amputated Mustafa, his body tilted to his remaining thick arm. His face fills my mind again, his words in my ears, such that I see him again, even smell him. I picture him scouting, waiting, plotting his slow revenge. He would have obsessed over his lost limb, brooded over it, stared at the place it used to be, wailed as he considered its loss. I pause, searching opposing passageways in the darkness. Would I or anyone else have done less?

Objects move in the early morn, shopkeepers unlocking doors, herders tending stock, groomers preparing their mounts. A dog runs past, yelping, chased by unseen foes. The sweet smell of baked bread mixes with odors of moisture and manure. Blood enters my mouth, trailing down my face from my ear, its texture silky, its taste metallic. I hobble forward, past the Bab al-Makkam and its muttering dromedaries, the darkened suq, the shuttered homes of the wealthy. A rooster crows nearby, another farther away.

The first cries of the muezzin fall as I reach the broad expanse of the Bab al-Faraj, brighter now in the dawn, its sediments of people stirring and unfolding, gathering with the start of the day. I halt, aware of how my injuries must look. I glance around for a place to wash but find nothing. Instead I join the rotation toward Mecca, the wait for the recitation of words familiar even in Arabic. I remember, as the supplication begins, the morning in Katma when I thought I had lost her, the prayers, the sight of her up on the roof. I glance up now but find nothing, only the gray edges of once white buildings, the stirrings of pigeons and doves. My mind, so compliant till now in avoiding thought of the necklace, bursts forth in unleashed agony, imagining her garroted, stabbed, or otherwise hurt, her body left to rot in the street. What had Mustafa said, that he had been helped by a kind man? I toss this about as I kneel in the mud. Blood wells in my nose, spattering in droplets on the ground just below.

I rise afterward, shaking. Others on the street watch. I cross the boulevard, edge around a dusty date palm and the debris spread beneath it, past deportees, dogs, and old women, past carts and donkeys piled high with cotton, until I stand before the hospital itself, its window holes open like eye sockets. Walking around to its back, I search for the house she'd mentioned, the doctor's house, only to find three adjacent dwellings: a nicer two-story, with a small balcony and pitched roof, and two smaller bungalows. All are shuttered, and dark, as if their inhabitants are asleep or wounded, or dead.

I knock on the door of the two-story, wait, knock again. My hand goes to my face, the dried blood that has stiffened. I catch sight of my injured arm, red beneath the wrapped cloth. My breathing is loud through my crumpled nose. I knock again.

No one answers. I glance at the hospital behind me, at the doors, the open window holes, the figures occasionally passing. Perhaps Araxie and the doctor are already at work. I wait, hoping to catch sight of her—even a glimpse will release me—but my distress breeds impatience, and I knock on the other doors, my fist hard on the wood. I expect no response and receive none. Everything is quiet. Eventually I turn, my heart thundering, my breath loose and shallow. I make my way to the front of the hospital.

A group of men stand in the hospital's doorway. The breaking dawn leaves the entrance in such darkness that I cannot see or identify them, only the red embers of their *sigaralar*, rising and falling, rising and falling, hands to mouths to dark sides. Some part of me sounds a warning, a message dulled by pain but shrouded even further by fate, by a certain inescapable ruin. I recognize the men's uniforms as I reach them, the olives and tans, the red epaulets and braids of Ottoman military officers.

"Well, my friend! We've been waiting."

I make a motion to retreat but stop myself. There are four of them, two of whom shift quietly, encircling me.

"We have been told you are a Turkish soldier, a deserter. Is that true, Mr. Khan?" The man flicks his dying cigarette into the street.

Some reservoir of strength fires within me, finding its way to my voice. "Who told you this?"

The man laughs. "Does it matter? Are you or are you not? Do you have papers?"

"I was a gendarme. I brought a group to Aleppo."

"Did you receive permission to stay, or to leave the service of the gendarmerie?"

"I did not."

"Then you will come with us. Your country needs you, at least what is left of you after your punishment. You see, Ahmet Bey, this is a serious matter." He moves closer to me, such that his face is more visible, tobacco-laden breath blowing in toward mine. I do not recognize him.

"In addition to deserting, you appear to have consorted with enemies of our country. This, as you know, is treasonous. You could pay with your life."

He gives a head signal to the other officers, two of whom grab my arms. I gasp at the pressure, the onslaught of pain.

"I see you've been injured." He evidently says or motions something to the officers, for the crushing grip slackens, and I am boosted upright. We begin shuffling down the walkway to the boulevard, half walking, half stumbling. Early-morning pedestrians crane to look.

"Tell me, Ahmet Bey," the lead officer says, twisting his head to look at my face. The insignia at his shoulder appears to be that of a colonel, though it is hard to tell in the darkness. "Was it worth it?" He offers a half-turned smile, as if we are privy to a great secret.

I do not answer. From up in a hospital window comes a voice, in languid Armenian. I look up, as do the others, to see a woman standing there, a stout, older woman.

"She is gone," says the woman, her voice chopped and broken.

17

A hand brushes my shoulder.

"Hey! Time to wake up!"

I turn, careful of my injury, surprised at the absence of pain.

My fingers trace my wounded ear. It is whole, likewise pain-free. I sit, eyes open to a spare bed with white cotton sheets, purple fluorescent lighting, a thin man with a scabbed nose. My eyes cloud, refocus. John Paul speaks.

"They're taking us outside again. Nap time's over."

It all comes crashing back then, the white walls and ceiling. The slippered feet of the asylum, the smells of excrement and ammonia. The metal bedposts perched above linoleum floors. I should be back—fighting, overcoming these soldiers—but I am here, only here. I close my eyes and lie down again, wishing the dream back upon me. Where have they taken her? What can I do? A renewed prodding interrupts, and I lift my arms at it, flailing. The bedsheet billows and cracks.

"Hey, now. Easy." Lawrence's drawl edges farther away. "I'm just waking everyone to go outside." He holds up his hands against me, a tamer facing a lion. "Actually, you have a visitor. If you'll follow me, you can see her now."

But the dream! Lights flash, settling as I stand, stars retreating to individual lights, three doors merged now to one. John Paul's head peeks from behind Lawrence, his eyes in narrow scrutiny. I clear my throat.

"Who is my visitor?" I ask. Is it she?

"It's your daughter."

I follow into the brightness of the dayroom, past others in line for the excursion outside. I see a head near the front, a glimpse of Sasha's oversized jaw, and I am frozen, the thought twisting and circling that this man had helped me, helped *me*. And for what? I remain still, then, slowly, step forward.

Victor/Sasha shifts his head. His eyes are dulled, diluted by pain, but the same—gray and oval, wide set under leathery brows. I find myself unable to speak, only to stare, the pressure in my forehead bringing pain to my cheekbones. He returns my gaze, his expression firm and without acknowledgment, but nor is there any surprise. I want to touch him, to laugh. Questions gurgle and die in my throat.

"Thank you," I say finally, my words thick with moisture. "Thank you for what you have done."

His stare remains, his expression unchanged. Others are there, giving ground, eyeing us both with some measure of curiosity. He does not look at them—only at me, for what may be seconds, perhaps minutes. I hear Lawrence calling, the scuffling of feet, the sniffs of growing impatience, but we remain locked, connected by current, until the barest shift of his head releases me.

I step toward Lawrence, past blank stares and mutters. My feet make a flapping noise on the floor.

"Are you okay?" Lawrence's brow dips lower than ever.

"Yes. Okay."

But unsettled by this past newly found. Those who had helped had not known of my transgressions. No one knew except Allah, if he still cared to watch. Except her. Am I now like the man who sees, too late, his own errors? These things, this certainty I have sought all my life, but now when they come they bring pain.

I am led through the outer door, the same glassed-in room. Violet rises when I enter, dabbing at her hair with one hand.

"Hi." She leans forward to peck at my cheek. The wrinkles around her eyes are deep and dusted in makeup. "How are you feeling?"

"Okay."

Her smile fades.

"How are you?" I ask. My voice is weak, as if my vocal cords have been damaged.

"I'm okay."

"Have you checked on Sultan?"

"I asked your friend Carl to do that."

"Have you told Lissette . . . of this?"

She looks away, then back. "I told her you had to be hospitalized, for observation. I didn't tell her it was here."

I nod. She has put me here, my protector. My Violet. But I must protect her. Protect them.

She presses her hands together. I struggle to stay in the present.

"And Wilfred?"

"He's okay."

"Tell me, please," I say. "Tell me Wilfred will never be put in a place . . . like this place. Tell me you will not bring him here."

She looks down. "He's okay," she says. "He'll be fine."

"But *tell* me. Make me this promise."

She stares at me, her neck flushed. "What promise, Papa? That his life will be grand? That he will never have issues? That the issues he has won't get worse? I don't think he would ever have to be put someplace, but if that's what's best, then that's what we'll do. I can't promise anything." She pauses. "Does it hurt you to know that? To know the truth?"

The truth. I shake my head, Wilfred's image before me, then John Paul, his arms swinging. "He is so young," I say. "His whole life is before him . . ."

"Papa, is it really Wilfred you speak of, or the idea of him? This perfect image you create for yourself."

I still my hands. "What?"

"You want him as your extension. Your surrogate to live your life over." She leans forward, eyes flashing. "Isn't that it?"

"What?" I say again. But she is energized now, her lips wet. Her face colors and shines like a flower.

"Papa. Is there that much you regret?"

I stare. My heart lurches.

"I've lived my life," she continues. "It may not have been the one you picked out for me, but it's mine. Are there regrets? Of course, but not so many. I charted my own course. I dug into *life*. If I had it to do over I would do things the same."

A shudder creeps through me, a cold twist like a knife. "And your child," I say, before I can stop myself from saying it. "The one you gave up. Is there not . . . Do you not regret . . . ?"

Tendons shift in her face. She is silent then, nodding, her gaze stuck near my collar.

She pulls a long strand of hair.

"I think of her every day," she says slowly, eventually. "I wonder about her, about her life, what she looks like, whether she is even alive. I named her Autumn—did you know that? I play her birth date every time I play Quick-Pick. Each day, I think I will go to her." She pauses again, and her face lightens a moment, so much younger, so vulnerable. "But I never have."

I stare, unmoving.

She smiles, the bone out in her jaw. "Perhaps you're right, Papa. Perhaps I'm more like you than I think."

I pinch my lips. I have blundered. Why must I do this? I did not intend harm, intend anything, actually—not now. Not this time. We stare past each other, her face closed like a wound.

"I wish only to help," I say softly. "With Wilfred. I know his suffering."

Her response again takes its time. "I know you do," she says in a dulled voice. "I don't blame you, you know." She looks up. She smiles again, and my smile follows hers.

She does not blame me. Her anger, recrimination—I deserve these and more, but she is calm, her eyes distant. Liquids pool in my throat.

"You are diligent," I say after some time. It sounds so formal, so awkward. "You are a good daughter."

Her face is marbled and pale. She rolls her lips, the words stuck behind them. "I haven't always been diligent," she says finally. "I couldn't be there at the end with Mother. I told myself that this time I'd be stronger."

"You are strong."

She offers a wry smile. "Sometimes." She pats her foot, shifts position. "You have your radiation appointment this afternoon. I spoke to Dr. Mellon about it. They're going to have someone here take you over."

I shake my head. I want to hear her, and listen. Is not duty love? Her left eye flickers, caught in the lights; for an instant it looks different, lighter than her other one. My heartbeat slows. "What?"

"I understand you had a nice visit with Mrs. Fleming." Her gaze is up and moving. The surface, regained.

"Yes. It was nice of her to come."

"Are they treating you well?"

"Yes, okay." My resentment rebounds. I am a prisoner, her prisoner. I fold my hands. "Please do not tell Wilfred."

Her stare is distant. She nods. I think she nods.

An HST sticks his head in the door. "Mr. Conn? It's time for your radiation."

Violet stands. "I'll say good-bye."

I rise, too, without speaking. Spots blotch my vision. I think for some reason of Recep, how he had sought me out, visited me in Georgia, how contrite he had been then, the owner of the murderous slingshot. How we all want absolution. I exit the admissions unit back the way we had entered, past closed doors and cupped seats, out into bright sunlight and a midafternoon breeze. The HST, who introduces himself as Royce, directs me into the back of a white minivan with South Georgia Psychiatric Center stenciled in green letters across it. I stare at the cage separating passengers from the driver. I climb in.

The radiation session is a replay of what I've been through before. I lie under the white machine and its big bulked-up arms, stare at the strange glass tulip scene built into the ceiling, converse with Claire, the pretty redheaded nurse. I note the scuff marks at the bottom of the door, the texture of the radiation bench, the way the tulips slope down to the water. I see the flaws in construction, the cracked threshold, the door that is not plumb. The sounds of the machine make a rhythmic beat, like an engine's gentle chugging. The room's ceiling tiles bulge in places, retreat in others.

The session ends quickly. Royce stands at the doorway. I glance down corridors, note exits. It is a movie—*The Manchurian Candidate*—and I am brainwashed, after all, sedated and confused as a part of some plot. Violet has deceived me, they have all deceived me—Carol, Lissette, Angela Lansbury. Why had we not had more children? I speak to them then, but they all look confused. "What language?" they ask, and the one smiles, "Is that Turkish?"

Turkish. We drive back, down Gordon Avenue and its ivy-covered trellises, past manses and wrought-iron fences, brick knee-walls, past the homes of people I knew in some life—the Hunts, the Clays, the Maguires. Carol's friends. Are their children now grown, their grandchildren? I think about Wilfred, see him before me, see the dark of his skin. Memories stream past, a line for work, two lines, one for coloreds. I am pushed from one line to the other. Am I colored? I did not know this. America's different halves, and I stand in darkness.

"This place was originally a military barracks." Royce's voice comes from nowhere, his first words of the trip. We are back now, among the pines and guard station. "It was redone ten years or so ago, but you can still see traces of the old buildings." He points to the left, to the area I have been told is a facility for the mentally retarded.

South Georgia Psychiatric Center. SGPC. I gaze at the buildings and the white clapboard chapel, the lack of fencing beyond. The entire facility is unfenced, other than the units themselves. The area behind the chapel is a neighborhood. A plumber I once knew had lived there, a competent man, methodical, effective at diagnosing problems and discovering why things would not work. Undersized pumps, defective piping. It makes me think back again, of becoming a plumber, how fascinated I was then with toilets and drains. So modern! So sanitary! They seemed to symbolize America—waste removed and diverted, hidden. Sanitized. A *convenience*. This was so long ago.

The van slows and stops. I disembark. The smell of cut grass comes to greet me, an odor of order and death. An urn near the drop-off sports the tombstones of dead cigarettes. A button is pressed, a current clicks in response. We enter the admissions unit through a blast of air-conditioning, and continue past the reception window, through locked doors, to the mostly empty treatment area.

Royce fingers his keys. "I think they're in the rec area."

We walk outside, back into heat and humidity. Heads turn at our entrance, return as quickly to cigarettes, to the study of ground and sky. A young black man I have not seen before lies stretched out across the Ping-Pong table. A group of familiar-looking men toss a basketball that clangs against the goal.

"There you go." Royce pulls the door shut.

The air smells of fresh-lit tobacco, the taste following behind it from decades long past. I stand for a moment, hand in my pocket. I am the man without a childhood—seventy-two years since I entered the United States—a builder, a worker. I have made parts of this country. My hands bear the scars and bent nails. I glance at the brick wall, the motion detectors arrayed on its top, gauging distances, measuring angles. I am strong. I could scale this, I think, my breath rising. I can still walk. There is no fence beyond. But then the deadening returns as though leached through the walls, and I am shackled, constrained. I see John Paul and Puff in a corner, engaged in conversation with a woman with bleached hair. I turn in defeat and shuffle over that way.

The group shifts, allowing me a place to sit down. The woman looks anywhere from forty to sixty, her face starched by sun and cigarette. She turns her head sideways, as if remembering an old injury.

"You know, I been wanting to ask you something." She pauses, staring. I do not remember our having previously met. Her lips part. "Where you from?"

I start. "I am from Wadesboro."

"No, I mean where you *from*?"

The others look on. I clear my throat. "I lived in New York. I moved to Wadesboro because my wife came from here."

"But your ancestors—are you Jewish? Italian?" Her face splinters and cracks.

"My ancestors were in Turkey."

"So you're a Moslem. But you don't wear one of those things on your head."

"I am not . . . I am not . . ." A sense of betrayal seeps through me. "I am an American. A plumber. I have worked all my life."

"I thought you were a builder." John Paul, now.

"I was."

"But you just said you were a plumber."

I start to explain. I progressed, I moved upward . . .

"Emmett." Puff's voice is a carburetor. "There's something I been wanting to ask you as well." He digs a finger into a moss-covered ear, pulls it out, digs again. "What you running from?"

"What do you mean?"

He shrugs. "Everybody's running from something—most particularly everybody that's here. I'm running from the bottle. John Paul's running from these things that creep up on him. Peg"—he turns to the woman with bleached hair—"what you running from?"

She smiles her thin smile. "Three ex-husbands."

Puff turns back to me. "How about you?"

"I . . . I run from these dreams."

"What about them dreams?"

"Something I did."

"Something bad?"

I look up at him. "Yes."

A silence intrudes. John Paul cracks his joints, pulls his arms. The scars on one wrist shine, curvy and graceful, shimmering like a painting or a newly born flower.

"Whatever you think it is, it's always something more." Puff's voice is so deep as to be barely heard.

"What?"

"The dreams or the bottle or the ex-husband—it's always

something deeper. Something that's the cause of all that. I mean, people don't just take to drinking, or dreaming, or whatever. Something *drives* 'em to it."

"Oh?"

"Yeah."

Another silence. Another crack of sinew and knuckle.

"My mother used to say that if you ate cabbage before going to bed, you wouldn't dream," John Paul offers.

No one responds.

Puff scratches his ear, pats his head. "I've done a few things myself." He opens his mouth, releasing a length of pink tongue. "Have you killed anybody?"

I swallow.

"I have," Peg says. All eyes turn to her.

"I killed ex-husband number two." She looks around. "I mean, it was self-defense. He went after me with a butcher knife."

Heads nod, gazes shift.

"People never know," John Paul says quietly. "The turmoil that goes on inside. I mean, the pain and everything, the reality of it. People don't understand. If you've never been through it, you don't understand."

"That Grady was a mean motherfucker." Peg flicks an imaginary cigarette. "Broke the dog's back with a metal flyswatter. Just plain mean."

"In the Bible they said it was demons," Puff says, his eyes squinted. "Demons."

"I know people whisper behind my back. I know they see the scars. Do I care? They don't *know*."

"One time he got drunk, Grady did, and went over to my

cousin Beth's house naked as a jaybird and just stood outside the door, ringing the doorbell."

"I had my first drink when I was ten. Boone's Farm Apple Wine—it's hard to get that anymore. Then beer, then rum. I never liked scotch, though."

"My father killed himself with a plastic bag. He'd been sick. I started graduate school the next day."

Peg nods. They all nod.

"I remember how Grady's body looked, after I'd done it. Pinkish and peaceful. But still drunk. Still mean."

"I only met my father once. He was a drunk, too—worse than me. That he was. And everybody knew it."

"Everybody thinks they know things. But they don't. They just don't."

A silence follows and I am thinking, suddenly, of these hells scattered beyond just my own. Little, big, black, white, old, new, tired, alive. Pulling, with a force wrought from God, curling, perhaps intertwining. I am alone here. Are they not also alone? Alone in our hells with no floor.

"Okay, everybody!" Lawrence's voice comes from around the corner. "Time to go in!" He makes his way over. He looks tired. "Come on, guys."

Legs lengthen, backs bend and tremble. Lawrence examines us. We form a line. One of the patients in front begins howling, his voice trailing away, and for a moment I am back with the line of roped men, the clinking sounds made as we walk with our weapons. The line halts, heads angled. How do I stop this? The others rush in, the attendants, the howls shrinking to yelps, to gurgles, to confused snorts and sniffs. Those in line grumble and spit. We move forward—I am one of them, now—separating as we reach the women's area, the men's. I sit on a couch, at a far end, as others take seats alongside me. I am thinking, thinking. Is it not time to sleep? Sleep brings me back, to prolong and protect. Protect what? It has lurked in my mind, a hidden white space, that if she existed, then her life is now gone. Perhaps she married. Almost certainly she is dead.

I attended a horse race once, in New York, with a colleague named Luther. He explained betting, how odds were calculated. It was difficult to understand. I think now, of these odds, the odds of my survival, the odds of hers. I picture her, as I had in the dream, as a teacher, a mother, graying. Why must I remember this, dream of her? Her life has been lived, as has mine.

Puff belches softly. A toilet flushes; captured air groans. The thought comes, quick down its pathway, that I might find her, that she is healthy, alive. I play with this fantasy, work it. I embrace it. I think of what I might tell her. Some things would be hidden—by her, yes, by me. I have done my best. Would she believe my forgetting, my remembering just now? It is long, so long ago. Yet so strange in its vividness, more real now than things present. The others have abandoned me. She is all I have left.

The notion stays with me throughout dinner, through mashed potatoes and creamed corn and John Paul's dissertation on fluoridated water. New patients arrive: a thin man with greased hair and mottled skin that bespeaks blood near the surface; an alcoholic-looking woman. Leo and several women have been released. The idea continues its roll. I plot my search, our reunion. I long for sleep, for her—she is in danger! Perhaps I will be released—my heart thrusts at this—and then, and then . . .

I find the phone, the phone that patients may use. I must ask for help, to look up Carl's number. I have lost my big glasses, and I cannot remember . . . Carl, I say, can you find someone? You, with the FBI. Her name is Araxie. Marashlian. I spell it—perhaps it has changed? She could be anywhere. He says he will try, for me, that I should not expect much. Where am I? he asks. I'm not sure if I respond. He sounds doubtful, and hesitant.

But I am undeterred.

18

I awake slowly, my mind stumbling to wakefulness, then not, then life once again. Footsteps plop in the soft distance, a mechanical something rattles and purrs. Water runs. I listen, puzzling. And then there is noise, and spiteful light. Doors scrape, beds creak. Objects move.

"Time to get up!"

Groans, from afar. I push a blanket off, rise to my feet. The surroundings are familiar, but not quite, white walls with metal beds, a low ceiling. A prone form beneath a blanket.

I finger my pajamas. I am in Wadesboro, the facility. *I have not dreamed.*

I turn. I run my fingers down the bed's metal frame. Have I dreamed but only now just forgotten it? I reach back. I have dreamed for days now, for weeks. Sweat dampens my brow.

A voice calls from the door.

"Get up, John Paul."

The figure enters the room, moves to the bed opposite. Rustling. I raise my head, turn. "John Paul, quit your faking. You're getting out of here today."

John Paul rises. His head twists, taking in the orange-skinned HST hunched before him, the floor, me, the floor again. "Out," he says quietly, neither question nor statement.

I sink back to my pillow. I stare at the ceiling. The dream is gone—*gone!* John Paul is leaving.

"Mr. Conn."

The orange-faced man again, the cratered patchwork of scars. Lawrence. He holds his hands back as if clutching a weapon.

"Mr. Conn, it's time to get up."

I lie rigid, my eyes fluttering, then closed. If I could only sleep again, then the dream . . . But sounds trickle. The creak of John Paul's bed, the shuffle of distant feet. A hand wriggles my arm.

"Mr. Conn."

I sigh, turning. Rising. My body is old and defeated. How could life leave me here? Exiled. Unfinished. I tread to the bathroom, engage again in the sad routine of elimination, the lukewarm shower spray, dazed and naked men. John Paul's back is to me, his hands soaping, his shoulders hairy and thin. I turn my head, thinking that soon I will sleep again, that waking will occupy only a few placid hours. This provides comfort. I towel myself dry, recover my clothes, stare with contempt at the mirror showing my gaunt, unshaven face, return in small steps to my room.

Breakfast. I avoid John Paul, sitting instead with Puff and some women. I say nothing, eat almost nothing. An incident occurs, someone yelling, the HSTs rushing, but I pay it no mind, old hand that I am now, a lifer—that is the word for it—stiffened and adapted in full to this place. This home. I shake my head slowly. I glower at the others who stare at nothing and slurp tepid coffee. I sling an epithet at them, my voice high and creaky. I want to wake them up, shake them! But few heads even turn.

I return to the dayroom to find John Paul marching ahead of me. He proceeds to our room and begins packing, rearranging, his body in motion in pistonlike jumps. I linger near the door before entering, ashamed now of my silliness, sit on my bed, and watch him bend and shift things. His lips form rapid words, chewed and unspoken.

"Oh, hey." Our eyes meet. He holds the brown suitcase that had been stored under his bed.

"You heard," he says, and his eyes shift a moment.

"I did. Congratulations," I say, and mean it. He should get out of here, go out into the world, live a full life. He is a young man.

"I'll probably be back," he says wryly, calmly, and for an instant he appears older, his face chalky and lined. He snaps the suitcase shut, looks around the room, jerks his head up, the old manic smile clamped back on his face.

"It's been great getting to know you! I wish you well with your dream, with everything."

The dream. I smile, and nod. If I could sleep now I would. "For me, too, John Paul. I wish you much luck."

We grip hands and I am surprised when he hugs me, his face against my breast, his arm crooked with force on my neck. We stay clasped this way for several seconds. He smells of soap and pomade. Then he is off, out into the dayroom, to the good-byes and well wishes of others, the sweep and shuffle of feet, the plunk of distant piano keys. Is it his mother who waits outside in her car?

I picture a thin, shrewish woman with spidery hands, John Paul's intent look on her face. What must she think of his coming and going? Has his condition improved? Stabilized—that is the word used here. Is she pleased? I stare at the empty bed, still crimped from his imprint. The room is still now, and silent. The voiceless TV flickers, shaded and distant.

I wander into the dayroom. There are others here, staring. Talking. I sit among them, yet I am alone. I do not wish to talk. Someone expels gas and I think of the things I endure now. A man laughs uncontrollably. Another plays with his fly. A cramping forms at the bottom of my stomach, burgeoning so that for a moment I fear illness beyond just despair. I steady myself, a sailor fixed on the shore, my mind returning again to the dream, the fight and arrest, the cold and bloody necklace. Ani had said she was gone. How could I . . .

"Medicine!"

A shifting. A queue. I hang near the back. I turn at what I think is the sound of John Paul but is not.

"Not today," I say softly, when the medicine is handed my way.

The nurse, a milk-faced girl, screws up her face in a nest full of protest. "But, Mr. Conn, they're what the doctor prescribed."

I remain steadfast. The nurse consults Lawrence, who attempts persuasion.

"I'll have to report this to the doctor."

"Okay."

"They may put you in the secure area."

I nod my assent. I want no more treatment, no medication. The drugs have stifled these dreams—I think this is so. I wish to sleep now but there is noise all around me.

I decline my medication again after lunch, the same protests following, the same threats. The day lingers. Recreation area, treatment team (why didn't you take your medication?), a session in which the facility's chaplains, an ancient husband and wife, lead off-key hymns and bang on the old piano, a call for art therapy (I decline) with an energetic young therapist. Patients come and then go. New patients are added, Sydney is led off. Finally, late in the afternoon, I am called to the door.

"Mr. Conn! You have a visitor."

I march past dulled glances. Violet is there in the windowed room, smiling, the weight of our last meeting stowed behind upturned lips. She offers a hug and I grasp her as at a life raft. Images flicker: the blond child fitting under my arm, the girl. The young hippie, beaded and defiant. She is life, passing. Aging. How long since I held her? I cannot shake the feeling that this time is the last.

"How are you feeling?" she asks after disengaging, after we've taken our seats.

"Okay."

"Did you dream?"

"No."

"Really?"

"I did not dream."

"Isn't that wonderful?"

"No."

A half-laugh escapes her. "Papa, I don't . . ."

"When can I leave here?" My tone is friendly, but firm.

"Papa, I spoke to Dr. Mellon this morning. They're still monitoring . . ."

"I want to leave. I want out, Violet. Please."

She shakes her head. Her face is the color of concrete. "I don't think it will be that much longer."

I look at her. She is Grace Kelly—no, Ava Gardner. I am old, my anger a vast plume now that rises so easily. "What is longer?" I say. Birds chirp through the wall.

"I'm not sure. A few days."

A few days. I do not wish to argue. "Is Wilfred home?"

She nods. I am—what? Anxious. Envious.

I bite my lip. I launch my request, despite this, despite everything.

"In my dream, there is someone."

Violet's mouth slips down at its corners.

"A woman. Someone I knew long ago." I pause. I wait for her gaze to reach mine again. Slowly. "I want to find out . . . what has happened to her."

She points her head down.

"Violet. Look at me!"

She looks up. "The nurse told me you refused your medicine," she says softly.

"Violet!" I almost shout it. I hunch forward. "Please."

She looks down, then away. "Papa. I think this is all in your head. It's the tumor, the disease. Remember Mother . . ."

The disease? What is she saying? "This . . . is *real*!"

"Papa."

My eyes cloud with pain. Carol—I am not Carol. I have asked for so little. But Violet couldn't know, wouldn't. I should be grateful for this.

I say into silence, "I must get back to things, then."

Violet raises her hands. "I shouldn't have said that. I didn't mean to insult you." She hesitates before grasping her purse. "You can make it a few more days—don't you think?"

"No!" My voice creaks. Oh, such a monster.

"I want you to do something for me, Papa." Her voice is low, and steady.

I do not look up.

"I want you to take your medicine. That will help you get out of here. I want you to get better."

"I am not going to get better. Can you see that?" I lift my head. "This is who I *am*."

Andre tilts his head in. He looks from one to the other. "Time for your radiation appointment, Mr. Conn." He bows his head in retreat.

It is *Sunset Boulevard*, Norma betrayed and abandoned—no, *The Phantom of the Opera* and its enraged, empty ghost. But it is neither of these. I stare at the spots on my hand, the marks of the years. I do not look at Andre, or Violet. I stand and walk out.

No one speaks to me. I speak to no one. I wander, alone, stung by my banishment. I try to nap but cannot, do not dream. I stare at John Paul's bed. I replay my argument with Violet, my rage lessened and laced now with shame. A voice calls for medicine and I am stubborn, still. Firm.

I use the phone that evening, after waiting for other conversations to end. Puff's instructions on what to feed a dog named

Button ("he likes his chicken ground up with his beef"), the starchy woman Peg's complaints about the food stamp office. It is finally my turn. I grasp the phone, unwind the crimped cord. I want to remedy things. I dial Violet's number.

Wilfred answers. His voice takes my breath away.

"Hello. It is your grandfather."

"Hey."

"You are well?"

"Yeah." He pauses. "I heard you were sick."

Hasta. "I am better. I hope to be home soon."

There is silence.

"And you?" I ask. "How is school?"

His breathing stops, as if a pipe has been disconnected. "Okay," he says finally. He interrupts himself to shout, the phone muffled, "It's Papa." A muted conversation—an argument?— ensues. Stones ping in my stomach.

He comes back.

"Wilfred," I say. There is so much to tell. I know his exclusion, his being the one that is different. A pariah. An outcast. And yet the promise of youth, of work and reward—he can learn this! He must not let guilt enfeeble him. Prejudice lies ahead, violence. He must persevere.

"Papa, I can't understand you." He calls behind him again, "His voice is like gibberish!"

More muffled, parallel dialogue. A scraping of hand on the phone. "My mom says we'll come see you tomorrow."

I shudder. Come see me *here*? I cannot get the words out, the words that will stop this.

The phone crackles.

"I hope you feel better, okay? I've got to go. Mom says she'll call you."

I hear the rasp of my breathing, the whoosh and sigh that were his. Gone now. Silenced. The handset is grimy and slick.

The pain from before knocks my head. How could she do this, bring him here—the one thing I have asked her not to do? She must think I am dying, that this has become the boy's last chance to see me. Here! I cannot bear it. Her patronizing, suffocating, self-satisfying love.

I return to my room. John Paul's bed is remade, left askew. I am shaking. I strip away clothing.

The bed creaks as I fall on it, the thin pillows spreading. My head cracks and rolls. I hear snatches of music—singsongs, from before. An imam asks why I have forsaken him.

Sleep takes a long time to come.

Shadows form, re-form. From somewhere in the distance a dog barks, fueling a sleep-filled anticipation—no dogs at the hospital! But perhaps there are, at least somewhere, for when I open my eyes I am back, listening to the whisper of hospital feet, the same murmurs and snores, the same sighs. I sit up in darkness, my head cocked to the sound of the HSTs, rousting and puttering in their early-morning rounds. I bend forward, straining against damp clothing. The other bed is empty. There has been no dream.

"Time to wake up! That is, if you're not already awake."

The shuffling, the routine. Is it gone now, the dreaming? A bland breakfast. The queue for drugs I refuse. The protests, the note scratching in charts. The muttering TV.

I find myself midmorning on a bench in the recreation area, breathing in fumes of tobacco, wishing for strong cups of tea. The sun is bright already, like the sky and the crags I had seen in the desert. I am thinking of her, of how we rode on my horse, her hands clasped about me, her hair falling free of the cap she wore then. Here, it is hot, too. I wipe sweat with my fingers. After a time I stand, grab a darkened basketball, push a low shot toward the rim, miss, shoot again.

No one watches, not even the guards. I adopt a crouch, alter the release. Is this not how one does it? I remember sports, from before, games of hiding and tag. The ball flies through the hoop. Single claps sound behind me. I retrieve the ball, shoot again. I am an American. Sweat wets my hands.

"Mr. Conn!"

I turn.

"You have a visitor."

I follow, back to the dim of fluorescent light, the stench of cleanser and people. Is it Lissette? Please, please, not the boy.

But it is Carl, his big belly jiggling. He wears a cotton shirt, a worried look. I am pleased, so pleased. We shake hands, regarding each other. We sit.

"Mrs. Fleming told me you were here." He looks away, as if ashamed to know this. His neck falls over his collar. "It happens," he says. "Us guys that have been in battle, that have seen so much. There's only so much you can take."

I am silent. His presence has clogged up my throat.

"Are you okay?" He looks like Marlon Brando, only fatter. He glances around. "This place is not as bad as I thought. I always pictured it as really old, with paint peeling and all, and crazies that ran when you entered." He shrugs his shoulders. "This is like the VA."

I nod, grateful. So grateful.

He studies me. "You're not looking too good, old guy. I guess not bad, for—what?—ninety-two?" He laughs, his teeth large and stained. The laugh brings back memories, good and then bad. I want to leave with him, sit in my house, drink my steeped tea, listen to him tell his stories.

"I think I've found your woman," he says slowly. "I honestly wasn't sure I could do it, or do it this quickly. But I still have friends." He smiles a certain smile, a smile with its meanings. He, too, is important. We, too, are friends.

He hands me a note card. I can only just see, without my glasses. I hand it back.

"What does it say?" I ask.

"It's the address. Don't you remember—the one you asked me to find?"

"Yes, yes. I cannot see."

"Oh!" The big laugh again. He holds the card far from his face. "Araxie Marashlian Merguerian, Two-fourteen West Ninety-sixth Street, apartment five C, New York, New York. Born 1901."

He looks up. "I think that's it. Is that what you wanted?"

I am numbed. "Merguerian?"

"Married name, eh?"

Her name exists. Could it be?

"Sometimes this data can be a little dated, but usually it's dead on." He pauses. "Tell me—who is she?"

I . . . I cannot find words. How do I tell him?

"Thank you," I whisper, as I whispered to another.

"You're welcome." He slaps his legs. "We soldiers help each other, even if we were once combatants. That's part of our code. We're like Grant and Lee, at Appomattox."

"Yes, yes." My words sound silly. Has he confused things? I do not know these men, these soldiers.

He hands the card back. "When do you get out of here?"

I close my eyes, my fists in my lap. His question brings it back again, unknowing Carl—my imprisonment. Violet. Wilfred. The present.

"Some days. They want to watch me, to monitor."

Carl rubs his big jaw. "Yeah, they always do. They think they can see something you can't. But we Americans, we southerners—we know ourselves. We wrote the book on denial." He shakes his head and laughs. "I guess I'd better go."

We stand. Carl looks down, stays on his side of the table.

"You get better soon, okay?"

I try to smile. "On my honor."

I watch as he exits, fingering the note in my pocket, bringing it out again, putting it back. I think to fling myself at a door, a window—how else to escape?—a *bülbül* trapped by its cage. The Armenians. Araxie. Death as near as the sun's certain rising. I take the note out, crease it. Refold it. The name is just different, but it could be, it could be . . . I rub my hand on it, even though I do not see the letters. It is blurred. She survived.

"Mr. Conn!"

I return the note to my pocket, my idea re-forming, squeezing in its embrace. It stays with me, this idea, pressing in its insistence, even as I endure another treatment team and its questioning (Now, why are you not taking your medication? Does this make you feel better? Why do you think you're not dreaming?), as I plow through a John Paul–less lunch. I find my glasses. I check the note three times as I eat. Others are dead, but she may be alive. Alive! I laugh aloud, ignoring the stares. I make for the phone, thumb through a smudged directory, punch out the numbers with my thin, shaking fingers.

"Br . . . ah, Peter?"

It is he. Seconds and words slip past but it is only a recording. I wait for the message's end. My stomach is buckling.

"Peter. It is Ahmet Khan. You . . . your uncle." I pause, unsure of how then to proceed.

"Uncle Emmett?" Peter picks up the phone and is speaking. My name—my Americanized name—spills forth with its syllables.

"Yes?"

"Hey, it's Peter. Sorry I didn't answer. I'm having to shield my calls, on account of the grant award. My phone's been beeping like a fire alarm."

I do not understand this. Still, I plod on. "Peter, I must ask a favor."

"Sure."

"Do you have a bicycle I might borrow?"

A pause. "Ah, yeah, sure."

"The doctors wish me to get exercise. I am wondering if you

could drop it off for me at the oncology center, the building behind the hospital that looks like a bank. Do you know it?"

Another pause. I wait—I am a poor liar. Carol could tell before I opened my mouth. But not Peter. Not Brains.

"Ah, yeah. I can probably do that. Do you need a helmet?"

I sigh in response. "A helmet. Yes, a helmet." I provide direction, ask him to leave the bicycle behind the building so that it is not in the way. My worry shifts from refusal to performance—what are the odds (again) of his execution? But he seems to understand, repeating my instructions back. Others shuffle behind me, waiting with impatience for their turn at the phone.

"Peter, I must go."

"Oh, okay."

"Thank you so much for your help."

"Sure. Glad to. I'll have it there. By the way—where are you?"

I pause. "I am in treatment."

"Hope you feel better!"

I put down the phone, shift past the others. Has anyone heard? Lawrence the HST floats nearby. He cracks his fingers, one on the other.

"How's it going, Mr. Conn?"

"Okay."

"Whatcha up to?"

"Nothing. My radiation appointment is soon."

"What's that?" He points to the note card, its edge in white guilt in my hand.

"An address." I do not offer it.

"Can I see it?"

"No."

"I need to see it."

I hand it to him. He squints at it, holding it far from his face, hands it back.

I am numb. I return to my room, retrieve my wallet. I glance at my watch. What do they *know*? He has seen the note—they will know the address . . . My hands shake. How many times must I betray her? I am ninety-two years old.

The radiation appointment goes off as scheduled. Royce picks me up again, drives me in silence, flirts with Nurse Claire, sits outside the radiation room. I am undressed, positioned, and rolled out on a table, all while my plan winds its way through my mind like a snake, twisting. Slithering. I eye doors and distances. I make minor adjustments. I question myself—do I really intend this?

It seems I do. Calmly, deliberately, my clothing regained in an adjacent bathroom, I put my plan into action.

19

The bike is there, black helmet on black handlebars. After pretending to need the restroom, I have walked out the side door, turned, and hurried around the building's back drive. There— between dumpster and barn-shaped shed—I strap on the helmet, swing into the seat, take one dizzying step, and am off, grunting against the chain's resistance. I am unsteady, even after having ridden all those years. I am an old man now. Slowly I pass the cedars and crepe myrtles, gathering speed, into the parking lot, out and away. I am free.

No one shouts at my exit, no horns beep or wail. I swing onto the sidewalk at Graham Avenue, back in the direction of town, my legs pumping, my breath shortened already. I imagine for a moment the scene at the oncology center, the searching, the realization, Royce on the phone, Nurse Claire frowning. A plume of guilt wraps my abdomen, broken by joy at the thought of escape. I am Steve McQueen—no, the big man whose name I forget. I am

America. I pedal faster, the air whipping my face, down Barton Street and its homes in shiny siding, past the Full Abundance Christian Center Full Gospel Church, past the school, the bike bumping against blocks of sidewalk stained mineral orange, out into the bustle of Jackson Street. Still no one follows, no police cars, no vans. I glance at the traffic. Sweat drips from my chin, fountainlike.

I pause on the opposite sidewalk, gauging directions. Despite my forty years here, the address I have scrawled is unfamiliar. Is this *West* Jackson? I press on, what I believe to be south and west, my legs burning, my breath noisy and ragged, sweat stinging my eyes as it slips down my face. Lights flutter, street numbers dance, ones becoming sevens, twos threes, sixes nines—are there cars behind me? Past the State Department of Corrections' Wadesboro Diversion Center, across a tangle of railroad tracks with lights like dual sentinels, past the Texaco station and its patched asphalt, along the neon-fronted Pic 'n Save, until I find the tiny sign painted red, white, and blue—the picture of a streaking canine. The Greyhound station. The home, as Carl says, of the gray dog.

The station has been formed from the remnants of a convenience store and gas station. Three lone plastic chairs, one red, one yellow, one off-white—the type seen in actual bus terminals—have been placed in the island where the gas pumps once stood. Weeds sprout in clumps in the concrete, below a single, curved lamppost unexpectedly tilting upward. Beyond the building is a tree surrounded by weeds six feet or higher. Yellow paint flakes from metal shingles, some rusty in the sun.

A bus pulls up, lights blinking, smoke billowing; it makes

a wide turn and stops short of the building. An elderly black woman and a young man disembark. I pull the bike to the side of the building, near a fenced-off shed that might once have housed produce. I expect a car to pull up alongside, blocking any exit, but there is nothing. My mind is clear. I hurry to the office, wiping sweat with my hands.

Several people stand before a cluttered desk, behind which sits an elderly woman with white hair and browned glasses. The room smells of ashes and dead smoke. A window air conditioner strains against the afternoon heat. The others in front of me—an old man leaning on a cane, a black woman with her hair in diagonals—form a line reminiscent of the queue for dinner or medicine at SGPC. The woman behind the desk pecks at a computer keyboard, mutters to herself, pecks some more.

"That'll be forty-five dollars," she announces in a husky voice. The old man switches hands on his cane, digs in a pocket for crumpled bills.

I glance at my watch, at the bus waiting outside, at people now milling around it—perhaps they have tickets already? I shift from one foot to the other. The woman in front of me poses one question, then another (Now, can you reach New Orleans without going to Tallahassee? Where is the best place to get dinner? Is it cheaper to come back Tuesday instead of Wednesday?), each met with an expansive, time-consuming response (No, she must go through Tallahassee. The food is best in Mobile.). I shift again, watch as luggage is loaded. Surely this bus will not leave with me standing in line.

The women finally reach an agreement, a fifty-five-dollar fare in which the purchaser first tries to use a credit card, then a check, and in the end produces cash from a faded coin purse. A ticket spits from a machine. Luggage doors clang. Surely the police are here now.

"I need to go to New York." The woman in front of me has not fully moved yet, still groping for something in a massive black purse.

"Okay, honey. You want to go today?"

"Yes. Now, please." The other woman eyes me, moves slowly out of the way.

"When you comin' back?"

"Oh, Tuesday."

"Okay." More pecks on the keyboard. She draws a labored breath.

"I can get you there in twenty hours—you'll arrive about twelve-thirty tomorrow afternoon. You'll change buses in Tallahassee, Jacksonville, and Charlotte. South for a few minutes, east, and then north."

"Yes. Can I take this bus?" I point outside.

She glances out the window, as if unaware of a bus nearing departure. "Sure, honey. You can take that bus. What's your name?"

I pause. "John Paul Edmonds."

"Edmonds. Is that with a *u* or an *o*?"

"Um . . ." I am a poor liar. "*O*."

More pecks, the laboring of the printer. "Okay, hon. That'll be ninety-one dollars."

I bring out my wallet and hand her the money. She smiles a brown smile.

"Thanks, hon. Have a good trip."

I leave the small office, my shirt stained and wet, the dampness turning to cold down my back and legs. I duck my head, checking again for pursuers, but there is only the bus driver, an aged man with a mustache twirled into points, and several large women whose backsides swing as they mount the grooved steps.

"Any luggage?" The mustache bobs up and down.

I shake my head. Inside, the bus is fuller than I expect, though I see empty seats in the back. I keep my head down as I edge down the aisle, the smell of the rear toilet mixed with perfume and stale chips. Blasts of cold air-conditioning increase my discomfort. Snippets of conversation make their way forward: ". . . yeah, then they had to just sew up my rectum . . ." ". . . well, she *said* she was Jesus . . ." About two-thirds of the way back I see her, despite my attempt to look past. Worse, she sees me.

"Uncle Emmett!"

I slide into a seat. Josephine rises, edges with difficulty past the woman beside her, slips back and plops into the seat in front of me, her arm curled over its top. Brainsetta.

"Hey!"

I force myself to look, willing my face to show friendliness.

"Where're you going?" Tiny hairs glint at the corners of her mouth.

"Ah . . . Tampa. They are sending me for more treatment." I wipe again at my face. "And you?"

"Oh, we're going to a rodeo." She waves a meaty hand at several women nearby, some of whom nod and grin. "Near Houston."

"I see. A rodeo."

She leans forward. "It's the finals. The national ostrich-roping finals." She lifts a plucked eyebrow.

I stare at her. I glance at her associates.

"Ostriches?"

"They say it might become an Olympic sport. I've been in training for months."

I rub my face. Josephine leans farther over. "So, what treatment are you having?"

"Some different radiation. An experimental-type thing."

She nods sympathetically. The doors to the bus close, a swirl of piston and hinge. The motor rumbles. Air brakes release.

She looks forward. "I guess I'd better get back to my seat." She smoothes the bulge of her hair. "It's great to see you. Hey, did you hear about Peter's grant? Isn't that unbelievable? Five million dollars. I'm still on a cloud."

"Unbelievable. Yes." I smile against a new gust of air. "Goodbye."

"Bye!"

She twists away. The bus pulls back from the makeshift station. I search again for sign of the police. I am shaking, confused. Is my confinement not known, by Josephine as well as the others? Did Peter not share my request? The questions trigger more questions, slipping me into the ether, in which one thing becomes another. I am an escapee, mental patient, dreamer, widower, father, grandfather, gendarme. Is there more? I should have been dead long ago. I am a stranger here. I am a murderer. Even now others stare, their lips pursed in accusation. Someone brandishes a portable phone—will they not call back to Wadesboro? Josephine and Peter, Brains and Brainsetta—by combining their tiny minds they must know. The police will check the bus logs, find the ticket to New York, uncover the assumed name. Lawrence has the address. The world's oldest escapee! Violet will be there, side by side with orange-clad HSTs; doors will slam, metal cages swing shut. They will beat me to New York, they will find her. And I will be lost.

I make my way to the restroom, enter, and set the latch. My pants are sodden, my skin bumpy like chicken flesh. I sit on the tiny toilet seat, the stench of disinfectant alive in my nostrils, the bus swaying and rocking. Someone knocks on the door. It must be the police, I think—this American efficiency! I stand and bump my head, searching with my hands for some other way out, but the room is tight, like a coffin. A muffled voice from the door ("Are you okay in there?") finally brings me to open it, to peer out in paranoia at a spindly old woman who gazes back through thick glasses and asks loudly, "Are you done yet?" I go back then to my seat, my hands on my arms, shivering with such intensity that my muscles begin to twitch in their own halting rhythm: murderer, murderer. Murderer.

We reach Tallahassee and file off the bus. Outside, a porter pulls luggage. I skirt the group, waiting, my eye out for HSTs or Violet or anyone else, but there is no one, only grimy walls and muttering people and the smell of rancid grease from the door leading inside. Petrified dollops of gum spot gray asphalt. A sign welcomes us to Tallahassee, the Capital City, the sign's end bent and smudged. A uniformed policeman leans against a far wall, his head turned away from the metal chair in which I sit to stare at a blank, coin-operated TV. I place my head in my hands, convinced that even a glimpse of my guilty face will betray me, but then the shivering starts anew, becoming so severe that in a panic I stand

and make for the snack bar, past video games and a Greyhound-topped gum dispenser, out a side door, and onto the sidewalk. There, only inches from streaming traffic, I change my plan. I must confuse and outwit them, as is done in the movies. I must vary my means of escape. A battered-face man bars my way but I step around him, ignore his request for a cigarette, edge down the street to the side of the building. A yellow taxi waits at the corner.

"Hey!"

I turn in resignation, captured at last. But it is only Josephine, hurrying down the sidewalk in a curious, crablike waddle. She pulls up alongside, her face bent and flushed, gasping for breath in a back-bending heave.

"Our bus is leaving. I just wanted to say bye."

She grasps me in an awkward hug, her neck bent forward to avoid crushing my chest. Beyond, on a marquee across the street, the words "free trans check" float above her.

"Good luck," she says.

She says this as she says all things, her mouth in U-lines; she is Brainsetta, but she is more. Her eyes gleam with a sly recognition. She knows. I am silent. So foreign, this relative, of Carol's, not mine, thrust upon me as had been Georgia, so absurd in her mannerisms. And now kindness, when I have shown her contempt. She knows. Not much, but she knows, and keeps silent.

"Thank you," I respond.

"You're welcome." She turns back down the sidewalk. A car barrels just past. I stare after her, thinking of fate, of providence. What if Araxie had been in another caravan? What if Carol had been assigned to a different ward? What if the British had left me, had not mistaken me for one of their own? The things that changed the course of my life—the war, the deportations, the injury—all carrying me with them like a seed in the wind. The deaths. America, working. Violet, and Lissette . . .

I find myself in the taxi. I glance around.

"The airport. Take me, please."

The driver grunts. The door slams, the steering wheel turns. Tallahassee races past—bricked and porticoed—to the accompaniment of the driver's snorts, as if the sights deserve derision but fall short of speech. His seat shifts, its beaded back like an abacus. Smells of mildew and marijuana rise. His chin is large like a whale's, reminding me of something I cannot quite place, twirling me back to the dream, to her, to memories now muddled, of the *klimbim*, the fight, the men who detained me. Do I remember their faces? I strain, in my memory—I cannot lose these things found! But it is useless, this straining, one either remembers or does not. A door opens or closes. I learned this long ago.

A grunt sounds before me, a meter clicks over. The taxi, the whale-man. Is he mute? We have arrived. He speaks then, a hoarse "Thanks, buddy" as I transfer crumpled bills to a wide, dirty hand.

The terminal is crowded, the fissures in my new plan quickly exposed. There is, of course, no direct flight from Tallahassee to New York, and my other options are through either Charlotte or Atlanta. The Charlotte flight arrives too late for me to make any connection to New York until morning. The Atlanta evening flight is sold out. I hesitate a shaky moment, then opt for Charlotte, determined at least to get closer. I hand over my driver's license, establish a record with my name, not any other. This will be checked, found. I am doomed. Yet determined.

I sleep on the flight, my stomach tightened in worry. I have flown only three times before in my life. My head slips in sleep, startling me into drool-filled awakenings, to a strange sense of motionlessness, as if we are characters in a play, only pretending to fly. I think of *The High and the Mighty*, but then I dream, in stray threads: of my hands at a throat (Mustafa's? John Paul's?); and then of home, with Lissette; with Wilfred, a baby. These stay with me, even after we reach the chaos of the Charlotte airport, in a spiral of such longing that I make for a bank of pay phones, hands trembling, and sit for some time. Calling cards, long distance—I do not understand these, or the woman who enters my ear and asks with impatience, "What is it you want?" But I am connected, finally, through a series of clicks.

"Hello?" Violet's voice carries through, light and familiar. "Hello?"

I wait for the phone woman—must she not approve this? There is silence. I am thinking, pleading, but I can say nothing. My voice is contained. I only breathe, some part of me hoping the sound itself provides comfort.

"Papa?"

Only silence.

"Pap-o?"

The phrase she used as a child, as lips formed, words came. Pap-o. I hear the break in her voice. But I am silenced, looking back from the grave. Is it not better—yes, best—that I go now? I must go. My hand replaces the phone in its cradle, banishing her voice back to nothingness, air. I stare at the phone and its hard plastic handle, the residue of makeup caught and held in its cracks. I remember Carol in the years near her death, calling strangers at odd hours. Just to hear voices, she said, when she no longer heard mine.

I rise, after a time, a small headache brewing. Travelers stream past. Some look my way and I think of SGPC, of escape. Paranoia slips back, the fear that waiting will bring capture, and soon I find myself at the Hertz counter, exposing my ID, signing papers, scanning a map for the route to New York. It is almost ten o'clock at night by the time I reach the car, my head now throbbing, the pain in my vision like spots on a cloud. I have difficulty locating the knob for the headlights—I must search for this. Then I exit. Am I still at the airport? But I find my way, somehow. Lights fade behind me.

I drive in silence, stopping only once for aspirin I suck straight from the canister. I am alone, abandoned. I am free. The car is strange and quiet, but I am careful. My mind clears and calms. I will find her. Memories come, too, spilling about, overlapping: Carol at the beach, a snatch of song from the forties. *The Creature from the Black Lagoon.* Sequential no longer, more like splatters of paint. I remember a compliment from a customer who loved his new toilet ("It is like a Roman fountain!"), the smells of diesel and sulfur. My first ride on a subway, the clacking and rocking and disorientation. And then further back: the taste of *döner*, of rakı. The noise a hammer makes as it falls on heated metal. I hold them, these memories, as I bring forth obscured others. Are there connections? There are absences. The childhood I constructed for myself, gone now like a used shell. The life I made here, my American life. So many people—how many people met in a lifetime, a long lifetime? And then her.

I drive on. I stop at a motel outside Baltimore, a neon-riddled establishment labeled the Starlight, its carport fronted by a half-zipper façade. I am surprised at the time; it is four in the morning. I have been driving for—what?—almost six hours? Memories and thoughts and the headache shield time. I check my watch again, check the clock behind the desk. Four a.m. The clerk, a sallow-faced girl with too much eye shadow and a ring in her lip, takes my money (nearly the last of it), and my name (Victor Sasha, this time). She hands me a key with a plastic tab, 117.

"Good night, Mr. Sasha," she says in a voice too low and graveled for someone her age. For some reason she reminds me of Violet, of her defiance as a young woman, re-fostering an inclination to call back, to give myself up, a temptation I wash away with another half-dozen tablets as I enter the room. I strip off the flimsy spread and fall onto the bed, my stomach growling, my head grinding as if saws have been let loose inside it. I kick off my shoes, unbutton my shirt, rise, fumble with the air conditioner, return to the bed. The unit motors to life, a buzzing whine that drowns out a neighbor's pornographic video and the insects outside. The throbbing of my headache changes to match the air conditioner's rhythm, thoughts sweeping past of what it would be like to die here, alone in the Starlight Motel. So many have died—why not me? Why not now?

I wonder what Araxie remembers. And then I sleep.

· 20 ·

The air conditioner rolls to the end of its cycle, freeing me from a struggle with a dream that melts away. Daylight slips between cracks in old curtains. I move my head, the ache lessened but unvanquished, as if it, too, has been sleeping but is now just awake. That which is left numbs the side of my head, a tingling that extends down my shoulder, so that when I rise I hold my head fixed as I did with the frame, a time that now seems almost decades before.

I flick on the bathroom light, examine my face in the mirror. The face that stares back has aged even since SGPC, hollowed and thin, its eyes dark and cratered. I am naked, my body fallen and old. My breathing has calmed, though. My eyes are shiny and clear. I can think again without the knives interrupting. I shower, rub my fingers through wetted hair, arrange myself back into my sweat-stained clothes. I edge out the metal door, key in hand, onto the concrete walkway, to the steps down to the parking lot. Into morning.

The red Chevrolet looks unfamiliar but my key turns in the ignition. I find a convenience store busy mostly with truckers, odors swirling of wet cardboard and coffee, doughnuts, aftershave. I forgo food for toiletries, spending my money on shaving cream, toothpaste, a toothbrush, a pack of disposable razors, a tank of gas. Back in the parking lot, bathed in exhaust and cigarette smoke, I examine bumper stickers on the pickups pulled up to the curb. *It's More Than Guns, It's Freedom. Horn's Broke, Watch for Finger.* Satisfied somehow, I return to the motel.

I open the bag of razors, bring out the shaving cream, scrape a new razor across my old, furrowed face. I pause when I finish, raise my head at the sound of a knock, but the sound fades and dies. I finger the blade, feel its edge as I shift it from left hand to right. I place it on my left wrist and pull slowly across, its depth just enough to nick a vein near the surface, from which oozes bright blood. I put my mouth to my wrist and taste metal and salt. I pull my wrist away, see a bubble re-form, and bring it to my lips, again and again and again, until only a clear liquid remains and then nothing, in its place a small opening, a depth of pink layers.

I brush my teeth, thinking of John Paul and his scars, of SGPC, Violet, Lissette, and then back—all mixed together, of some things perhaps lost. I create mental tests for myself. When was I born? What was the knife maker's name? What tunes did Omar play at the *klimbim*? I think again of Wilfred. Do I remember anything new? I exit the room again, return the key to a slot before the small, darkened office. The zippered façade is still half lit, in neon. I cross the parking lot to the car.

The traffic is full now, trucks bleating and whining. I see police cars. I think, Do they seek *me*? I imagine telling them that

I, too, was a gendarme. I grip the wheel with both hands. I keep to my lane. Cars appear behind me, slowing, zipping around. I feel more comfortable after a while, my driving easier, more mechanical. I take my time. The day lengthens. My stomach gurgles and pouts; I turn the radio on but it is loud. I turn it off. Thirst beckons. I think to count signs as I once did with the children, and the memories soon follow, flowing up with such strength as to blot out light, even life: the great wooden doors at the hospital in London; a chess match in which my enraged opponent ate the pieces he captured; Carol, pale-faced and sick on our voyage to America; the strange Western clothes she had me wear at the time. I was a new man. I was starting a new life. More memories follow of the city's great swirl, its darkness and closeness, the way the wind swept and howled and tossed hats like stray birds. Lissette's tiny body, light and warm next to mine. The strangeness of southern Georgia, the odd accents, the heat. And then voices. Carol's upper register, John Paul's baritone, calling to me and the others. I can just make out words that erase, like a dream. Violet, Dr. Wan, even Wilfred. They compete, talk, talk over their own talking. If they would all only quiet, I could hear them, perhaps remember. Her voice was smooth, yes? I strain to catch it. I see signs for New York and think I am a fool, for this search at the end, an old man's hopeless quest. And yet elation cuts through me. I grip the wheel tighter. I am a child before Christmas, alive in my greediness.

And then it happens. Blue lights behind me, the single whirl of a siren. I pull, deflated—so close!—to the shoulder. Two policemen. They take their time exiting, the lights winking and mocking, my mind leaping back fifty years to another time the police stopped me. At night then, New Jersey, coming home from a job, 1940. I had only just learned to drive. I had purchased a car, a Chevrolet. I was so proud, then. A man was with me, another plumber, Ranesh. We were made to get out, place our hands over our heads as they searched through my car. They made us strip down. They had sticks. Ranesh protested and they hit him, just once. They poked at our clothes. They pulled down our underclothes and placed the sticks lengthwise along the cracks of our rears, prodding, not deep. They laughed with thick laughs and said niggers shouldn't be driving. I could not see their faces. Then they left. I told no one of this. For a time I could still feel the cold rod on the edge of my buttocks, still awake thinking of standing naked along a highway. Then I stopped thinking of it. I have not thought about it in years.

The men reach my window. I try to lower it but do not know how. I exit the car, carefully following their directions. They are young, their faces greasy. Must I strip? I am a *citizen*! But they only ask questions. Where is my license? Why am I driving slowly? Am I really . . . ninety-two? I must touch my nose, count backward from 100. I think, English. English. I stare at my skin. Has it not lightened with age? One turns to the other, saying, I usually call these in, but . . . All as my mind gallops. Do they not know? Have they not heard? They ask again where I am going, and I answer softly: To see a friend. They scratch their heads. It is hot. They say, Be careful, to drive at least forty-five, that someone probably should drive me around at my age. Then they leave.

I slump in my seat. I have forgotten now how to drive. Are they gone? They are gone. A fly buzzes about me. Slowly things return, the key, the ignition. The motor turns over. I pull onto the highway. My speed builds. I am free—unrestrained and still free!

My head bobs in relief. My hands stick to the wheel, sweat pasting my shirt to the Chevrolet's red cloth seat. I search again for blue lights. I will find her, I say to the dashboard, the speedometer. Cars are about again, whizzing and rocking. An ambulance zings past and I must empty my bowels.

Has time elapsed? I have stopped, sipped some water. New York is closer. The last of my money I must spend on the tolls. I remember my first bank account, the concept so foreign—to give someone my paycheck, a week's worth of work. Whom would I trust so? No one, but Carol talked me into it. And then the Depression, the bank failures. I walked by the bank and its columns two times each day, often more. Our bank did not fail, but still I wanted my money, to touch and rub my fingers on the hours of my life. Later, in Georgia, I would go and sit at the bank and ask to see my account balance, to be reassured. Sometimes I took money out just to put it back in. I am exposed without cash—I have felt this way since my youth. There are the cards, the machines that give money, but I have never worked these, never trusted them. I pull my wallet out now, finger its edges, toss it onto the seat. In the end there is nothing. I will be naked before her.

Things grow more familiar. The traffic is slow now, there are horns and brake lights, blue spurts of exhaust. How long since I lived here? I calculate but lose track. The flood of cars makes me anxious, the freeway clogged like a drain. There are signs for food, for lodging—all in English. Did I expect something else, perhaps Turkish? I remember how strange I found signs at first, how incomprehensible. My struggle to learn English, to sound out the strange symbols. The day I took the wrong train, when I mistook

E for F. The foreman who shook his head and made strangling pantomimes. I would go home to ask Carol: What is brain dead? What is jackass? My children mocked my odd accent, "Not *eef*, Papa, *if*." "'We go to *the* store,' Papa, not 'We go to store.'" I worked at it, worked. I became proud of my English. I follow the English signs now for bridges, Manhattan. My fuel gauge shows empty. I know E from F.

I make my way. I miss an exit, backtrack. It is all so confusing. Carol and I lived in Queens, not Manhattan. First an apartment, then a row house. I remember our steps, our neighbors the Manellis. The Ruggieros on the other side. The day we brought Lissette home. The day a storm wrecked our railing. Was Araxie here, too, then—a mere train ride away? I work the window down, acrid smells of exhaust, food, and smoke entering the car. The memories that trail behind these are pleasant. How strange it all was then . . . how wondrous! The buildings, the subways, even the cars. The smell of people and machines, the bread lines and protests still years away. The smell of possibility. There were people of all colors, descriptions. What did they do? Where did they live? Could I ever have imagined this? I found work. I survived, even the Depression. I did not wish to leave, but Carol insisted it would be best for the children, old as they were then. It was the beginning of her decline. And so we left. It seems so long ago.

I am here now. Manhattan. A chill rides my spine. It is the same, but different, clogged with trucks and yellow taxis. Crazed people on bicycles. Glass and chrome and neon. Noise—was it always this noisy? Like a great anthill, the ants stacked and marching and noisy, noisy ants. The sky is browned with their output. Pedestrians throng at corners and seep between cars. I know the address but still I must find it. I make several false starts and stops. Horns peal like bells as cars stack up behind me. Will my gasoline last? I am close, I think, close. The voices and headache are silenced and slain. So near! I can feel it. I tilt my head out and shout at tall buildings, at the bottoms of water towers I installed as a young man. Fear follows, not of death or injury but, worse, of disappointment. The address may be dated, Carl said. She would have to be . . . eighty-nine? Ninety? I search my memory, for the last thing I said to her, the things I wish to say now.

The car stops, the gas gone. I pull to one side. Horns shriek anew, a fat man bent and yelling. I open my door to the street. I search for signs, the light fading. How far? Still some blocks. I begin walking, my legs weakened. I must pause and rest often. The smell of food comes, Turkish food, *pide* and *güveç* and even *şiş köfte*. I am back then to the desert, huddled around a campfire, warming my hands before a hearth. Buying kibbe near a fountain. I smell smoke from a narghile—even *sucuk*! But my hunger and thirst are less clamorous. I reach Ninety-fourth Street and must rest on a stoop. Cars rumble, people chatter. I listen, breathing deep, smelling again, tasting. A woman yells at someone—a husband? a lover?—and laughs a harsh laugh. Someone throws out garbage as I had at the *klimbim*. From somewhere comes the patter of water turned from a tap, trickling, draining. I sit, and savor it.

21

A vestibule. Dim, inside. There is no doorman. I find buttons, numbers, the names adjacent. But it is wrong—the name at 5C is Gilbert. I stare as my stomach folds. I walk outside, then return. Is the address wrong, the building? I am tired now, and weak.

I push the button. There is silence, then a voice, a young voice. "Yes?" This voice does not know me.

"I am looking for Araxie. Marashlian." My voice comes from the crypt.

The button offers no response. Then, "Who is this?"

I close my eyes. "Ahmet Khan."

There is something. A sigh? Finally, "Please come up."

An elevator cage, a hallway smelling of food and tobacco. Number, numbers, and then a door, partly open, a woman's frame in yellow light.

"Come in." The light falls, her face becoming just visible.

I am lifted, transported, to desert and hilltop and a thousand dream places. It is she, still a teen, one eye blue, the other somber and dark. She is different, updated, her hair short, the dark makeup so common. She is dressed all in black. Her skin, too, is darker, as if the rigors of the trek have marked her. But it is she.

I say nothing. My mouth moves, syllables half forming. I am back in the ambulance with the tumor's arrival, the first wisps of dream coming, but, no—I am here. I shift my feet. A word—the word—winds up through my throat.

"Araxie."

The girl looks down. "She is dead," she says softly. "It will be four years in May."

We stare at each other.

"I am Augustine, her granddaughter. And you . . . are Ahmet Khan."

Her granddaughter. My name. My voice of its own accord, rumbling. "Yes."

She flips her hair. "Ahmet Khan," she says again. "She said you would come."

Things weave in and out. I am there, I am here. At the end the past is so great it intrudes like an army. I find myself in a chair, though I do not remember sitting down. She is seated, too, speaking, but I am only looking, thinking. Granddaughter. I think to touch her. So alike as to be one.

"Grandmother lived here for forty-two years, then my mother. My mother died six months ago."

"And your father?"

"He died when I was two."

Her fingernails are short and black. She gnaws on her forefinger.

"Do you have other relatives?"

She shakes her head, defiant, almost. Even this, this gesture . . .

"What did your grandmother tell you?"

"She told me you saved her life."

I spin again, through a world raw with violence. The women at the fire, the men on their ropes, the mother and the child and the horse's hoof. Mustafa.

"What life did she have?"

The girl nods, older in this way—maybe eighteen? Nineteen? "She had a remarkable life." The blue eye flickers. "She lived a long time. She was blind, at the end, but still vital. So vital."

"What . . . what happened to her?"

I think she will not know this. Why would Araxie have remembered, recounted to her these old, death-filled horrors? But the girl—Augustine?—only nods and clears her throat.

"She was taken," she begins. "A man, Hussein, abducted her, took her by force from the house where she stayed.

"Another man was there. Mustafa. He wanted to rape her, but Hussein wouldn't let him. Instead, Hussein ripped the necklace from her neck, and told Mustafa where to find you."

The memory swims back. She is reciting, but yet . . . The pain swells in my ear. My nose is crushed, my teeth broken.

"They stayed with his sister for some time, maybe a year. Grandmother worked at a new hospital. She tried to escape once, but was captured. She married him—Hussein—after that. She was given no choice."

I am dizzy, suddenly. Falling. She is . . . she is . . .

"It was either that or die," she continues. Her voice is like a bell. "He made that quite clear. And, although I considered the latter, the will to live proved too strong."

I . . . I . . . She is speaking, this descendant, but I hear only Araxie. Her voice! Even . . .

"We lived for several years in Aleppo. I bore him a son. We called him Hossan. Hossan died when he was two—an illness shriveled his body to only paper and bone. Hussein died two years later.

"I never loved him—Hussein." She pauses. "I tried. He was not wholly bad. But in the end it was I who killed him."

She wipes at her face. I rock as if on a ship.

She looks away, in the direction of the shaded window at the end of the room. Colors are switching, reds now, and greens. Her hair is thick. It is *she*.

"After the war, a number of Armenians returned to Turkey. I waited, but eventually I, too, wished to go back, to find people, to see if any of my relatives had been spared. Hussein would not leave. Eventually we did travel, but to Der Zor, to see his relatives. In those days, traveling was dangerous. There were brigands and bands of outlaws that preyed on those on the roads. A day or two after we left Aleppo we were attacked. Hussein was injured—he suffered a broken arm, as well as a serious head wound. After the bandits departed, with all of our money, Hussein took out his frustrations on me. He had this club, this hardened, petrified woodlike thing, and he beat me with it, using his one good arm. I can still hear the grunts of his efforts. I lost several teeth, suffered broken ribs in the process. At some point something snapped within me, and I responded." She pauses, her face still turned to the window. "I pinned him down, grabbed one of the blankets from our bedroll, and pressed it into his face. He fought, but I was stronger, given his wounds. I suffocated him." She pauses again. "I left his body by the side of the road."

Her gaze shifts to me. "Somehow, I made it to Harput, or what was left of it—I don't remember the journey. Only a handful of Armenians remained, of what had once been a thriving community. All our homes had been taken by Turks. An old Turkish woman answered the door to my house. I remember yelling at her, screaming like a madwoman, people opening doors and staring. I managed to locate a couple of distant relatives, an old aunt who had stayed, some cousins who had survived the deportation and returned. With their help, I obtained a job teaching Armenian orphans at a missionary-run school in Mezre. I stayed there a year or so, until the Armenians were evicted again.

"After the Greeks attacked and began making their way through Anatolia, the same things began to happen: the rounding up of Armenians (the few of us still there), the suspicion, the persecution of all Christians. I determined to die this time rather than face a new deportation. Fortunately, the missionaries at the school protected me and a number of the children. After the Turks retaliated and forced back the Greeks, the missionaries were permitted to leave and take some of us with them. Some of the children were left behind—I never understood why, or on what basis selections were made as to who stayed and who went. I remember offering to stay, pleading for the other children; I suffered enormous guilt about it for a long time. I still see their faces sometimes in my dreams."

I draw a deep breath. I want to ask, to explain. How could I have forgotten?

She smiles again. "I arrived in this country on October twenty-first, 1922. I was twenty years old. Do you remember how we used to speak of it, of what America would be like? It was nothing like what I expected, with its grime and its noise and its people and customs, but at the same time it was everything. It gave me a chance to remake myself, to start over, to become whole again. I had seen so much. I didn't know what to think. I told myself I had been scarred by life.

"The missionaries that brought me to America were Presbyterians, from Boston. We went there after our arrival in New York. The children were placed in an orphanage, and I was offered a job teaching them. It was hard—I spoke not one word of English. I was homesick as well, for my family, for Anatolia, even for Aleppo. There were a number of other Armenians in Boston, so this helped. We would get together occasionally, compare notes, speak our language. An older lady, Mrs. Piranian, would make *choereg* for us—it was heavenly! We spent most of our time searching for loved ones, trying to find relatives who survived. I located some cousins eventually, the Elmassians, who had been in New York but moved to California. They were on my mother's side. I visited them once, in about 1927 or so. We stayed in touch for a while, but eventually lost contact. I never heard anything about any of my other relatives. I assume they all perished.

"I thought of you often during this time. Even when I was married to Hussein, I thought of you. I imagined myself escaping, stowing away on a boat—do you remember?—traveling to America to find you. I was certain you had survived, even when I heard you were taken prisoner. I don't know how I knew this, but I did. After the war, when I had returned to Harput and Mezre, I would often go for walks in the streets, even in the areas where Armenians were not welcome, thinking that I would catch a glimpse of you, that you would be there. But I never saw you. When I came to America, I looked for you on the streets, in Boston, in New York, even in California. I spent some time one day at Ellis Island, going through records, checking the boat logs of ships. I never forgot about you, not then, not ever. It's why I knew you would come.

"I met a man, eventually, an Armenian man, in Boston. He was a nice man, a kind man. His name was Levon Merguerian. We married in 1928. He was in the shipping business in Boston— they shipped goods to Europe, brought raw materials from South America. He did quite well for a while. Then he lost his job. We struggled, as did many, counting our pennies. But we survived. We had two children, Sarkis and Simone. I cherished them, as I did Levon, for I had always felt rootless and alone.

"Levon died in 1978," she continues. "His health had deteriorated." She swallows, a tiny ripple in supple flesh. "I thought about you a lot after he died. I don't know why—I was almost eighty by then. I found as I grew old that my thoughts often went to that time and place. Occasionally, before my sight went, I would encounter other people I had known before, almost as if I had lived a previous life. I was in Harrods once, in London, when a woman came up to me and called me by name. I recognized her when she spoke—we had worked together at the hospital in Aleppo. I ran into one of my childhood friends in a restaurant in New Jersey; we hugged and kissed and caused a big commotion. Another time I was on a subway in New York when a man jostled my shoulder as he passed. I looked up, and remembered. This man had raped me—he was one of the gendarmes. I don't remember his name, but I hadn't forgotten. If I'd had a weapon, I might have killed him right there.

"But I thought mostly of you. I thought of this day, when you would come to me. I have waited for you, for there's something I've needed to tell you, something you should have been told all those years ago. But first, tell me—what do you remember?"

She smiles. I suck in air. She looks so familiar. The hair, the thin nose. So much has happened.

"I remember too much," I say slowly. "It has been buried, so long, but now it comes back like the sun. I remember your eyes, the first time I saw you. I remember how captivated I was, how I could think of nothing but you. I remember our time in Katma, when we shared the small room. I remember waking to find you missing, only to discover you up on the roof. I remember when you were sick, on the road to Aleppo. I remember the necklace I gave you, the look in your eyes."

I swallow. "I remember other things, too—unpleasant things. I have forgotten for most of my life, but now I remember as if I were there once again. Things are fresh and raw, like new skin. It has . . . it has led me to find you. I have thought of nothing else."

She laughs, a deep, throaty laugh, the laugh of a much older person. Silence slides through and I am buffeted by memory, by the way her hand pulls her hair. She is so young. A sliver of light slips like fog past the window.

"Did it really happen?" I ask.

Her smile fades, her lips pressed and thin. "Oh, it happened," she says, her voice low and alive. "Don't let anyone tell you it didn't. It was, it remains, *genocide*." The word spills from her mouth.

The room falls to silence. The anniversary, the magazine article. Young, and yet old.

"I read a story once," she says, "about a man who could remember everything, including even his remembering. He would be surprised every time he looked in the mirror, even if it had been only seconds before, because he remembered details so minute his features would appear changed as he became slightly older. He found it difficult to think or act, to do anything in the abstract, so absorbed was he in the details and remembering. The point of the story seemed to be that to think is to forget, to filter from the mind the unnecessary. I have told myself this, repeated it to myself. I have called it our gift from God. This headlong, heedless survival."

I squint. I am speaking again, about memory. How I have heard that each time we remember, we change the thing remembered in the smallest of ways. I bubble with words, with these things left unsaid. I tell her, "This memory that comes now, after so long withheld—it is sharp, like a dagger. I feel the sand in my face. I smell the death. But I mainly see you. I tell myself that some things—beauty and love—transcend."

"Beauty?" Her voice shakes, her face twisting with years. "I suppose I was beautiful once. It cost me dearly. How I wanted to blend in, to be unnoticed! The eyes you mention, the exotica, prevented this. They cursed me with their uncommonness. I stood out, to Turks, to Armenians, to Syrians, to other children, to men and to women. I could never hide, despite my attempts. I prayed, back when I thought God still listened, for deliverance from this malady, for one eye to magically transform itself to be uniform with the other. At one point I even considered mutilating myself, but I soon came to realize I was already disfigured. I suppose that but for my eyes you might never have noticed me, and as such my life might not have been spared, but they caused me much pain. Although their purpose is for seeing, they allowed me only to be seen. In the end, I was not ungrateful for blindness.

"There is something else about my eyes, though, the hidden something I must tell you, the burden I've carried so long. My eyes are, if anything, a testament to my pedigree, a proof of my deception. For you see, I am not an Armenian—I never was. My father was a Circassian, an Ottoman from somewhere near Thrace. My mother was a Turk from Bitlis. When I was born—perhaps it was because of my eyes, at least I've always thought so—I was abandoned. An Armenian family took me in. I was raised as a Christian, in an Armenian family, but I was born a Turk. The story I told you was partly true—my Armenian brother *had* been taken in by a Turkish family, my Armenian mother did die before the deportations. But so did my father. The man you shot that night was not my father. I knew him—he was a trader from Harput, a kind man who had helped me stay safe on the journey—but he was not my father. I'm not sure why I told you he was. I think I thought it would make you feel guilt, bind you to me somehow. Perhaps it did. But in that I've deceived you for almost a century. And for that I ask your forgiveness."

Another silence intrudes. I clear my throat again, shuffle my feet. She asks for forgiveness, when I am the monster.

"I never met my natural father," she says eventually. "My natural mother lived in Mezre, but refused to acknowledge me. Even when I returned from Aleppo, when I sought her out, she would not speak to me. She had married, had a number of children.

Perhaps she thought others didn't know about me, but they did. She had tears in her eyes when she shut the door in my face. Those tears alone have allowed me to forgive her. My brother"—and here her voice trembles, wavering up to a new pitch—"my brother was killed while I was in Aleppo. An accident, or so I was told. A cart fell on him." She pauses. "He was only eight or nine." The smile returns to her lips, pained now, her chin lifted upward. "Ironic, isn't it? I survive a death march, and he is killed by a falling cart." She allows the smile to fade. "I've never understood life. After a while, I quit trying.

"I've always found it interesting that there is no blood test—nothing that I know of—to distinguish Armenians from Turks, Christians from Muslims, saints from sinners, the good from the bad. In the end, who really knows—maybe God? I find it funny that the people at my job called me 'Turk.' I never told anyone my story, except my family, never told anyone anything. I don't think I look Turkish, whatever that is. But we were right, Ahmet, about America, about its beauty, its opportunity. Here you can change your name, alter your identity, construct the someone you wanted to be. A few things remain, seared so deep as to defy alteration. Will your children know your heritage? Your great-grandchildren? Will they know what you did in this life? Maybe there are some things that should be passed on, that should never be forgotten." She pauses. "I think so."

She looks up. "That's it." She is changed now, a granddaughter. She flicks her hair in embarrassment.

I open my mouth but no words break and follow. It comes back to me, this, these two different people. One dead, one young and alive. I heard . . . I saw . . .

I sway in an emptiness. I know now. I know.

"Thank you," I say. "Thank you for telling me. Your grand-mother, she would be proud."

"Can you forgive her?"

I tremble. The horror of it all holds my tongue in its place, but she nods her acceptance and says, "She said she'd forgiven almost everyone through the course of eighty-plus years. She held no bitterness for the Turks, or for God. She'd seen so much."

And me—the one that forgot—how can I be forgiven? I have failed to express, to even voice my regret. I stare at this child. I am tired now. So tired.

She tilts her head. "I wasn't sure you would come. I thought you might be imaginary—you know, her imaginary friend. But she was so certain. She told me this, all my life. It's kind of weird, but she knew."

All this time. Only hours away.

There is silence. "Do you miss her?" I ask. "Your grandmother?"

Her eyes cloud now, the blue and the brown. She nods and looks away, out the length of the far window.

I examine her, the dark makeup smudged.

"There is something I need to give you," she says. She stands and turns.

I follow as if on a path. There are rooms, clothes, food on a stove. An ironing board and refrigerator. She digs through a pile of things, blankets and clothing, before pulling out something in triumph. She offers it to me, this object, this worn bit of cloth. I examine it, rub it between my stiff fingers. There is something, something . . .

"She said it was yours. Your shirt. She said to thank you."

I exhale, my face quickly broken, the room slow and spinning. Faces pass before me, so many, detailed—I cannot keep them apart as they move close together. I strive to form words but the floor falls. Slim hands grip my shoulder. I say, or I want to, I must tell them. Please tell them. Lights flash in circles, like those of an ambulance. Odors shift, of ambergris, alcohol.

I am moving once more, my direction uncertain. I tread air and water. There is pressure against me. And then I am seated, a voice in my ear, a hand pressing again on my shoulder. My arms are trembling. Sweat falls, or urine. The voice in my ear grows more pronounced. Understandable.

"Mr. Khan."

"Yes?" My voice is thick and aged. Where am I?

The voice is close, a face near. One light eye, one dark. A dimly lit hallway.

"Are you okay?"

"Yes, yes. Okay."

"I think you had a seizure. Should I call a doctor?"

"No, no. No doctor. I am fine." I rotate my head. "I have these sometimes." My voice gathers strength.

"Are you sure?" she asks.

"Yes, yes." I attempt to stand, make it halfway up before falling, shake my head, rise again. There are voices, others. "Is he okay?" Is it her?

I am in a lobby, facing buttons and numbers. Then outside. I am thinking, I have found her. And yet . . . It is cold, in the darkness. My hands clench and reach from my pocket to my face. Please.

Moths dance on streetlights. Cars honk, far away.

A breeze creeps up from behind, rustling leaves or street trash
Someone is asking me questions, shining a light.
I am rocking, rocking.
What is your name? I form the words, but in Turkish.
The headache thrusts and stabs.
Then just the rocking. The whisper, and rocking.

22

I am dreaming. We are back in Aleppo, Araxie and I. We are in a line of people, moving. Moisture hangs in the air.

We stand on a ship, its decks flat and wide. Gulls flap and call in the breeze. We pause at the rail and look out at the crowds, the people behind on the shore. Working, watching, their faces small and obscured—who are they, these people? The cypresses narrow from this distance, the city in dust.

On board there are sailors and crew. People march down steps toting large loads. The ship is now moving. The sea swells beneath us. I look at her, I cannot help but look at her. My heart beats in time.

I hear voices from somewhere, some future. Men rustle. "Can we move him?" A pain pricks my side.

But then quiet. It is quiet here, on the ocean. The waves are small, the sway the push of a hammock. She is leading me somewhere, a room, deep below. There is the thrill—the old thrill—of being with her, of freedom.

She opens the door. There are others inside. They stand as we enter, a ripple of foreheads. I pause, surprised. My head knocks.

Again come the voices. "Easy now, Mr. Khan." "You're okay." "Lie down now."

But I recognize these people. They are there, from the trek. The man I shot at the fire, the baby's mother at the river, the women dancing, the prisoners on ropes. There are hundreds, melting, giving way—the pregnant woman left behind on the road, the others floating up in the river. And more. I see Ani, Dodi. But still, giving way.

And then Carol! Her nurse's outfit, her smile fixed and bright. She is looking away, out at boats on the water. She starts to say something, then stops. Behind her come others—Lissette, then Violet. I stare at my daughters. What . . . what is this dream?

They stand there, expectant. I struggle to wake. I must ask their forgiveness, but my voice will not come. I am mute, dream-mute. My throat burns with the effort.

Their eyes begin closing. First those in the back, then row upon row, like blinds being pulled or sails furled and drawn. The ship bucks and slides, crashing them one into another, fading but not eliminating. They do not disappear. Still, the lids shut—now Ethan, the black man. John Paul, his wrists high. Wilfred, a smile forming. I twist away but still look. Carol, eyes closing. All shut now, all shut.

Until only she remains. She stares, like the blind. She is younger, with eye shadow. I say to her, I want to say . . . But it is late. It is late.

ACKNOWLEDGMENTS

Many thanks to many people, including Perry Mustian; Kenneth Fuller, M.D.; Gerald Kadis, M.D.; Steven Johnson, M.D.; my Turkish and Syrian traveling companions Will Butler, Bryan Desloge, and Bill Law; Peter Garretson, Ph.D.; Jeff VanderMeer; Paul Shepherd; the folks at Putnam, including Halli Melnitsky, Victoria Comella, Ivan Held, and the wonderful Amy Einhorn; my agent, Scott Mendel; and most of all my wife, Greta, who puts up with all of this.

I am deeply indebted to others' descriptions of the Armenian tragedy (many of them recollections of relatives who survived the brutality of the trek), including David Kherdian's *The Road from Home*; Peter Balakian's *Black Dog of Fate*; Mae Derderian's *Vergeen*; Antonia Arslan's *Skylark Farm*; Micheline Marcom's *Three Apples Fell from Heaven*; Grigoris Balakian's memoir, *Armenian Golgotha*; Margaret Ajemian Ahnert's *The Knock at the Door*; Rafael De Nogales' *Four Years Beneath the Crescent*; Donald E. Miller and Lorna Touryan Miller's *Survivors*; Clarence D. Ussher's *American Physician in Turkey*; and others. These works reflect the resilience of the Armenian people amidst unbelievable suffering.

AUTHOR'S NOTE

All my life, people have asked if I am Armenian. I've always replied that I am, that most names ending in "-ian" reflect the old Armenian word meaning "son," though my Armenian heritage is distant—my paternal great-grandfather fought for the Confederacy in the U.S. Civil War. Until I reached my thirties I never thought much about my ancestry, until one day someone asking this same question also asked if I had read Peter Balakian's book *Black Dog of Fate.* I hadn't, and did. I learned then the awful fate of the Armenians at the beginning of World War I, and of those, including Peter's grandmother, who survived the forced trek into Syria. I was mesmerized, and read more. How could this horrible thing have happened, and so few (including me) know anything of it? I read survivors' stories, transcripts of oral histories, memoirs, and history books. I learned of the denial of the Turkish nation, and of the fact that to speak of the Armenian deaths as genocide remains a crime in Turkey to this day. Eventually, I hit upon the idea of writing a novel about the deportations, but approaching it from the point of view of one of the policemen, the gendarmes, who escorted these groups from the country. Several years later, *The Gendarme* was born.

After finishing the first draft of the novel, I placed a newspaper advertisement seeking a Turkish-speaking person to read the manuscript and evaluate my use of Turkish words. A husband and wife, graduate students at the local university, responded. I explained the story, including its sensitive topic, and they agreed to review it for a small fee and get back to me in a few weeks. The next day, however, they returned to my office, explaining that after further consideration they would be unable to complete the task. The subject matter was, they said, too controversial. I later found another graduate student to review the manuscript, a young Turkish man who provided suggestions I found valuable. I asked, at the conclusion of our discussion, if the novel had offended him. He paused a bit and responded that, yes, there was an element of affront to it, particularly in the presenting of things from a Turkish character's point of view. When I asked him to elaborate, he said that it was difficult for modern Turks to understand the fixation of the Armenians and the West in general on this episode in history, that a war was on, that bad things happened in wars, including bad things that happened to the Turks in this war. The Turks and Armenians had experienced other conflicts before this. He said that modern Turkey has moved on.

I thought about this later when, in an effort to trace a general path taken by the deportation caravans, I spent part of August 2008 in Turkey and Syria. I'd completed several drafts of the novel by this point, and wanted to see the area I'd researched and written about, to travel the routes, even to feel, to the extent possible, what those deportees almost a century earlier might have felt and experienced. In 1915, at the beginning of World War I, something close to panic gripped the Ottoman Empire, a fear that the sizable Armenian minority in Turkey was aligned with their Christian brethren the Russians in opposition to the Turks in the war. A few reported uprisings prompted a massive and brutal response. Those not killed were forced to join the caravans proceeding south and east to the Syrian desert and then to the city of Aleppo. I followed this path almost a hundred years later, from Cappadocia in central Turkey over the Taurus Mountains, on to Antakya and then into Syria. Traveling paved highways in an air-conditioned van, I tried to imagine what it would have been like for old men, women, and children to make this journey on foot, along dirt roads in late spring and summer. They would have had to leave almost all of their possessions behind. The sun would have been searing, the paths dusty and arduous and long. Water would have been scarce. Disease and lack of food and thievery would have taken their toll. Some would have walked hundreds of miles. Others would have had to be carried. It was easy to see how many would have failed to survive it.

Three friends accompanied me on my trip. While my companions were aware of my research, I was cautious with our Turkish guides and most of the people we met about discussing my heritage and specific interest in the region. I found that the guides, although quite knowledgeable on all things historical, made scant reference to World War I, and no reference at all to the Armenians. When asked (usually by one of my companions) why the country was 97 percent Muslim, as opposed to, say, the population in Syria or Lebanon, they mentioned reciprocal Turkish-Greek relocations after World War I, an event they described as hard on both sides but necessary, given the times. Although I found Internet references to Armenian heritage tours in Istanbul, few tourists seem to have followed the route of the caravans, perhaps in avoidance of the topic, and the sadness, anger, and shame that surround it. Treading the same path where many suffered and died is disquieting, even devastating, particularly when things now look so serene. Are bones buried beneath the dust, corpses of children who died from deprivation? My interaction with modern Syria's border officials was both lengthy and difficult, but the visit to Aleppo itself was rewarding, as one can still envision the excitement this exotic metropolis must have presented in 1915 to those few deportees who made it. Taking pictures of the Syrian plaque that commemorates the genocide and watching an Armenian Church service provided me with a surprising sense of closure, an affirmation that these horrific events are at least recognized somewhere, recorded instead of wiped from the earth through disavowal and silence.

In 2009, Turkey and the Republic of Armenia reestablished diplomatic relations. Part of their agreement to do so included the establishment of a joint historical commission to probe the facts of the early twentieth century. With the one hundredth anniversary of the Armenian deportations only a few years away, and the vote on Turkey's admission to the European Union also looming, perhaps old wounds will be reexamined, past wrongs addressed, and long-delayed solace offered. Or will a whitewash continue? Some will argue (à la my Turkish-speaking friend) that it is time for those of Armenian descent to move on, that events that happened a century ago shouldn't dictate current policy or affect strategic alliances. Is the labeling of events as "genocide" so important? There were, in this case, provocations: Christian Armenians and Russians forced many Muslim Turks from the Caucasus in the late 1800s; there were uprisings in 1915, though small, by several bands of Armenians. Any war produces paranoia regarding native populations—witness the internment of Japanese Americans during World War II. But clearly the Armenians were annihilated in Turkey, a population of over one million simply no longer there. Few would say we should forget the Holocaust when its events are a hundred years old. Should those culpable in Rwanda, or Kosovo, be excused for their actions taken in "time of war"? Genocide represents perhaps the ugliest of human deeds, the mass killing of often defenseless fellow beings. Our actions and policies should be to stop it, whenever, wherever, and however. To stop it we must publicize it. Saying it didn't happen is a mere recipe for recurrence.

People sometimes ask, Why would you want to write about this, or even know of it, when your immediate ancestors were not part of the tragedy? I have no simple answers. In some ways the distance is helpful, permitting me a novelist's audacity in attempting to probe the mind of one most would consider a perpetrator. In other ways it is deadening, a balm stifling emotion and fostering apathy and appeasement. Remembering is living. Forgetting, as Ahmet Khan learns, has its costs. Decades on, even centuries on, our shared history remains vital, the connection, however tenuous, to some tribal sense of before. Time stretches and calms, but still we reach, for we belonged then. We want to *know*. Sometimes that knowledge is painful, or inconvenient, or even damning. But it is essential. It exposes us for what we have been, and can be.

Mark Mustian
Tallahassee, Florida
January 2010